ONLY AT THE CAVERN

Book Two of The Cavern Series

By

ANNA ALEXANDER

AnnaAlexander.net
Newsletter
http://eepurl.com/Q0tsz

Captain Marco DeWinter is a cop on a mission when a brush with death lands him in the hospital. Regulated to mandatory time off, he begins to re-examine his priorities and entertain the idea of his sexy ER doctor having him on the receiving end of a set of handcuffs. Ever since Marco discovered Dr. Jasmine Jovanovich's secret life as a dominatrix, he's been eager to feel the bite of her Stiletto in his back as she makes him worship at her feet.

Jasmine agrees to be his guide into the darker pleasures, and is delight when he dives in with the same enthusiasm as he does his police work, that is until he makes her question her "Cavern Only" policy, and wants to blur the lines between her professional and personal life. When Jasmine is caught in the fallout of one of his cases, Marco must convince her that not only can she trust him to keep her body safe, but her heart as well.

Dedication

For my family. Always.

Find Anna Online

Website
annaalexander.net

Facebook
facebook.com/pages/Anna-Alexander/282170065189471

Twitter
twitter.com/AnnaWriter

Newsletter
http://eepurl.com/Q0tsz

CHAPTER ONE

MARCO DEWINTER YANKED the watch off his wrist and stuffed it into his back pocket, then sat on the offending object for good measure. The damn thing wasn't doing him any good reminding him that his contact was late.

He reached for his cup of coffee and scanned the immediate area for the thousandth time. Sure, meeting an informant in the middle of the night in the darkest recesses of the city park was incredibly cliché, but when the guy wore a costume straight out of a science fiction movie, carried a sword and was overly protective of his privacy, locations were limited. It was either the park or a dark alley, and that idea was just as groan-worthy.

A few hundred feet from his post, the fountain marking the entrance to Denny Park babbled. The running water was one of the first signs spring was on its way and the weather was warm enough to keep the pipes from freezing.

And as always, in just a few weeks one of the local high school students was going to have the brilliant but not original idea to dump a case of industrial-strength bubbles into the water and turn the park into a scene straight from an old-time sitcom. Then some poor rookie shlub was going to be saddled with the task of preventing more juvenile stunts with thrice nightly patrols of the park, not with the intention of preventing real crime, like drug dealing or prostitution, but because the mayor liked to keep the fucking park looking pretty. An annual ritual that exemplified the city's resources in action.

In all actuality, though he'd never admit it out loud, Marco enjoyed the giddy sound of splashing water. The city was beautiful in the spring when the soft-pink burst of cherry blossoms forced through their green prisons to embrace the light of the sun. Scrubbed clean by the rains of winter, the city sparkled like a freshly polished diamond. A sense of expectation hovered in the air, much like how one felt at New Year's when the clock crept ever closer to midnight. Old skin was shed and possibilities abounded.

As the scent of flowers from the nearby arboretum and fresh mulch tickled his nose, he bit back a smile. It had been far too long since he had stopped to smell the roses. Would he even remember how to if he tried? Pursuits of relaxation weren't meant for men like him. Men who lived every day entrenched in the harsh realities of living and were tasked to clean up the mess of mankind. Perhaps when he grew old and his bones creaked, he'd take the time to relearn the texture of a flower's petals, but for now that was a forbidden luxury. Another in a long list of items trapped in the illusive promise that was called tomorrow.

He took a healthy swallow of lukewarm coffee, not because he was thirsty, but he needed to occupy his mind with something, anything, before he did something that gave away his impatience, like pace about in aggravation or start to fantasize about other ways he could be spending his Monday night. Or with whom.

Don't go there, man. Don't go there.

He shook his head and blinked hard against the memory of a petite, curvy doctor with long dark hair covering her lace-encased breasts that jiggled as she flicked a riding crop through the air.

Goddammit. He crossed his legs and pressed his thighs

together in an attempt to stem his growing erection. A hard-on was the last thing he needed.

"Captain. I apologize for my tardiness."

"It's about fucking time," he mumbled and jumped to his feet. "I was thinking I'd been stood up. I was about to post all over Facebook what an asshole you are."

The Chameleon chuckled and stepped out from the shadows. "Again, I apologize. I would have stopped and gotten you flowers, but that would have delayed me even further."

"I hope you brought me something better than flowers." Marco tipped his head back to look up at the man he hoped carried the key to what he'd been searching for over the last three years.

There weren't a lot of men Marco had to tilt his head up in order to look him in the eye, but the Chameleon was one of the biggest son of a bitches he'd ever met. The man was a mountain, standing over six-and-a-half feet tall with shoulders so wide, he'd have to turn sideways to enter a room. Their breadth seemed even more impressive when balanced out by a broad chest and lean waist. His head was covered by a cowl, and a tunic lay over his torso. It was made out of an unusual material that refracted light and made his body look as if it disappeared. Funny thing was, the costume wasn't the most unusual thing about him.

The Chameleon held out a large manila envelope. "I hope this suffices."

Marco set his cup down on the bench and tried not to rip the envelope to bits with his excitement. He reached inside and withdrew a tidy stack of paper about an inch thick, including eight-by-ten color photos and charts of dates and locations.

"What exactly am I looking at here, Cam?" he asked, wishing he had better lighting and a desk to look over everything with a fine-toothed comb.

"As you know, Smithwick has homes and hideaways located all over the world. He never stays in one place for very long, but I've deduced that he has four locations in western Washington that are his favorites. One is in the Cascades, one on the coast and two here in the city. He keeps a small group of men as his personal security detail. No one is allowed direct contact with him without going through them first. Using your notations, I've pieced together as many photos with names as I could. In the last two weeks, his extended security detail has tripled. Either he knows he's being stalked or he's working on a big project."

"I suspect it's a combination of both." Marco flipped through a few of the photos of a gated house that appeared to be located near the university district. It made sense since a large portion of Smithwick's empire was built on drug sales, and a college student was an easy score. "Is there any way you could use your super speed and sneak in and place some cameras and recording equipment on the property?"

"Do you have a warrant for that?"

"Of course not."

"Then no." He crossed his arms over his massive chest. "I told you, Captain. I will not break the law for you."

"It's for a good cause."

A stony silence was his only reply.

"Fuck," Marco grumbled. "I bet if I had tits you'd say yes. Or how about long, dark hair and light-purple eyes. Huh? Is that the kind of girl that'd make you agree?"

Cam allowed a small smile. "Not even then."

"Yeah, right."

Marco knew exactly the kind of woman who floated the Chameleon's boat. The second time he had met the Chameleon, he had immediately recognized the strong jawline and piercing stare of Lucian Kilsgaard. Lucian and his wife Amaryllis, who fit the description he had just mentioned to a tee, owned not only one of the swankiest restaurants in the city, but also the most notorious nightclub. The Cavern catered to the darkest desires of its patrons, and Amaryllis controlled the circus with a masterful hand. Marco doubted there was very little the man wouldn't do for his wife.

Only because he suspected that both of the Kilsgaards, and potentially more of their family members, were all gifted with superhuman powers, he didn't press the issue of the man's real identity. He witnessed firsthand what happened when someone crossed the family, and he didn't want to become a stain on the asphalt.

"If it gives you any comfort," Cam said, "the technology Smithwick's using for protection is state of the art. The motion sensors are so sensitive, they pick up the slightest movement. Even when I used my super speed."

"Was that at all of the locations?"

"Ya."

"Fuck again. Looks as if I'll need to figure out an unconventional way to spy on my friend."

"Do not fret, Captain. You will succeed."

"Thanks for the vote of confidence." He secured the envelope and slipped it into the inside pocket of his jacket. With a small sigh, he scrubbed his hand down his face as his mental checklist expanded with the latest information.

"When was the last time you've slept?" Cam asked.

"Can't remember."

The Chameleon regarded him with a tilt of his head. "What happens afterward? After Smithwick is captured, what is next for you?"

What's next? What kind of a question was that?

"I go after the next bad guy."

"And after that?"

"I do it again. That's my job."

Cam sighed. "Is that all that your life is about? Your job? What about a home? A family?"

"I have a home. One I like very much. And I have a sister who sometimes thinks she's my mother. That's plenty of family."

"And what of a woman? A mate? Someone to care for you and for you to care for her?"

"I have a girlfriend." He picked up his coffee cup and pointed to the green logo on the side. "She's even a mermaid. She's there whenever I need her and gives me exactly what I need."

"*Everything* you need, Captain?"

The way he phrased the question sent chills down Marco's spine, much in the same way those similar words had done when Lucian's wife spoke them a few weeks prior. Then he had been chasing a vigilante who had led him to The Cavern. He had needed the man's name, but Amaryllis disagreed, saying the name was what he wanted. She told him he would be back when he was ready to get what he needed. Minutes later he had run into a vision straight from his kinkiest fantasies and hadn't been able to maintain his focus since.

"Women don't fit into a cop's life, especially this cop's life. You of all people should understand that."

"I do." Cam nodded. "All too well. For years I was defined by my position. Nothing mattered except my job and my ability to perform with the utmost perfection. I do not regret any action I took, but I do regret the cost of time I spent away from focusing on my personal life. The time I spent away from family, especially since I will never see them again. I cannot get that back."

"Sorry to hear that," Marco murmured.

The origins of the Kilsgaards and their small familial clan were a deeply guarded secret, and he had spent quite a few hours trying to solve that mystery. The only thing he was able to deduce was they weren't human. Whether they were mutants or, gulp, aliens, he wasn't certain. But he'd witnessed at least three of the members move with a speed and strength that were off the charts. Wherever they were from, it wasn't local.

Cam nodded. "You are a good man, Captain. We—I, I mean I, worry that you may be burning yourself out before you've had the chance to really live. You deserve your happiness."

The slip-up made Marco chuckle. "I'll keep that in mind. Thanks for the intel. I really do appreciate all you've done."

"Let me know if I can be of assistance again." He raised his finger. "And remain within the boundaries of the law."

"Will do, Oprah." He turned to leave. "Say hello to the missus for me."

He looked back over his shoulder with a smirk that slowly faded as he realized he was all alone.

Damn. Just what in the hell was the Chameleon?

With a shake of his head, Marco left the park. Across the street from the park's entrance was the building that housed The Cavern. Pink and blue lights lit up the exterior walls and the block-long line of people waiting to get inside to let loose with their inhibitions. His gaze traveled to the second floor and the rows of false windows. He had a damn good idea what went on behind those walls, and the thought made his head swim and stomach roll even as the blood pooled thick in his cock.

Was she up there, right now? Was there a man at her feet, naked and willing, begging, to do everything she asked of him?

Fuck. He pressed the heels of his hands to his eyes. The female-talk with Cam must have affected him more than he realized. Ever since he had set foot into that blasted nightclub, he'd been plagued with what ifs and maybes. His focus was fractured and now was not the time to deal with distractions.

He was so close to catching Smithwick, he could practically smell the little bald-headed bastard's expensive cologne. Three years of his life were not going to be wasted because he developed a hard-on for a woman who could probably kick his ass and make him enjoy it.

He withdrew a pack of gum from his jacket pocket and pulled out a stick. As he strode down the street, he chomped on that gum as if it were made out of rock and kept his gaze locked on the black SUV parked a block down the road. He approached the car on the passenger side and opened the door.

Cassidy Coulter threw him a smug grin. "The night's still young, Captain. And we're technically off duty. We can go inside for a drink. Maybe catch a show?"

"Shut up, Coulter." Marco slammed the door shut.

The lieutenant had all the looks and charm of a blond surfer-dude who thought of nothing but the next wave, but the man was sharp and caught all the subtle clues that made him an excellent detective. Jesus, how long had he watched Marco stare up at The Cavern with goo-goo eyes and drool running down his chin?

As an occasional attendee of the club, Coulter knew first hand exactly what went on inside those walls. Hell, he'd probably participated in the festivities too. Perhaps even with her.

Marco snapped on his gum and pulled the packet of infor-mation out from his jacket pocket. "Head back to the station. We have work to do."

"What did he bring you?" Coulter asked as he pulled out into traffic.

"Names, some photos, but most importantly, locations. He

found four dugouts in Washington, two of them in the city. And all of them have had their security upgraded to über-high tech levels. Even with his super speed, he was almost caught on their cameras."

"Damn," he whistled. "Makes sense though. If I had a guy with super powers after me, I'd be as paranoid as hell."

Marco grunted in agreement and began to snap photos of the documents with his smartphone.

Smithwick wasn't the only one who was paranoid. The crime boss had his long, evil fingers in a lot of pots and it wouldn't surprise Marco one bit if those grimy digits extended into the police force, especially after the way his team had been called off the case the previous month. It was only after he had presented new evidence, compliments of the Chameleon, and had solved the vigilante case that he had been permitted to resume investigating Smithwick. If there was the slightest chance someone would fuck with his evidence, he was going to keep a backup.

Coulter took a left onto First Avenue. "Sanchez called. ATF wants in on the case."

"I hope Sanchez told them to fuck off. In as nice a way as possible, of course." He added with a grin.

"He did." Coulter chuckled. "We won't be able to hold them off. Asswipe would hand the case off to the feds in two seconds if he had the opportunity."

"Well, they can wait until I'm done. I am not going to risk one of them screwing up and destroying everything I've worked on. Anyway, I don't think Smithwick will be doing business for much longer. Damn, this is good shit." He snapped another photo and shook his head. "If only Cam wasn't such a goddamn choir boy. This case would be closed."

Coulter hummed in agreement. "So…" he said a few blocks down the road. "Did he do anything cool?"

"Did who do what?"

"You know. The Chameleon. During your meeting. Did he run really fast or pick up a car with his bare hands?"

He looked at his lieutenant as if he had smoked crack. "Why the hell would he pick up a car for no reason? And where would he find one in the middle of the park?"

"Because he can. I don't get to attend your secret meetings, and the only time I've seen him use his super powers was when we almost captured Smithwick last year, and then I was too busy dodging bullets to see anything."

Marco shook his head as he returned the documents to their envelope then slid them inside his jacket pocket. "Our boy doesn't roll like that. He's not a show-off."

"Man, wouldn't it be cool to have super powers?"

"I don't know." He recalled the haunted look in Lucian's eyes when he talked about his family. "I think sometimes that power is a burden."

"Says those that have it to those who don't."

"True that. True that." A figure to his right caught his attention. "Hold up, Coulter. Pull over."

Well what did we have here?

They had left the swankier part of town and were traveling through the darker, more sinister neighborhood that consisted of the waterfront area and shipyard. Dive-bar after dive-bar lined both sides of the street, offering a refuge for those looking to get wasted or for human companionship, or both if one had enough cash.

Under the tattered awning of a pizzeria stood a tall, lanky man with shoulder-length brown hair. He wore the typical northwest uniform of a flannel shirt and torn jeans. In the light of the lone street lamp, his fancy gold watch flashed with his arm movements as he chatted up a small group of men, and his cherry-red Doc Martens shined with a high-gloss.

Son of a bitch. Trevor Konkle was out on the streets.

The last time Marco had seen the petty crook was during his arraignment for his part in the kidnapping of Fiona Corrione the year before. At the time, she was the girlfriend of Lucian's cousin Dhavin who Marco suspected had been the bearer of the Chameleon mask at the time. The kidnapping had been arranged by Smithwick to use as leverage against the superhero who was interfering in his drug-dealing business. Since she had been taken into the city, Marco and his team had been called in to facilitate her rescue. The mission culminated in an eye-opening turn of events that had him witness the power of the Chameleon and his first look at the crime lord, who until then had been hidden behind the logos of dummy corporations and hired thugs.

Smithwick might have slipped through his fingers that night, but the war was long from over. And now one of his associates was strolling through town, acting as if he were king of the world.

"Hey," said Coulter as he followed Marco's line of sight. "Isn't that Trevor Konkle? I thought he was serving a nickel for the Corrione kidnapping."

"He was." Marco pulled out the laptop located underneath the dash and logged into the police database. "Look at that. Time off for good behavior. He was released last Wednesday."

"How thoughtful of parole to let us know."

Marco grunted in agreement. "Wait here. I'm going to congratulate our friend and see what he's up to."

"I don't know, Cap. Konkle wasn't the brightest bulb on the chandelier, and he's looking way too cocky for a man who was involved in that clusterfuck last year. Most of Smithwick's men who were involved that night are either dead or have gone missing."

"All the more reason to have a chat. He must have been given some encouragement to show his face."

"Or he really is as stupid as we thought he was."

Marco wouldn't say that. The man had kept his trap shut during the entire trial, and Smithwick valued loyalty.

"I know that you know that you can't bother the man without probable cause."

"I'm not going to question him. I'm just going to say hello." Marco stuck his gum in a stray piece of paper and dropped it in the cup holder, then flashed his lieutenant a big smile. "And ask him what his plans are for the future."

"Captain."

Despite Coulter's protests, Marco jumped out of the car and maintained a respectful distance as he followed Konkle down the street. The parolee nodded to those he passed, handing out what looked like a business card to anyone who would take it. The action reminded Marco of the men who stood on the sidewalk in Vegas and handed out calling cards for "strippers."

As they approached the corner, Konkle turned to glance over his shoulder before he stepped off the curb. He caught Marco's gaze and his eyes widened in shock for several seconds, then he took off as if he were trying out for the Olympic sprinting team.

"Here we go," Marco grumbled, then gave chase without a second thought.

Down the street and through the back alleys they ran, and damn, the boy could fly, keeping at least a block or two between them. Marco was in no way a fitness slouch, but this definitely was not his normal workout on the treadmill.

Konkle took a right between two phó restaurants and ran out into the middle of the street. The wail of screeching tires made him jump back as a SUV stopped scant inches from taking him out at the knees. Coulter jumped out from the driver's side, and Konkle turned, ducking into the alley next to the x-rated movie theater.

Marco kept right on his heels, following him into the shadowed enclave only to draw up short as he found the dead-end road empty. He tried to slow his breathing to be able to hear for any telltale sounds and pressed his palm against the fire raging behind his sternum.

There. A squeak from overhead. Marco looked up and spotted Konkle's red Doc Martens disappearing over the roof line at the top of the fire escape.

Marco immediately went after him and climbed up the metal ladder. He paused before his head cleared the last rung at the top of the third story. Ever so slowly, he peeked over the one-foot-tall retaining wall. After several tense seconds, he completed the ascent.

The roof was blocked off to the left and before him by neighboring buildings. Their fire escapes were empty and all the windows closed up tight. Unless the kid had sprouted wings and knew how to fly, he had to be close by.

Ten-foot-tall neon letters ran across the length of the roof like Las Vegas showgirls. Marco laid his hand on his gun and crept closer to the letters. From the corner of his eye he saw a shadow come at him and jumped back as an icy burn erupted across his chest.

Konkle jumped from his position behind the closest letter with blade in hand and swung his arm. The knife glinted in the light like a pink wand as he feinted and slashed through the air like a deranged wizard.

"Fuck," Marco spat as a back-handed swish caught him again but this time in the forearm. "Knock it off. I just want to talk to you."

"Fuck off," Konkle screeched and swung again.

Marco blocked the attack, latching on to Konkle's wrist as he turned his body into the slighter man's torso. Konkle responded by going batshit crazy, flailing and jerking his limbs in a thousand directions. The only defensive move the academy taught to fend off this style of fighting was to get low and avoid being stabbed in a critical location.

Marco hooked his ankle around Konkle's leg and kicked, knocking them both to the asphalt. Konkle landed first with a loud grunt. The knife skittered to the side with a ting before he twisted, rolling them over and over across the sticky blackness. The short lip of the roof scraped up Marco's back as he went airborne over the side. Only his grip on Konkle's lapels kept him from tumbling the three stories to the street below.

The tips of his shoes scraped against the brick as he tried to scramble up the side while staring into Konkle's wild eyes. The man's beer-scented breath washed over his face in hot, misty puffs that made his eyes water. Above the sound of their ragged breathing he heard the sickening sound of seams popping.

"No, no, no, no," Marco groaned as the shirt gave way.

His gaze zoomed in on the moon, hanging high in the sky like a giant light bulb that grew smaller and smaller as he fell. He threw out his arms, clutching at nothing but air until his hand hit the ladder to the fire escape. His fingers curled around a bar, slowing his descent until gravity bitch-slapped his body mass, causing his grip to slip as if his hands were slathered in butter. The slight reprieve slowed his momentum down just enough so that when he hit the roof of Coulter's SUV, the pain that radiated up his legs only made him scream three soul-wrenching curses as opposed to a million. His knees buckled and he tumbled down the windshield, across the hood then down to the wet pavement with a solid thwack to the head for good measure.

Flashing lights sparked in his vision, making it appear as if the stars were winking at him in appreciation for putting on a dazzling show.

"Captain," Coulter's muffled shout sounded as if his head were stuffed inside a pillow. "Captain, speak to me."

"Fuuuuck," he might have said. At least, that's the shape he felt his lips make.

"Stay still, Cap. Don't move anything."

Sure. No problem. At the moment he didn't think he could even make his eyelids blink.

Since memories from his past weren't flashing before his eyes, he figured he wasn't dying. And least yet. From the neck down to his feet, he felt as if he were submerged in a vat of stick pins, and his vision blurred in an out like a camera lens trying to focus.

Shit. Was he paralyzed? Was he going to spend the rest of his life as a lump of flesh in a bed? Was Smithwick going to walk as he lost his ability to do so?

Fuck that. Even if he had to drag his ass across the ground by his teeth, he was going to take that rat bastard down, and that shit-head Trevor, too.

Over the pounding in his head, he heard the wail of sirens, and the flashing lights turned from yellow to red.

"Jesus, Coulter," he slurred. "You called in the goddamn hose draggers? Do me a favor, run the car over me. I don't want them to see me like this."

"You fell off a roof," he shouted. "Of course I called them. Stop moving. Put your arms down. You might make things worse."

His limbs functioned? Hey. Great.

A dark shadow fell across him. "Lieutenant, what'da we have?"

"Nothing," Marco growled. "I'm good."

"That's why there's so much blood, right, Cap?"

Blood? Ah fuck.

"Coulter," he gasped as his vision dimmed. He battled against the need to close his eyes. Death was not going to take him without a fight. He had too much unfinished business. Too many people to protect. Which reminded him… "Coulter."

"Yeah, Cap?"

"If I—if something happens. My house. Bedroom closet. Black box. Blow it up before my sister finds it."

"Anything good in there?"

"Does the trick."

And with his thoughts lingering on his pitiful porn collection, the darkness sucked him under.

CHAPTER TWO

M ARCO LIFTED HIS eyelids, which felt as if they were stuck together with glue, and instantly regretted the action. Damn it. It wasn't like him to leave the blinds open to the morning sun.

Wait a minute. Those weren't his blinds. And this wasn't his bedroom.

"Sorry, Cap. I'll get the light." A blurry blob that resembled Coulter crossed to the window and lowered the blinds.

"Where am I?" he croaked.

"The hospital. Don't you remember last night?"

Last night... "Fucking Konkle."

"You do remember," Coulter exclaimed in delight.

Yeah, he did. Well, most of it anyway. The biggest standout was the inability to feel his limbs.

Well, he was definitely feeling something now, if one counted the sensation of having their entire body feel as if they'd been starched and pressed to death. Man, an eighteen-year-old on Viagra never felt this stiff. However, if he was able to feel discomfort, that must mean he wasn't severely jacked-up. Right? Dear Lord, let that be right.

Fear threatened to choke him as he drew in a breath and focused on his hands tucked under the thin blanket. He concentrated on wiggling his fingers and almost shouted for joy when he felt the over-bleached sheet scratch against his palm.

He carefully tested the muscles of his back and flexed each section all the way down his legs to his toes. Despite the fact that his mouth felt as if he'd been sucking on cotton, his head swam and there was a ringing in his ears, watching the fabric at the foot of the bed roll with the movement of his feet more than made up for the hit by a shit-ton of bricks sensation.

"Captain DeWinter. I have questions for you."

And just like that, all his goodwill went right into the crapper.

"Commander," Marco addressed the diminutive man who came to stand to the right of his bed. "You came to see me? I didn't know you cared."

The twitch of his mustached mouth suggested that the statement was correct. "When one of my officers is injured on the job, I care very much."

Of course, L&I took precedence over common decency and care for your fellow man.

The commander adjusted the lapels of his suit jacket as he puffed out his chest. Here it comes. "Captain, explain to me how you came to be in this condition."

Sure. He was going to divulge all the details like a choir boy confessing his sins in church. Even if he did remember them all.

"Honestly, Commander, it's all a little hazy. I'm sure Coulter filled you in on what happened."

"Lieutenant Coulter told me his version. I want to hear yours."

"Well…" he didn't dare look to Coulter for assistance, especially when the truth was there had been very little, okay, absolutely no reason to have given chase in the first place. He wasn't ashamed to admit to himself that it had only been his pride and overzealousness that had driven him up to the roof. An offense the commander wouldn't hesitate to use to rip him a new asshole. Coulter was good at keeping his mouth shut, but what scenario had the lieutenant come up with?

"Well, what?" the commander snapped.

"I'm trying to remember," he growled. "These drugs they have me on make it hard to think. I, uh, we, were driving down First and I spotted a known drug dealer roaming the street and appearing as if he was off to make a sale. I followed in order to observe his activities better, and the second he saw me, he ran."

"Why did you pursue him?"

"He dropped a dime bag as he ran."

"Drugs were not found at the scene, nor on your person. Did you leave it on the street?"

"I picked it up on the run. It was in my pocket. He must have stolen it back. I remember him coming at me with a knife."

"Was this before or after you followed him onto the roof?"

"Roof?" He blinked with as much innocence as a guy like him could muster. "I don't remember a roof."

The commander's eyes rounded. "You don't remember falling three stories?"

"Is that what happened? No wonder I feel like shit."

"Captain—"

"Excuse me. Why are you causing my patient distress?"

The sultry voice drew Marco's gaze to the door. What little energy he had evaporated like water on a hot griddle as heat thickened his blood and raised his temperature.

Dr. Jasmine Jovanovich appeared every inch like the professional she was with her long, brown hair plaited down her back and a set of green scrubs and white lab coat hiding her killer curves. But in his mind's eye Marco envisioned her looking as she had the last time he had seen her walking the halls of The Cavern. Then she had been dressed all in black from her neck to her toes. A corset had cinched in her waist, emphasizing her plumped up breasts that had been covered in a sheer mesh fabric that had done nothing to hide her pretty nipples.

"Distress?" The commander arched an imperious brow. "The captain is not distressed. Are you, Captain?"

Marco blinked the kinky vision away and subtly shifted his hands underneath the blanket to cover his growing erection. "Nope. Not at all."

Dr. Jovanovich strode into the room with a purpose and grace that immediately put Marco on edge. Her eyes danced with amusement as they narrowed. The woman was up to something.

"And you are?" she asked the commander.

"I am Commander Asante," he answered with an extra little shimmy to his shoulders. Did he actually pop up on tip-toe to appear taller?

"Lovely to meet you, sir. I'm Dr. Jovanovich. Now if you will excuse us, I need to examine my patient. You may wait out in the lobby."

"I'll be fine right here, Doctor. Go right ahead."

"No."

It was a simple word, softly spoken, yet Asante started as if she had shouted at the top of her lungs.

"No?" he sputtered. "What do you mean no?"

"You may wait in the lobby or anywhere else you please. Not here."

"But he's my officer."

"And he's my patient."

Ooo, Marco liked the touch of possessiveness in her voice when she said the word "my." He liked it a lot.

Dr. Jovanovich lifted her chin. "Commander Asante, I understand that he is your employee and was injured while on the job, but I will be giving Captain DeWinter a thorough examination, and I cannot have you hovering over my shoulder. When I have more definitive answers to his condition, I will inform you immediately. I am sure you understand my need for space, Commander Asante."

Each time she said his name, a tick flinched near the commander's left eye and his hands fluttered by his sides. The man swallowed hard with a nod. "Yes, ma'am."

Marco's eyes widened and his cock leapt beneath his palm. He risked a quick glance around and breathed a slight sigh of relief that he wasn't hooked up to a monitor that would reveal his accelerated heart rate. Damn, the woman was sexy when she put the commander in his place in that smooth-as-butter tone of voice. Even Coulter had the look of a besotted man with his softened smile.

She fluttered her lashes. "Leave now, Commander."

"Yes. Yes." He walked out of the room without a backward glance.

She turned that superior stare toward Coulter who jumped. "Oh, um, I'll be right outside if you need me, Cap."

Coulter's departure was at a more leisurely pace than the commander's. When the door swung shut, the doctor sighed and turned toward him with a satisfied smile. "Was that the Commander Asswipe I hear you guys talk about?"

"Yeah." He chuckled then fell silent as she stepped closer. Right. Examination. Just how thorough was this examination going to be? "So, Doc. How you doing?"

Fuck, he winced. Could that sound even more like a pick-up line?

Her smile widened. "Better than you at the moment, I'd say. Chasing criminals up on roof tops. I thought your last name was DeWinter, not America."

"I'm just doing my best to protect the public. I live to serve."

The soft hitch of her breath sent another lick of heat to his groin. The sound was so slight, but he heard it, saw the way her body stilled for the space of a heartbeat at his choice of words.

Part of him wanted to stammer out a retraction, but he held his tongue. He did live to serve and had given his life to his community. However lately the only person he wanted to serve was her, and he was more than aware of what it took to satisfy the good doctor.

The idea was ridiculous, for certain. He was a man. A cop. An alpha who was comfortable telling others what to do. But for the last month, in the dark of night when he wasn't staring at police work until his eyes crossed, his imagination began to spin fantasies of what it would be like to serve Mistress Jasmina. To kneel at her feet, naked, braced for her command and to follow as she wished.

Between chasing Smithwick and entertaining lascivious thoughts of Dr. Jovanovich, his mind had been going nonstop. It was a wonder he hadn't dropped from sheer exhaustion.

"Well." She tapped her pen against the clipboard before setting it on the side-table, breaking the spell of possibility her little catch of breath had evoked. She reached toward the control panel on the bed and raised the back to a sitting position. "Let's begin. The lacerations you sustained on your chest and arm are superficial and only required a few stitches. When I admitted you last night, your partner said you landed feet first on the roof of his car before tumbling to the ground."

"You were here last night?" he interrupted.

"You don't remember?"

"Obviously not."

Her brow furrowed as she answered, "Yes, I was here last night. If I want to keep my job, I do have to show up to work."

"Oh. I—uh. I thought you might have been out last night. You know." He lowered his voice. "Out."

She dropped her gaze and her tongue flicked out to wet her lips. "I'm in the middle of an eighteen-hour shift."

The knowledge that she had been at the hospital and not playing at The Cavern perked him up like a shot of caffeine. "That's a long day. You look great. Fresh. Pretty, like you're just starting your day. What's your secret?"

Her lips twitched as she fought a grin. "Frequent moments of amusement from charmers such as yourself. As I was saying, we took x-rays of both legs and your hips, and fortunately for you, nothing is broken. I'm going to check your ankles and feet again. Now that the pain medication has burned off some, I want to see how you're really feeling. Please place your hands on top of the blanket."

"What?" his voice cracked with alarm. "Why?"

"I have my reasons. Place them on top of the blanket. Please." The words were polite, but her tone suggested he'd better do as she said or else she'd find a way to make him.

He gulped hard and carefully slid his hands out from beneath the blanket, taking care to make sure his erection was properly hidden.

"Thank you," she murmured then moved to the foot of the bed.

She pulled the bedding back to expose the lower half of his legs. Bruises marked his skin, and his ankles appeared to be twice the normal size. Her fingers were gentle as she prodded the tissue around one foot.

"Do your legs ache?" she asked.

Nooo, it wasn't his legs that were aching at the moment. "No. Not really," he choked out.

"Any pain when I do this?" She pressed against his right ankle, making him wince but he forced the sensation away.

"Nope."

"What about this?"

Agh! "Nope."

"By the way your fingers are flinching, I beg to differ. Stop trying to be a tough guy. I can't determine the extent of damage if you are not being truthful with me. Do you want to leave this hospital tonight or next week?"

Was she going to be around the entire time? He mentally kicked his ass. "Sorry, Doc. I thought you'd be impressed by a guy who isn't a wimp."

"I'm impressed by a man who can follow orders."

"I've noticed that," he muttered before conceding, "The second time you pressed hurt worse than the first."

"Thank you." She rewarded him with a caress up his shin then continued asking him questions as she smoothed her hands over his feet, tickling in places and digging in deep with her thumbs in others as she gauged the extent of his injuries.

The mixture of pleasure and pain sent a heat through his body that soon had sweat beading across his forehead. It took all his efforts to keep his hips still and not rub his hard-on against the bedding for some measure of relief. It didn't help matters that as she bent over, the front of her scrubs gaped just enough he was able to see the top of the lacy white bra cupping her full breasts. With each move of her body he silently prayed the entire garment would miraculously melt away and reveal all her creamy skin to his gaze.

"Good." She stood upright and tugged the blanket back into the place. The action tightened the bedding over his lap, revealing the outline of his erection.

As she circled the bed, he tried to press his hips as deep into the mattress as possible to minimize the pup tent and prayed she didn't notice.

"I'm going to check your lacerations now."

He couldn't keep his eyes off her face as she peeled away the bandage on his arm. How many times in the past had he spoken to Dr. Jovanovich when he had come to question a victim or suspect for one of his cases? Not once had he stopped to notice just how beautiful she was. Details of his job had made him only see the professional, cut-to-the-chase woman who neither stood out nor faded into the background.

Funny how a chance meeting in the dark highlighted the woman underneath the green scrubs. The bit of sunshine that filtered through the drawn blinds highlighted the auburn shades in her brunette braid and matched the color of her eyes. The tinge of pink blush on her cheeks complimented her olive complexion and the roundness of her features. When she was in full concentration mode, her lips softened into plump little pillows he want to stroke with the tip of his tongue. Damn. Why hadn't he noticed her sooner? He could have…

What? He could have asked her out? Fit time with her into his schedule while he was hunting Smithwick? Did a woman with her tastes even engage in an activity as mundane as dating?

Dr. Jovanovich was so out of his league. His past experiences with women were either the occasional casual fling, never lasting more than a few dates, or a one-night stand here and there. And then there were the years spent pining for a woman who had only looked at him as a friend. Brett Briggs's marriage to Lucian Kilsgaard's brother effectively ended all dreams of her coming back to the city and finding a place in his arms. Once he had come to terms with that reality, the only time the thought of female companionship crossed his mind was when he was horny, and his hand was sufficient enough to scratch that itch.

Now here stood the doc. A woman who he was certain carried a PhD in male/female relationships. A woman who could chew him up and spit him out and make him ask for more His idea of wild-crazy-sexy probably didn't rate a raised eyebrow on her Richter scale.

But he wanted to find out. He wanted to sample a tiny morsel of what he knew Mistress Jasmina could provide almost as badly as he wanted to see Smithwick behind bars.

The flutter of her fingers as she worked loose the bandage across his chest made him bite back a moan of pleasure. Only the sight of the red slash running from the center of his sternum to the edge of his left nipple tampered his desire.

"Looking good," she murmured. "An inch deeper, the story would have been much different. You were lucky. Many times over."

"Thanks," he mumbled.

The examination continued with a check of his vitals and a glance into his eyes with a bright light. She nodded in response to whatever she saw, then reached out, spearing her fingers into his hair. With the same gentle touch she used with his feet, she rubbed and pressed all over his scalp. With the bare curve of her neck mere inches away, the clean scent of her skin mixed with the mellow sensation of her hands made his blood hum in his veins. He detected no other perfumes or artificial scents, just pure Jasmine.

He felt his lips part and he wanted to lick along the ridge of her collarbone. He wanted to sink his teeth into the plump pillow of her bare earlobe, just to hear that quiet little gasp of air again.

She hit a sore spot on his scalp and he hissed. She moved her touch lower to press against the stiff muscles at the base of his skull and this time he could not contain a groan of pleasure. The woman was killing him. "You've got magic fingers there, Doc. I think you missed your calling as a masseuse."

To his disappointment, she stepped back with a tiny smile

flirting on her lips. "Your physical injuries will heal just fine. What I'm mostly concerned about is what's going on with your brain."

"Are you questioning my mental capacity? Gee, thanks, Doc."

"Maybe." He loved the way her eyes lit up with her amusement. "In all seriousness, head trauma is not something I take lightly. I don't know how hard, or on what exactly, you might have hit your head when you fell. You could have a brain bleed or swelling I can't detect with a regular exam. As a precaution I'm going to have a CT scan performed. If all looks well, you can be released this evening."

For the first time since he woke he became concerned. "If? I don't like the sound of that word. What happens if *if* doesn't look well?"

"We'll cross that bridge when we get to it. My gut tells me all is well, but I want to be certain. It's my job to be thorough, Captain DeWinter."

"Marco. Please call me Marco." *And preferably in a throaty moan as you ride my cock.*

He shoved the image aside. "I get it, Doc. I do. You're good at your job. So if the x-ray of my head looks good, I can walk out tonight?"

"Not exactly. To prevent further injury, you need to keep off your feet for a week."

"A week?" He struggled to sit up. "Sorry, Doc, but I have to work. I'm just as dedicated to my job as you are to yours."

She pushed against his chest, forcing him back down. "I can see by your injuries that you are dedicated, but you have to allow your ankles to heal. If they give out, you risk greater injury to the rest of your body. Including your thick skull. One week. I'll tell your commander two knowing full well you both will dismiss my orders. But if I see you back in the ER because you broke your ankle or cracked your head open, I'll tie you to the bed myself."

"Is that a promise?" he asked, and this time he didn't hide the blatant rasp of desire that deepened his voice at the mention of her binding him in any fashion.

To her credit, she didn't blush or stammer. Instead she held his gaze with the same calculating look on her face she had when he had spotted her in The Cavern the month before. Right before she dug her nails into his side and threatened him bodily harm if he breathed a word about her alter-ego.

"Do not test me. Captain." She collected her clipboard and began writing notations across the pages. "A nurse will be in shortly to prepare you for imaging. After the scan, we'll send you something to eat. Lucky for you, it's green Jell-O today. I'm also going to write you a prescription for Lisinopril."

"What's that for?"

"Your high blood pressure."

"I have high blood pressure?"

Her snort of laughter was so charming. "Why am I not surprised? It's one-sixty over a hundred, and it's held steady since you've arrived."

"I take it that's not good?"

"Only if you want to suffer from a stroke. With a change in diet, medication and a decrease in stress, you should be able to manage it."

"Decrease my stress? Fat chance. You did see who my supervisor is. There's a better chance that I will actually take the entire week off like you want."

"Captain." She folded her arms across her chest and nailed him with a stare that struck him right in his overworked heart. "I hate to break it to you, but you are not invincible. You might have survived a three-story fall today. Do not make the mistake of thinking you will survive the next. You're a grown man who does not need a lecture, so instead I will make a wish for you. I hope over the next few days you'll take a moment to put some priorities in order. Despite being an asshole on occasion, you're a good guy."

He swallowed past the lump that had formed in his throat. "Would you miss me, if I was gone from this world?"

After several slow blinks her lips twitched. Ah, there it was. That tiny hint of a smile that warmed her eyes. "Of course. You bring me some of my most interesting patients. But I think there is someone who will miss you more. You've had a visitor pacing the floor for the last hour."

A visitor? "Who?"

She went to the door and waved to whoever was waiting in the hall. A young woman came barreling through the doorway. Dark shadows made the red rimming her eyes appear even more harsh, and sections of black hair spilled from her ponytail in a tangled mess. She wore her waitress uniform from the diner, the apron still tied around her hips, confirming that she had raced to the hospital in the middle of her morning shift. Hours of work missed that Marco knew she couldn't afford.

Ah fuck. Abby. He closed his eyes on a groan. "I'm sorry."

"You should be, you asshole." His baby sister drew up short by the side of the bed. Anger burned across her cheeks in red patches and her nostrils flared as her gaze took in his condition. She glanced back at the doctor. "Are you sure he'll live?"

The doc shrugged. "For now."

"Good." Abby punched him in the biceps.

"Ow," he hollered. "Careful. I'm tender."

"I'll tender you." She slapped him again. "What the fuck were you thinking?"

"Language. Please." He glanced over his sister's shoulder to see Dr. Jovanovich ease out of the room with her little smile. "I was doing my job."

"Yeah, right. Cassidy told me everything. You almost died chasing after one of Smithwick's men. And a lackey at that."

"But I didn't die."

"You could have." She flopped down on the mattress near his hip. "Marco, you have to stop. It's been three years. Smithwick has money and men and weapons, and you only have the stupid city police force."

"And Coulter, and the rest of my team."

"Cassidy isn't enough."

"Well they're all I've got," he growled then released a weary sigh. "You know I have to finish this, Abs."

"Why does it have to be you?"

"Because I'm the best. And I won't stop until he's caught." He reached out and pushed a lock of her hair behind her ear.

"It won't bring them back, you know," she whispered in a small voice as her dark eyes grew watery. "And I don't want you to join them."

Along Abby's forearms she carried the scars of the auto accident that almost took her life. She refused to cover them up, answering any who questioned her with stark honesty that they were the direct result of drugs and stupidity. The drug use was compliments of her boyfriend. The stupidity part she claimed for choosing to stand by him even when he made the shift from user to seller. And when he hadn't sold enough to satisfy Smithwick's henchmen, they had forced the car she had been riding in into a highway barrier at seventy-five miles an hour. Of the five people in the car, only Abby and her best friend's boyfriend walked out alive. Or at least Abby had. The boy would be confined to a wheelchair for the rest of his life.

His little sister had gone from a starry-eyed young woman to a jaded adult in the blink of an eye. It was the investigation of the crash that led the police to their first solid lead to the mastermind behind the rising drug scene in the city. And it was then that Marco vowed to personally stop the man who dared to hurt not only his family, but also the families of others who suffered under Smithwick's manipulations.

Marco never declared himself a saint, or the self-appointed savior of the city, but he never backed away from a challenge. That wasn't going to change now.

"I know it won't bring them back, Abby. But it's my job to protect this city the best way I can. I can't stop when I'm so close to nailing him."

She sniffed. "You've been saying that for over a year."

"It's true."

"Damn straight it's true," Coulter said as he entered the room. "I heard the doc tell Asante that you're out for two weeks. That sucks."

"That's what she said. She knows that's not going to happen."

"Marco," his sister chided.

"I said I'd try, but the woman's smart. She understands the game."

"And she's hot too," Coulter added. "Why have I never noticed that before? And she looks familiar."

No way was Marco going to say where Coulter would have seen her. "Because we've been to the ER on other cases many times before. So you never told me what happened with Konkle after I fell."

Coulter chuckled and clapped his hands together. "Physically, he got away, however, you tore his shirt when you fell. The section that came down with you had his cellphone in the front pocket."

"Yes," Marco hissed. "Tell me there was something good in it."

"We're working on it." He slid a meaningful glance at Abby. "Benny's trying to download as much information as possible before service is cancelled. What he's found so far looks good."

"I want a full report immediately."

"No," Abby all but shouted. "No work. Dr. Jo told you to rest. I heard that much from standing outside the door."

"Dr. Jo?"

She nodded. "She said I could call her that. I like her. She was the only person who would answer my questions and not treat me like a child."

"Abby—"

"No. You're going to heal and become stronger. And you're going to remember that life isn't all about work. When I was hurt, you made me get off my ass and reconnect with the world. Now it's your turn. You owe me."

He started to scoff, but when he saw the fear and worry in her eyes, his chest caved in and grew hollow. That look reminded him so much of their mother, and he had certainly given her enough cause to worry about his welfare throughout his wild youth. Cancer took their mother before he graduated from college, and their father had moved to Arizona unable to remain in the home they had shared. His sister was really the only family he had left.

"I will stay off my feet for a few days," he conceded as he reached for Abby's hand. "But I have to stay in contact with my team. I'll go insane not knowing what's going on."

"Fine. And I'll be with you the entire time to help you out around the house."

"You don't have to do that. I know you have work to get to."

"We shall see." For the first time since she burst through the door, she smiled. "It'll be fun. Maybe we'll find you a hobby."

The door opened and Dr. Jovanovich stepped in, followed by an orderly. "Ready to get your head examined, Captain?"

Hmm. Doc's question might be more accurate than the joke she intended. Not only was he willing to take time away from work, he also had an idea of how he could best occupy his thoughts during his "vacation."

He felt his lips stretch into a predatory grin. "I am putty in your hands, Doc."

CHAPTER THREE

J ASMINE RAN HER finger over the label on the medical folder and shook her head. Marco DeWinter. The man had more charm than one person had any right to. With the touch of gray in his black hair, square jaw and slim build, he looked like James Bond, but he dressed like a college English professor. A sexy combination in her book. He had that rare ability to calm the most frantic person one moment and put a major smack-down on another the next, all while wearing a smile the entire time. Whenever she saw him, he was always cool and in control.

Well, almost every time.

Laughter bubbled in her belly as she recalled the look on his face when he had stumbled upon her at The Cavern. Of course she had been equally mortified at being found out at her favorite hangout. Her nights spent as a dominatrix were not something she announced to the general public. If her family discovered her secret, the term "freak out" would be a gross understatement. As for her work colleagues, the frat-boy mentality was not something she wanted turned in her direction. To the other doctors, she was a void. She came, did her job and left with a minimum of fuss. That was why the nurses loved her. She didn't question their ability and they didn't question hers.

Once the shock of being discovered had faded, she had enjoyed needling the captain. For all he had seen as a cop in the big city, his bug-eyed expression conveyed just how much her appearance had stunned him. As well as intrigued him. The hard-on he had sprouted both that night and when she had examined him, made no mistake of his interest.

Poor man. His innuendos might suggest he was willing to play her game, but he hadn't a clue what it meant to be truly submissive. However the battle to win his compliance was bound to be epic. Men like DeWinter never relinquished total control. He had a single-minded focus on his job, blinding him to everything else in existence. That type of focus, while admirable, did not lend itself to the giving up control to another.

In the fifteen years she had been engaged in the lifestyle, she'd met her fair share of men who talked a good game but changed their tune after the first few encounters. She had quickly grown tired of men using her to itch their kinky scratch and then wanting to turn the tables and show the "little woman" who was boss. Experience had made her picky about whom she touched and who was allowed to touch her. It was going to take more than a killer grin and a verbal promise to obey to earn her respect in the playroom.

Pity though. He was quite hunky.

She handed off the good captain's file to the admin, then retrieved two walking casts from the supply closet before heading toward to his room to see him off. After another twenty-four hours with no change in his health, the captain was free to go home.

Fortunately for DeWinter, his sister was more than ready to force him into resting for at least a night or two, and Jasmine was not above encouraging the girl to be more demanding in the execution of her orders. He was a harbinger of all the signs of a man about to hit the wall. Stroke, heart disease, mental exhaustion. Whether he appreciated it or not, his sister's bullying might just save his life.

The door to his room was closed and she knocked to announce her arrival. The deep-voiced reply to enter sent a smattering of goosebumps up her arms. She'd have to be dead not to appreciate the sexy huskiness in the tone.

She cracked open the door to see him sitting on the edge of the bed, buttoning up his shirt. The edges of the white button-down framed the bandage that stretched across his chest. Around the gauze and down his belly lay a soft pelt of dark hair. She would have been be surprised if the captain engaged in the habit of manscaping. Most of the men she saw in the club were waxed or shaved to baby-soft perfection. She had no preference either way. Sensual torture could be administered just the same whether on bare skin or with a little fur.

"Oh, hey, Doc." He interrupted her daydream of running her fingers through his chest hair. She really needed to keep her focus. "I thought you were my sister."

"She went to bring her car closer to the entrance."

"And probably planning diabolical ideas about how to get me to stay off my feet. I saw how she hung on to your every word."

"She's a smart girl. And she loves you."

He emitted a disgruntled harrumph, but his eyes sparkled with reciprocal affection. He nodded to the boots in her hands. "What are those?"

She smiled and set them on the bed by his hip. He had showered since she delivered the good news of his positive CT scan, and the clean scent of his soap cut through the antiseptic smell of the hospital room in the most pleasant way. If they were anywhere else, she'd take the risk and lean over to inhale the delicious scent right from his warm skin followed by a tongue bath over the pulse point on his neck. Talk about giving a new meaning to the term "bedside manner."

Focus. Focus.

"These are walking casts. I know you're going to pitch a fit about being wheeled out in a chair, with these babies on, you'll have a good, showy excuse for why you can't walk out of here on your own. You can take them off once you get home."

"What makes you think I'm going to pitch a fit?"

She raised her brow.

"I may politely disobey your request, but I don't pitch fits."

"Right. Just sit tight. I'll strap them on for you." She rolled a stool over to begin her work. "If you'd like, I can wrap your head in bandages and put your arm in a sling. Make you look really heroic."

The contemplative look on his face made her smile. He sighed and shook his head. "Nah. Don't want to go for overkill."

Through the fabric of his pants, his calf muscle bunched against her palm as she positioned the cast into place. From beneath her lashes, she studied the way the denim of his jeans fit around his thighs. The captain had more of a runner's build than a body builder's. He was lean and toned in all the right places, but not what one would call ripped. More like The Flash than The Incredible Hulk, at least from what she remembered from her brother's comic book collection.

What she liked best about his body was how warm he was to the touch. He radiated heat like a furnace. When she had reached the twenty-sixth hour of her shift in the middle of the night and the thermostat had been turned down low, she had been half tempted to climb into the bed beside him for heat.

Sigh... He really was nicely put together.

"So. Doc..." his voice trailed off.

Her breath caught as tingles tripped across her neck in warning. Had she been caught admiring his physique?

"Do you have plans this week?"

A grin tugged at her lips. Was he fishing for information about her visits to The Cavern? "Nothing out of the ordinary."

"Oh." His free foot swung to and fro. "Would you like to join me for dinner one night?"

The request brought her upright. Her eyelids fluttered with her confusion. "Dinner?"

"Yeah. Dinner."

She narrowed her eyes. "Are you asking me on a date?"

"Uh." A flush of pink raced up his neck. "Yeah."

Oh, Lord. "I don't date patients."

"Well…then it's a good thing I'm not your patient. You're not my regular doctor. It was only timing that had you on duty and available when I came in."

"I don't date," she said and tightened the last strap of the boot with a little extra force to make her point.

"Play then?"

Her breath caught at his choice of words. "What?"

"Isn't that what you call it in the club? Play?"

Whoa.

Every molecule in her body froze, except for her heart that pounded like a bass drum in a marching band. Was he seriously suggesting what she thought he was?

As slowly as ice forms on a lake in winter, she pushed herself up into a standing position. With him sitting on the bed, they were now at about the same height. It didn't put her in the most powerful position, but at least he no longer towered over her.

"What are you saying, Captain?"

His Adam's apple bobbed and he swayed in his seat. "I'm asking you if you want to play. With me."

Intrigued wasn't quite the word to describe how she felt hearing his stuttered statement. The man actually had the balls to ask her to dominate him in her place of work. He was either brave, cocky or stupid.

She had to admit, if only to herself, the idea did have a certain appeal. But so did racing Ferraris down I-90. The speed, the danger, the rush of pushing the envelope were what made life worth living. Just as the fiery crash into the mountainside ended it just as fast.

Wait a minute. Why was she even taking a second to think about his request? She doubted the captain knew what he was asking of her. If he thought she was one of those so called Doms who engaged in one-and-done encounters, or got off on causing pain and humiliating others because of their own selfish need to make themselves look stronger, disappointment was all he was going to get. She wasn't a bully.

She also wasn't a Dom who was looking for a slave. Work, family and her need for control were all separate facets of her life and had their place. One life did not cross paths with the other. The subs she worked with knew her rules and shared the same desire. If they hungered for more, she did everything possible to match them with another Dom more capable to fill that need.

Somehow she didn't think the captain was looking for a permanent or semi-permanent encounter, but she'd play his game, for now. Once she made it clear what it meant to submit, he'd never ask her again, and their working relationship could continue as normal.

"How exactly do you want me to play with you?" she asked and folded her arms across her chest.

"I, uh…I don't know." He broke her stare and shifted in his seat. "I've never done anything like that before. I don't know what I like."

"It's not about what you like. It's what I like and what I make you like." She tilted her head and made a great show of looking him over from the top of his thick, dark hair to the blue casts on his feet, lingering on the bulge that strained against his fly. She stepped between his parted knees until a mere breath separated them. "Do you want to fuck me, Captain?"

Again with the hard swallow. His pupils dilated before his gaze flicked around the room. A moment later he drew in a breath and looked her square in the eye. "Yes."

Now it was her turn to swallow hard. Despite her intentions to refuse to feel anything for the man, heat spread throughout her body in a mellow burn she felt in her face and between her thighs. She liked that he didn't stammer that time. Conviction was such a sexy attribute.

All the more reason to refuse his request. "No."

"No?"

"No." The stare-down continued.

His brows jumped after several tense seconds. "No? That's it? Just no?"

"Correct, and before you ask, I'll explain why. In my world, it's not about the sex. It's the give and take of control. Yes, sex is sometimes involved, but it's not the be all and end all of the relationship. My submissive places his entire being in my care. Every choice is taken from them but one. Whether or not to follow my orders. Once that decision is made, they will either reap or suffer to my liking. In my hands I will expect you to learn exactly how to please me. If I ask you to fall on your knees, you hit the ground. If I want to bind you with ropes and have others play with my toy, you will sink into their touch. If I want to take you up the ass with a dildo, you will immediately bend over and spread your cheeks for my possession. You, Captain, are not a man who is capable of that loss of control."

"And if I was?" he panted. Red graced his cheeks and a his brown eyes shimmered with desire. His chest rose and fell with his quickened breaths. "What if I was that man?"

Then I'd make every moment the most exquisite torture of your life.

Her fingers bit into her biceps before she stepped back with a sigh. "Then I would find you the right person to make that happen. If you were truly willing."

"Why not you?"

"Contrary to what you might believe, I'm a one-sub woman. That position is already filled."

"Oh." His posture deflated. "Is it that guy? That man I saw you with that one time?"

She nodded.

"I'm sorry. I didn't know you were in a serious relationship."

"I'm not, well, I mean, it's not serious. In a traditional sense." What was she saying? She didn't owe him any explanations.

"Do you love him?"

His question stopped her short as the sentiment was completely unexpected coming from the captain. Not that she didn't believe him capable of compassion or other emotions as deep and complicated as love, but he was such a no-nonsense tough guy. Did the fact that she might be in love with someone else determine whether or not he'd continue to press his case?

The lie tickled her lips, but she refused the temptation to take the easy way out. "Yes, I love him. But not in the way you think. The both of us have a need only a rare few understand. I have earned his trust and it is a gift I cherish. So, yes, I love him, but we are not in love."

"I understand." His shoulders slumped and his fingers gripped the edge of the mattress as a muscle ticked in his jaw. "He's lucky to have a friend like you. Have to say, I'm jealous."

As far as compliments went, his words were not the most eloquent or unique ever to have been spoken, yet she felt his sincerity like the warmth of a fire on a cold winter's night. It ignited a desire to see to all of his comforts and take away that lonesome puppy-dog look from his handsome face. *Touch me*, his dark eyes seemed to plead. *Hold me. See me as I have seen you.*

She looked down at the floor and cleared her throat. "I'll see if your sister has arrived and bring your prescriptions."

The squeak of her sneakers on the tile as she turned and ran out of the room sounded as if the walls screamed, "Coward," at her retreating back. That hint of vulnerability was exactly what she looked for in a submissive. That tiny crack in the armor. The suggestion that they knew they were wanting. The indication that they hungered for instruction licked at all of her hot spots.

What if? Ah. A dangerous phrase. What if she took what the captain offered? What if she was able to mold him into the perfect sub who worshipped at her feet but was capable of functioning on his own when she needed personal space?

And what of Army, her current submissive? She meant what she said. The love between a Dom and their sub was precious and when she had taken Army, she promised her devotion. The hours and patience that went into cultivating the level of trust required in their relationship were not something she'd disregard because someone interesting crossed her path.

"Let him go, Jaz," she murmured and went in search of Abby. It was time for the captain to go home.

TWIN FROSTED GLASS spheres rested atop pedestals on either side of the asphalt driveway and glowed a mellow gold in the dark winter's night. Every time she drove between them, Jasmine always felt as if she were in that old movie *The Never Ending Story*, and she had to pass the Oracles' test or be burnt to a crisp. Given the mood she was in, blue lasers and fire would be the most likely outcome on this pass through.

During the last twelve hours of her shift, the skies did their best impression of Snoqualmie Falls, and a few choice assholes decided to drive as if there weren't two-inches of standing water covering the highway. Fortunately the ten-car pile-up had occurred after the morning commute. God help them all if it had been at the height of rush hour.

On any other night, she'd shake off the trauma of such a trying day by kicking back with a huge glass of Syrah and a steamy romance novel, or be buried deep in the crowd on the dance floor at The Cavern. Escapism was a powerful tool and she made it her passion to utilize every trick imaginable to deal with the pressures she faced every day. A night spent with her family was not among those techniques.

In truth, she'd rather be anywhere else in the world than walking up the stone steps of the home of her mother and step-father. Twice before she had tried to avoid these monthly dinners, and twice her mother had called nonstop for over an hour before showing up at Jasmine's doorstep. What was more important than family time? Why must she make her mother cry?

The lesson Jasmine learned was to make sure she was scheduled to work on as many of those nights as possible, and to never have a submissive in her home. Thankfully her mother hadn't realized the incense that had been hurriedly lit was to cover the scent of sex and sweat and was not for ambiance.

In all fairness, Oksana and her husband Bruno Brodsky were lovely people. To those they weren't related to. And the males of the family. Carry an extra X-chromosome and the expectations and attitudes reverted back to the happy, fun days of the middle ages. Nothing had disappointed her mother more than Jasmine's choice to go to college instead of going back to her Czech homeland and finding a husband. One would have thought she had announced she'd become a drug dealing mass murder the way her mother had carried on.

"Why you do this to me?" her mother had wailed. "Why must you break my heart? Was I not good enough example of how a woman should behave? You will find more joy in raising a family. Not in school. The boys in that school will spit on you. Smart girls are no attractive. Bruno, Bruno, explain how she is wrong."

Had Jasmine not expected the temper tantrum, she might have been hurt by her mother's reaction, but by then the argument had been so old hat and flat out wrong, she tuned out the crying and dreamed of the freedom of being out on her own.

She knew it was fear that made her mother believe a woman was incapable of surviving on her own. After her mother's family escaped from the Nazi stronghold on their village During World War II and made the decades-long migration across Europe, the women depended solely on the men to keep them alive. That dependence continued when they reached the United States and they were tossed into a culture they in no way comprehended. Housework, child rearing, those were skills they knew and understood. They were safe within the home. A belief that was passed on from mother to daughter and on down the line.

The notion had become so ingrained in her mother that when Jasmine's father had passed away, Oksana jumped on the first plane to the old homestead and married one of his cousins. Jasmine did have a few female cousins who put up a good fight against the archaic philosophy. Some even went on to attend college. However the only degree they had graduated with was an Mrs. with a minor in baby on the way.

It was sad, really. Jasmine sighed as she pressed the softly lit doorbell. Instead of being proud to have a daughter who was not afraid of forging her way in this big, scary world, her mother tried to obliterate the very fire that made Jasmine special. Good thing she had long ago stopped trying to earn her mother's approval.

The door swung open, revealing a petite woman decked out in a bronze-colored taffeta cocktail dress with a rhinestone belt encircling her plump waist. A strand of pearls adorned her neck, matching the drop earrings. She was an homage to Doris Day and June Cleaver, with a bit of Jeanne Copper from *The Young and the Restless* tossed into the mix, which was fitting since her mother practiced her English by watching daytime television.

"Jasmine," her mother cried with a smile that fell as her gaze traveled up and down her body. "What are you wearing?"

"They're called clothes, Mother." She stepped across the threshold and dropped a kiss to her mother's cheek.

"You are wearing the denim jeans on a special occasion. You could have at least put on a pretty dress or a skirt."

Her mother was lucky she found time to shower and put on something clean and wrinkle-free. "What are we celebrating tonight?"

"Emil has signed a new client. The boss was very happy."

"That's fantastic," she exclaimed with a plastic smile on her lips. And so completely typical.

Yes, let's throw a party because her brother did his job. He was a salesmen for a security firm, hired exclusively to land new clients. If her memory was correct, this was his third sale since he had been hired six months ago. *But hey, way to go bro for doing what you're paid to do.*

"Follow me, Jasmine." Her mother took her by the hand. "You can borrow some of my clothes. And lipstick. Men like to look at a woman's lips."

As if she didn't already know that fact, she silently smirked. *Hey. Wait a minute...*

She stopped in her tracks. "What men will be here to care if I'm wearing lipstick?"

Her mother's cheeks bunched so high with her grin, they almost obscured her eyes. She clapped her hands before her breasts. "Your brother is bringing a friend."

"Oh, Christ," she groaned.

"Jasmine Elena." Her mother made the sign of the cross and kissed her fingers. "Language."

"I'm sorry, but—I—ugh." What was the point? No amount of excuses, no amount of arguing was going to change the course of the next few hours. If she wanted to find a modicum of peace, it was best to pick her battles. This moment was not one of them. "I'm sorry."

"My baby daughter." Oksana slipped her arm around her shoulder, guiding her toward the living room. "I only wish for your happiness."

I am happy.

"Emil says this Mitchell is a good man."

"And Emil knows this how?"

"He works with Emil. He is a, uh how do you say, technical person. He makes work what Emil sells."

Jasmine waited for her mother to continue, but when nothing more was said, she nodded. "Sounds like he's quite a catch. By the way, is Emil bringing, what's his girlfriend's name? Angela?"

"No, no. Angela was three months ago. This last one was Andrea. She too is not the right girl. But he is young still. He has plenty of time to find the one."

Yes, Emil at thirty-five was still young, but she was an unfulfilled old maid at age thirty-two.

She broke away from her mother to greet her step-father who sat in his favorite chair. "Good evening, Bruno."

"Jasmine." He tilted his head up to receive his kiss. "Hmph. Your brother owes me twenty dollars. He said you will not be here tonight. I knew you would not break your mother's heart by missing another dinner."

"I make the ones I can. You know that."

He peered at her over his glasses. His bushy gray eyebrows rose above the frames like caterpillars. "*I* know. You are a good girl, when you remember your place."

The doorbell rang, saving her from making a smart remark that she knew would cause her more grief than the outburst would be worth.

Oksana ran to greet the newcomers while Bruno held up an empty highball glass. "Jasmine. Fix me a Scotch."

"My pleasure." She took his glass and walked the three feet to the small bar nestled in the corner of the room. The tink of the crystal stopper being pulled out of its home was drowned out by the sound of her mother's chatter combined with the husky murmur of men responding in kind.

Now that he was older, Emil sounded so much like her father, she sometimes forgot he was gone. Her brother looked like him too, tall and lean with charcoal black hair that was so straight, no amount of hair product could completely tame the strands into submission. With his sharp nose and heavy brows over small, dark eyes, his features embodied that eastern European sternness, until he smiled, which was all of the time. And why not? He was *the* son and the sun of the family. The hope for the clan to carry on their lineage. The only thing that kept Emil from getting too big a head was her willingness to knock him down a peg. There was no bigger competition than having a baby sister show you up.

As she poured the amber liquid into the glass she could hear the creak of the La-Z-Boy as Bruno hefted his thick weight to a stand and the solid thwack of his hand hitting flesh as he hugged his stepson tight and pounded him on the back.

"Emil. Good to see you, son," he greeted as if he hadn't seen him in years, when in fact she knew from Emil's social media feed that the two had gone to the football game together the week before.

"Papa. This my friend I was telling you about, Mitchell. Mitch, my stepfather, Bruno, and this is my sister, Jasmine."

Jasmine issued a little sigh and fixed a pleasant smile on her lips in preparation of meeting the latest victim in her mother's matchmaking scheme. She turned around and met the blue gaze of her brother's friend and felt lighting strike her in the head.

Holy shit.

She gasped in horror and her fingers relaxed. The tumbler of Scotch hit the berber carpet with a thunk, splashing liquor over her Sketchers.

"Jasmine?" her mother wailed and rushed toward the kitchen as her stepfather and brother looked at her as if she'd gone mad.

"Sorry. Sorry," Jasmine said and bent to pick up the glass while surreptitiously eyeing Mitchell. Or as she knew him, Army.

Army? Her Army? What the hell was her submissive doing in the home of her parents?

Granted, he looked just as shocked as she felt. His mouth fell open and when she met his gaze again, he dropped to his knees just as she had trained him.

Her eyes widened in warning and she gave the slightest shake of her head.

"Oh, I," he sputtered then gestured with a weak hand. "Can I help in any way?"

"No no," Bruno said. "Let the girl clean up her mess."

Heat hit her cheeks and she looked to the floor. Mess was an understatement. Here she knelt in her jeans and v-neck sweater with her hair in a loose ponytail and not a speck of make-up to hide the embarrassment she felt burning her face. Part of her allure as a mistress was the mystery, the fantasy. Men knew the moment she appeared in her costume that she was going to transport them away from the everyday and make all of their wishes come true. The only fantasy her current state of dress imparted was of clean dishes and a vacuumed floor.

Oksana rushed back into the room with a damp towel, which Jasmine accepted with a thank you and set about soaking up the liquid with the same focus she used in setting a broken bone.

"Can I get you a drink, Mitch?" Bruno asked.

"Uh, sure." He climbed to his feet. "Whatever you're having is fine."

"Good. Three Scotches, Jasmine," Bruno ordered and settled back into his chair and Emil filed suit on the coach.

She looked up and met Army's—no, Mitchell's confused gaze. She offered a tiny smile and mouthed the word, "later" and gestured with her head for him to take a seat. He nodded and followed the directive.

Since Mitchell was the guest, she served him first and watched with a sad heart as his hands trembled when accepting the glass. She could only imagine what he must be thinking. To serve her was an honor he never hesitated in thanking her for, and now here she was, waiting on the men without receiving a single word of gratitude in return. His gaze bobbed between her and her family with indecisiveness carved in his brow.

Clearly, he didn't know how to behave around her in this atmosphere, for she had taught him well. He never moved a single muscle in her presence without her say so, and now he was supposed to forget the last year of his training and act as if they had never met? She didn't blame him for his confusion and felt horrible he was placed in such a position.

After delivering her brother his drink, she offered Mitchell another smile of encouragement and left the room to assist her mother, and hopefully give him enough breathing room to regain his bearings.

The savory aroma of meat and spices enveloped her as she entered the warm kitchen. A pot roast rested in the roasting pan, and steam rose from the skillet of sautéed schnitzel. Without a word of direction, she went to work on preparing the asparagus for its turn in melted butter. Vegetables were the task of the daughter. The entrée, the mother. The roles were always such and were known by all the branches of the family. The home was a little factory with the womenfolk assigned their positions the moment they became able to control a knife.

Mere seconds went by before her mother looked at her from over her shoulder with a brilliant smile. "Eh? That Mitchell. He's a handsome man."

"Yes, he is." Beautiful, really. Especially when that muscular body was suspended from the ceiling and sweat matted the hair on his belly as he cried out in release.

What would her mother do if Jasmine regaled her with that little tidbit? A grin tugged at her lips as she imagined having to initiate CPR on the tiny woman. It wasn't that funny, really, yet she couldn't help sucking in a snort of laughter.

"Emil said he was in the military, but I can't remember which part."

Jasmine offered the appropriate sound of interest and held her tongue again. Mitch's nickname was Army for a reason. At The Cavern, subs in training had to earn the right to be called by their real name, and when they had first met, he had just finished his last tour of duty. Once he had returned home, his family and community looked to him for leadership, not realizing he was more comfortable taking orders. The struggle to find balance between the two worlds was what brought him to her dungeon. By giving him an outlet to revel in his submissive nature, he was able to handle the stress of the expectations others placed upon him.

He had actually earned the use of his given name eons ago, but he liked hearing her use the nickname. He said he knew what was expected of him, which gave him great comfort. That had been so far in the past, she had forgotten what his real name was.

Dinner was ready, and everyone took their place around the table. Bruno sat at the head, Emil to his right with her mother at the other end. Of course Mitch was settled on her stepfather's left, in the chair beside hers.

The moment she entered the dining room with the platter of asparagus, Mitch's spine snapped to attention. The tension didn't abate as dishes were passed from left to right and he kept looking to her as their fingers brushed with a plea in his eyes for some form of guidance. When everyone's plate was filled, Bruno commanded them to bow their heads in prayer.

Jasmine used the opportunity to risk placing her hand on Mitch's thigh and squeezed the thick muscle. From the corner of her eye saw him peeking at her and she hoped he could hear her mental shout for him to relax. A soft sigh escaped his lips and she felt the warmth of his palm before he covered her hand in a tight grip followed by a pat and she recognized the signs of the stress leaving his body as he pulled his hand away. Message received.

She knew him so well. Knew where to stroke to make him beg for more. Knew where to strike the whip for his ultimate pleasure, what to say to make him hard in an instant. How much cum he produced when she sucked him to climax. Yes, she knew him well.

Or at least, she thought she did.

"You're the oldest of five?" she repeated when her mother asked about his family. She didn't know that. She also didn't know he had graduated from Western, or that he had a degree in computer engineering, or played on an indoor soccer team. Simple facts garnered by a few basic questions made at the dinner table. After all of their time spent together, her only knowledge of him was about his body and its reactions, not about the man himself.

The tender meat tasted like unseasoned tofu on her palate as she realized how shallow and stagnant their relationship had become. Why hadn't she asked him more about his life outside of the club? Her contracts with her subs stated that their interactions occurred only within the confines of the club's walls. A stipulation both parties agreed upon, for it suited each other's purposes. But to what end?

Had he been aware that an invitation to join his co-worker for dinner with his family carried the possibility of an impromptu blind date with the man's sister? Why had he agreed? Was he looking to be in a more traditional relationship? Could she be that woman for him?

"Jasmine." Her mother's voice snapped her from her musings. The raise of her brow warned her to stop mentally checking out. "Mitchell was just complimenting your vegetables."

"Yes." He cleared his throat. "This is an excellent meal."

"Thank you," she replied with a gracious smile.

"All of the women in the family are good cooks," Oksana said. "We take pride in providing for our family. Make our men happy to come home after a hard day at work."

Jasmine restrained an eye roll. What an absolutely prehistoric statement.

"All except for Jaz." Emil chuckled around a mouthful of beef. "She works too much—ow." He jumped in his seat and glared at Bruno who ate without a hint of knowledge as to what had made Emil react as he did. Jasmine suspected it was a swift kick to the shin to keep him from ruining her chances at landing a husband.

Mitchell didn't appear to notice and rounded on her with enthusiasm. "What *do* you do for a living?"

She rolled a baby carrot across her plate and cleared her throat. "I'm a doctor in the emergency room at Schuster-Siegel Hospital."

"You're a doctor? I didn't know that." He caught himself and hastily added, "I mean, you look so young to be so accomplished. Do you enjoy it?"

"I do. It's very rewarding."

"I bet." He smiled and she felt her lips curl to match his warmth. "What do you like best about being a doctor?"

Oksana interrupted, "Jasmine, let's not bore our guest with the tedious details of your job. Besides, your work is only temporary until you find a husband and settle down. To make a family of her own is her passion, Mitchell."

"It is?" he asked her with a puzzled frown.

"No."

"Yes," Bruno interjected. "Jasmine. Clear the table and fetch us our dessert."

With a curt nod, she stood and picked up her and Mitch's plates, avoiding his gaze as she kept to her task.

For the rest of the meal she kept her mouth shut with only the occasional single-word answer, if required. It was the longest forty-five minutes of her life as she listened to her parents feed Mitch misconceptions as to who she was as a person and her life's goals.

The more her parents spoke, the more relaxed he became during the conversation, even to the point of holding out his cup in her direction while she poured coffee before she had the opportunity to ask him if he wanted any. When she gave him the look she reserved for when he presumed to know what she wanted of him, he blanched and his hand shook. In one evening her family had undone months of training.

Once the kitchen was cleaned and the men were partaking of their brandies, Jasmine was more than ready to go home. "Gentlemen, if you will excuse me, I have to work in the morning and must be off. Mitchell, it was nice to meet you."

He jumped to his feet. "I must be going too. May I walk you to your car?"

"Yes, yes." Her mother beamed. "That is an excellent idea."

She kissed her family goodnight and allowed Mitch to help her slip on her jacket. Together they walked side by side in silence. She passed her vehicle and led him around to the bushes bordering the driveway.

Mitch spoke first, which surprised her. Another example of how he had forgotten he wasn't to speak unless directed to. Of course, they weren't in the club to remind him of his place. "I can see why you are the way you are. Your family is very...old fashioned."

"That's a way to phrase it," she muttered then drew in a breath. "Mitch—"

He shook his head and his breath quickened. "I'm Army. Your Army. And I don't like that look in your eyes right now."

She licked her lips. Best to cut right to the chase, no matter how much it hurt. "I can't be your Mistress anymore."

"No," he shouted before she finished the sentence. "Why? I don't understand."

The look of distress on his handsome face broke her heart. In a sense she was punishing him for something that was not his fault, but the damage was done. In time she hoped he realized that she was granting him the best gift she could provide. Still the pain of loss burned through her. She stood on tiptoes to throw her arms around his neck, drawing him into a fierce hug.

"I love you," she stated emphatically and fought the tears blurring her vision. "And it's because I love you that I have to let you go."

He shook his head, burying his face in the crook of her neck as his arms closed around her as if she were a tether in a storm. "Why?"

"Several things. One, you've lost all respect for me after seeing the way my family treats me."

"That's not true."

She shushed him and drew back to frame his face between her hands. Her thumbs stoked the curves of his cheeks and her throat grew tight at the sight of his tear-filled eyes. "It is, and you know it. Well, maybe not all respect, but enough to make a difference. But that's not the only reason. Mitch, I am doing you a grave disservice. I'm holding you back from what you really want."

"You're what I want."

"Maybe. In the beginning. But I realized tonight that we've grown complacent. We've fallen into a routine that was comfortable, but you want more. You need more."

He shook his head again and she stilled him with a press of her palms against his cheeks. "Look where you are, Mitch. Why did you come with Emil tonight? You must have known he was trying to hook you up with his sister, and you were interested enough to accept the invitation."

Beneath her hands, his skin heated and he broke his gaze to

stare at the ground. "I-I'm lonely when I'm not with you," he finally admitted in a small voice.

"I know. At least, I know that now. We had an agreement, and you've kept it beautifully, as have I. But it's not enough anymore. You want what I can't provide and to keep you from it would be entirely selfish of me. You are a great guy and are entitled to your happiness."

His lips pinched together and his breathing continued to escalate while his eyes danced about. She recognized the signs of panic as he tried to hold it together.

"Tell me," she commanded with a sweep of her thumb across his lips.

"I'm scared," he whispered. "What if I don't find someone who understands me as you do?"

She nodded. "Change is scary. But I'm not casting you out on your own. I will find you the perfect Mistress. I promise. I'll find you one who will help you soar, not just keep you aloft. No matter what, I'm still your friend."

He released a stuttered breath and hauled her against him in a hug so tight, she struggled for air, yet she clung to his shoulders just as strongly. When the need to breathe drove her to move, she turned her head to brush a string of kisses along his cheek. Her lips settled on his in a gentle kiss. His mouth softened against hers and he kissed her back without any of the heat and hunger of lovers. This was a kiss of friendship. A kiss of goodbye.

Mitch pulled away with a little sniffle and smoothed a hand over her head. "I'll never forget you."

"Of course not. I'm going to make sure your new Mistress rides your ass like you deserve."

He chuckled and gave her one last quick hug then walked her to her car, opening the door at the sound of the lock disengaging.

She waved at him through the window and as she drove down the driveway, watched in the rearview mirror as he climbed into his own vehicle. Once she turned onto the street, a sob broke free and the tears she held in check streamed down her cheeks.

Mitch wasn't the only one afraid of change. The selection of a new submissive wasn't easy. And after the year she had spent with Mitch, his replacement was going to be a tough act to follow. Also, the connection they once shared was gone forever. Even if they remained friends, as she hoped, that deep level of communication was a loss she grieved as strongly as a death of a loved one.

She reached for the packet of tissues in the glove box and swiped at her eyes. No sense crashing her car because she couldn't see the road.

Once she was safely ensconced in the comfort of her home, she was going to bust open a bottle of wine and toast the end of a beautiful friendship with the honor it deserved.

CHAPTER FOUR

"CAPTAIN DEWINTER." A sultry feminine voice made the skin across the back of his neck tingle as if she had caressed him with the tip of her fingernail. "What a pleasant surprise."

Fuck.

He'd recognize that voice anywhere. Sexy, foreign, and far too smug for his liking. Damn it. The swallow of Jack Daniels lodged in his throat and for half a second played tag with the insides of his nostrils before sliding into his gullet.

He had thought he was hidden deep enough within the bowels of The Cavern to avoid detection. He should have known better.

"Mrs. Kilsgaard," he said, then turned to face the owner of the club.

Amaryllis Kilsgaard stood so close to him that if she took a deep breath, her breasts would press into his chest. As was her fashion, she was dressed for sin in a royal blue halter dress that displayed a generous amount of cleavage accentuated by a sapphire the size of a silver dollar resting above the cleft of her breasts. Lucian was either a very stupid or very confident man to allow her to roam about in such an erection-inducing outfit all on her own.

"I'm so happy to see you," she squealed and threw her arms around his neck for a hug.

Happy was right, she practically vibrated with glee. Her lavender eyes sparkled and she bounced on the balls of her feet as if she had just received the best present in the world.

A normal man might have been flattered by her enthusiasm, but in his experience with Mrs. Kilsgaard the only reason she'd have for being so excited to see him was she was up to something. She seemed to have a sixth sense about people that was damned right eerie, and usually those prophecies concerned him.

She reached out with her hand to smooth an invisible wrinkle from the lapel of his blazer. "Would it be fair to assume you are here in search of what you need?"

Yes. Maybe. Hell, he didn't know anymore.

The first time he had walked through The Cavern's door was when he had been on the trail of a vigilante crime fighter named the Claymore, who at the time he had believed to be Lucian. It wasn't, but before he left without the information he had come in search of, Amaryllis had predicted that he would return when he was ready for what he needed. Whatever it was she believed he was in need of, he hadn't a clue, but now here he was, skulking in the corners, nursing a drink and mustering up the courage to face whatever was to be found up the grand staircase and inside the playrooms. Specifically, he was looking for Mistress Jasmina.

"I see I am correct," he heard Amaryllis say and felt heat sear his cheeks as he realized he'd been caught staring up at the second floor landing.

"I'm not sure what you mean." He took a sip of his drink. "I've been ordered on a temporary vacation and thought I'd, uh, I'd stop in for a..." He trailed off as she looked upon him with pity curling her lips down as she shook her head at his lame attempt at finding an excuse as to why he was there. "I don't know why I'm here," he finally admitted.

She looped her arm around his elbow and hugged it against her breast. "There, there, Captain. Allow me to help clear that stubborn, male-addled induced fog cluttering your mind. I heard you were recently injured."

"Where did you hear that?" Only those in the department knew of the incident.

"Oh, please." She batted her lashes. "Between the Chameleon and the Claymore, very little happens with the people I care about without me knowing."

"Why should you care about me?"

"You helped save my cousin-in-law. And you inadvertently helped save a man I love as a brother. Whether you like it or not, Captain, you have been adopted into the Kilsgaard family."

Was that type of consideration a blessing or a curse? "Thanks?"

She giggled and guided him to the bottom of the staircase. "I take it you sustained your injuries while on the case of a mutual enemy of ours?"

"Yes."

"Was it worth it?"

"At this point, yes." More than worth it, if he was to be truthful.

Konkle's cellphone contained texts and phone numbers of several people in Smithwick's operation. In the two days since he was released from the hospital and trapped in the loving care of his sister, Coulter and their team were able to decipher a human trafficking scheme involving several massage parlors in the area. In a month's time a shipment of girls was scheduled to arrive from various Southeast Asian countries and then filter into the general population as masseuses before being dispersed across the country to the highest bidder. Konkle's job was to bring in clientele to sample the girls' ability to please before they were put on the bidding block. The best girls were auctioned off while those who struggled or fought were killed. According to intel, the auction was to be handled personally by Smithwick himself, who was currently biding time in Asia and coordinating the collection of the girls.

Until Smithwick returned, all Marco could do was sit on this thumbs and work on the other cases his team handled. After all, Smithwick wasn't the only bad guy in town, but in comparison to the shit Smithwick stirred, those tasks were child's play. And since he was still supposed to be on bed rest, all he had was time on his hands and the constant replay of Dr. Jovanovich trying to scare him off from pursuing any further talk of them hooking up.

Did she honestly think the idea of making him worship at her feet made him any less eager to fall on his knees for her? Quite the opposite in fact. However, the way she spoke of her submissive certainly had derailed his wishes. It had been plain to see she had great affection for the man, and he wasn't so shallow as to be a jackass and try to come between them. All that was left was for him to envy the lucky SOB.

Which was why he was here at the club at this exact time of night. If she had a regular guy she played with, it was reasonable to think they had a standing appointment. Maybe if he was able to see her, see them, in their symbiotic-whatever-you-called-it glory, he might be able to allow the thought of the doc performing all kinds of kinky acts on him to fade into oblivion. He hoped to God that would work. If not, foresaw a future of thinking, hoping, aching to make his fantasies become a reality until he went mad.

They reached the second floor landing and his eyes scanned the area, searching for any sign of Mistress Jasmina.

"Looking for something, Captain? Or someone?"

He sighed and shook his head. "I don't know. Maybe. I think I may be going crazy, Mrs. Kilsgaard."

She smiled and again he had that feeling she was seeing right into soul. "I think you are at a crossroads in your life. You know you need a change, but your mind refuses to listen. Instinct, however, has led you here. A place where you know you will receive what you need."

There was that word again. Need.

"And what do I need?" he asked in a gruff voice.

The smile widened. "You need to see a demonstration of what can happen when a man allows all thought to leave and live in the moment. Lucky for you, Mistress Jasmina is about to put on a show."

He stilled as his heart slammed into his ribcage. "She is? I mean, Mistress Jasmina? Who is that?"

Her eyes narrowed and she tilted her head. He held his breath as she looked him up and down before she replied, "Mistress Jasmina is a dominatrix. She is currently between submissives and is assisting another dominatrix. It should be very educational."

Between submissives? Since when? He strove to keep his tone casually interested. "What happened to her regular submissive?"

"I don't know all of the details, but from what I've heard, she felt he had learned everything she had to offer and what he needed was someone who could take him to the next level. She was quite saddened by the entire ordeal."

"That's great." Jasmine was single? The thought sent a shot of excitement through his body as if he swallowed electricity.

Amaryllis raised a brow. "Excuse me?"

Shit. "I mean that's great she was able to see that her sub required more and she cared enough to see that he got it. Not a lot of people would do that."

The surprise brow lowered, and he felt his heart climb into his throat as she hit him will that all-seeing stare. "Yes, Mistress Jasmina always puts the needs of others before her own. It's one of the reasons why I love her so, but sometimes I wish she did take more effort with seeing to her own needs."

Marco nodded, afraid that if he uttered another sound, it would give away why he was really at The Cavern.

"Come." Amaryllis tugged on his arm. "This will be quite a show."

The room she led him to had already began to fill with people. Couples and trios sat upon couches or lounged on the floor in various degrees of undress. Amaryllis brought them to a stop behind a loveseat where a man and women were engaged in a hot and heavy lip lock. The man pulled the bodice of the woman's dress down to roughly cup her breast in his hand where he tugged at the nipple while she squealed in his embrace.

Marco felt his eyes bulge at the display, but a quick glance at Amaryllis confirmed she barely gave the couple a bit of attention. He swallowed against the rather prudish reaction of being shocked and scanned the room for Jasmine.

There she was. Waiting in the corner dressed in all of her black leather and mesh finery. A short, flared skirt swirled around her hips and a matching bustier cinched in her waist and pushed her breasts up to form a shelf. Instead of the restrained braid he usually saw her wear, he dark hair was down in all of its sable glory. Although she was on the short side, the black suede high heels made her legs look impossibly long as she climbed up the three steps to the stage and the couple standing at the center under a spotlight.

"Who are they?" he whispered as the lights in the rest of the room dimmed.

"That is Mistress Madeline and her submissive, Megabyte," Amaryllis whispered back. "He purposely disobeyed her orders because he likes to be punished. But she's going to turn the tables on him. He doesn't know yet that Jasmina will be the one to dole out his punishment. Since they do not have a connection, she won't be swayed by his protests for leniency. He will also see the price he will pay by playing his silly game."

Mistress Madeline instructed Jasmine to undress her submissive as she twirled a long, blonde lock of her hair between her fingers. Fully clothed, the man appeared to be average. Mid-thirties, receding hairline, neither good-looking or ugly. He was your average Joe about town. Marco's impression of him didn't change as he was stripped down to bare skin. His physique was soft but not doughy, and hair covered his chest, arms, legs and belly. From the juncture of his thighs, his erection, again average, rose to half-mast.

While Jasmine removed the man's clothes, his mistress watched with a cool, detached expression. In her hand she held a whip, the end skimming the floor as she lazily swung the length back and forth. Every once in a while she trailed the handle over her midnight-blue corseted torso and upper curve of her breasts, flicking her tongue over the end in a teasing caress.

Judging by the delighted smile the sub struggled to contain, Marco saw how he thought he had played his mistress well. For a guy who was having his wrists bound and strung up by a hook hanging from the ceiling, he was looking very pleased with himself. That was until his mistress passed the whip to Jasmina with a wicked grin curving both of their lips.

A chair was brought up onto the stage while Mistress Madeline beckoned to someone out of Marco's range of vision to join her. To his surprise, it was the man he recognized as Jasmina's former submissive who stepped into the spot she directed behind her.

"I don't understand," Marco murmured before he caught himself.

"That is Army, Jasmina's former submissive," Amaryllis answered, not understanding the context of his query. "He agreed to assist in this punishment. Even though they are no longer a couple, he still wishes to please his Mistress."

"What kind of a name is Army? And Megabyte too for that matter."

"Don't you know? Here a submissive has to earn the use of their given name. Until then, you answer to the name bequeathed to you by your Master."

Bequeathed? Fuck, in this world, he was completely clueless.

A hush fell over the crowd and his attention was drawn back to Jasmina. She kept her legs straight as she bent at the waist and very slowly slipped off one boot then the other. The submissive sucked in a breath and Marco too recognized the subtle signal that she was about to unleash hell.

One step, then another brought her closer to the trembling man. She ran the end of the whip from his chin down to his groin and tapped his cock. "I'm allowed to do whatever I wish with him, Mistress Madeline?"

"Whatever you wish." Madeline guided Army's hands around her waist and encouraged him to touch her as he pleased.

He wasted no time and went straight for her breasts, diving his hands beneath the cups of her corset and squeezing the mounds with rough fingers. She cooed and reached up and behind to guide his head down for him to ravish her neck with biting kisses.

The hanging submissive released a whimper that turned into a cry as Jasmina released the whip and struck him across the back then let the leather fly three more times in quick succession. She walked up behind the man to press her breasts against the pink welts and grabbed his hair in her hand.

"Watch her and take your punishment," she growled in his ear. "See what happens when you disrespect your mistress with your childish games. Watch as another man takes what is supposed to be yours."

Madeline sat down in the chair and hooked her leg over each arm, spreading her thighs wide apart. Her skirt was rucked up to her waist, exposing the slick folds of her bare sex. She motioned to Army who fell to his knees and dived into the offered treat.

Jasmina took a step back and readied her stance for another strike. As she raised her hand, she glanced out into the audience, her dark gaze landed on Marco and her eyes widened with surprise. For several seconds they breathed as one, his fingers curling around the back of the couch in front of him as he waited for her next move.

"Well, well, well," Amaryllis sighed and nudged him with her hip, breaking the spell.

Jasmina's gaze narrowed and her upper lip ticked with a snarl. Marco silently apologized to the hanging man, afraid that whatever emotion his mere presence ignited within her was going to be taken out on his hide.

MARCO DEWINTER. THE man was like a virus she couldn't shake.

What was he thinking, up on his feet and standing in her club watching her at work? And hanging on to Amaryllis as well? Grrr.

She already told him she wasn't interested in being his intro into the BDSM lifestyle. Or was he here to scout for another Mistress? In her domain? If so, he was even more arrogant than she imagined and long due for a lesson in respecting her wishes.

Crack. Crack. With a flick of her wrist she created matching welts on each of Megabyte's butt cheeks. She wove a crisscross pattern of fine pink lines from shoulder to hip then worked the back of each thigh. Between lashes she glanced in Marco's direction and took great delight in how he flinched with each lash. Sweat glistened on his forehead and he was all but panting as she delivered her punishment.

Madeline did her part, moaning her pleasure as Army used his talented tongue on her clit.

"That's so good," she cried and pulled at her nipples. "I'm going to come all over his face."

Army groaned and his head moved back and forth in an effort to bring Madeline to her orgasm.

"Oh yes. Oh, yes!" Her head fell back and her thighs squeezed Army's head.

Jasmine dropped the whip. She stepped forward and ground her rough corset-covered breasts against Megabyte's ravaged back. She reached around his waist and found his cock, rock hard and slick to the touch.

"Look what your arrogance cost you," she said and worked his cock with her palm. "Her orgasm could have been yours. That could have been your mouth tasting her flesh.

A sob broke past his lips. "I'm sorry. Sorry."

"Are you? I don't think you deserve a Mistress as fine as Madeline."

"No! I'm sorry. I'll be good. I promise. I promise."

"I don't think you've learned your lesson yet." She squeezed the base of his cock and stemmed the tide of cum from erupting. "Army, show Mistress Madeline what she could be playing with instead."

Madeline reached for the straining fly of Army's jeans with

eager hands. She licked her lips as she drew out his erection, hard with a shiny, plum-shaped head ready to release his cum at her command.

"Ooo, she likes this new toy," Jasmine taunted and matched the strokes of Madeline's hands on Megabyte's cock. "Do you want to see your new toy come, Mistress?"

"Absolutely." She reclined back in her seat and resumed palming her breasts. She nodded at Army. "Stroke your cock."

Immediately he complied. "Like this, Mistress?"

"Yes. Good boy. Make it feel good, but don't come until I say."

"Yes, Mistress," he grunted.

"That is how a sub behaves," Jasmine said in the weeping sub's. "Your sole purpose is to please your Mistress. Look at the strain on his face. Look at the how tight the muscles are on his forearms. He wants to come so bad, but he will wait. And wait. And wait. The anticipation is maddening, isn't it?"

From the corner of her eye she scanned the audience. Gazes were torn, switching back and forth between Army masturbating before Madeline and Jasmine's hand pumping Megabyte. But the only person's attention she was really interested in was Marco. His eyes never left her, touching on her from the top of her head to the points of her bare feet. He was with her, feeling her. It was as if he were the one in her arms, bearing her marks on his back, throbbing in her hand. Waiting for her command.

"Come, Army," Madeline barked. "Come on my tits."

A strangled cry broke past Army's lips as he released a stream of cum on Madeline's breasts. She twirled her fingers in the milky liquid, rubbing it into her skin. When the last drop fell on her pink nipple, Madeline sent him a pleased smile and nodded her head. He dropped to his knees and bowed his head, awaiting his next instruction.

"See, Megabyte. He came on what was yours." Jasmine quickened her strokes. "He got to come on your Mistress' tits. And you get to come on the floor. Come for me. Now."

Megabyte bellowed and shot several jets of cum at his Mistress' feet. Jasmine searched again for Marco and their gazes locked. "Come," she said again.

Marco's eyes widened and he jerked as if he'd been poked in the gut. He hunched over the couch, his jaw clenched tight and his lips pressed in a firm line. Those dark eyes of his glittered up at her with want, hunger, and the need for more.

Heaven help her, she wanted to give it to him.

Between her legs she was completely drenched. Her sheath pulsed and flexed. She wanted to fuck and be fucked with a level of desperation she never felt before. The muscles in her thighs twitched ready to jump off that stage, march over to Marco and throw him onto the floor. She was desperate to lick his cum from his belly and ride him into the ground.

The click of Madeline's heels on the floor snapped her back into the right frame of mind. She jumped back and shook her head to clear the cloud of lust toying with her control. Yes, a sub was meant to provide their Master pleasure, and yes, she sometimes referred to her men as toys, but she never treated them as objects. She took her time learning exactly how to extract the last bit of enjoyment from her subs before allowing them to penetrate her body. It wasn't like her to want to use Marco in such a manner.

Madeline approached her sub, who swayed in his bonds and sucked in great gulps of air. She tilted his chin up with her finger and leaned in until the tips of their noses touched.

"This is your only warning, Megabyte. I don't suffer fools, and your games are not welcomed here. I accepted you as my sub because I saw a need within you to be seen. I still believe that, and I can make all your wishes come true. But on my terms. If you are ready to be the submissive I need, I will see you on Saturday at nine sharp. If not, don't come back. Understood?"

"Yes, Mistress," he stuttered. His voice sounded hoarse and he kept his gaze directed at the floor.

"Thank Mistress Jasmina for her instruction."

"Thank you, Mistress Jasmina."

Jasmine trailed her fingers across his shoulders, horrified at how badly her hands trembled. She curled them into a fist. "You're welcome."

Madeline gave the signal, and three of the club's stewards climbed onto the stage to assist with bringing Megabyte down from his restraints. The lesson was over, but the aftercare was just beginning.

As the men worked on Megabyte, Jasmine walked over to Army who sat on his knees, exactly as he had been instructed.

She ran her fingers through his short, blond hair and cupped his cheek. "You did well. I'm so proud of you."

His eyelashes fluttered and against her palm the muscles of his face flinched with a brief smile.

"Every Dom here is going to want you now."

He sucked in a sharp breath and his startled gaze flew to hers before he remembered his place and dropped his head.

"You may speak," she said.

"Do you think so?"

"Ah, honey." She smoothed her thumb over his wrinkled brow. He had had such a difficult start at the beginning as he struggled to accept his true nature. And just as Madeline had seen something in Megabyte, Jasmine had seen the man Army could become. It saddened her to see how he still didn't see it in himself. "You have no idea. I've already had several people asking me if they can take you on. After this demonstration, I'm going to be hounded until I choose someone worthy of you."

The happiness that infused him was like a million-watt light bulb, straightening his spine and shining from his eyes in a golden glow. His smile was wide, and no matter how hard he tried, he simply could not contain his joy. She rubbed his head again and commanded him to stand.

"Come on, Mitch. Let's go unwind." She grasped his biceps and led him off the stage.

Just like that, his submissive posture disappeared and he looked at her as one would a best friend. "What about you, Jasmine? Do you have my replacement picked out yet? I saw the line parked outside your dungeon when I arrived. It was crazy."

News of their separation had spread through the club as quickly as an embarrassing photo on social media. The line of eager subs in the hallway outside her personal dungeon had shocked her. She knew she was good but not that popular. So many faces, yet at that moment she couldn't remember one of them. The only face haunting her at the moment belonged to a certain police officer with salt and pepper hair and dark eyes that pleaded for her to show him the way.

Did she have the courage to take him on the journey or would she play it safe with someone already accustomed to the lifestyle?

She looked up at Mitch and drew a deep breath. "I think I do."

CHAPTER FIVE

MARCO'S STOMACH GROWLED the second he stepped through the front door of his home. Abby was cooking something yummy and by the scent he could tell that it was meat and delicious. Since he had skipped lunch, she could have made tofu and bean sprouts and he still would wolf it down. Thank goodness she had taken a break from her usual healthy diet.

"Hey," he called out and hung up his jacket on the coat tree. "What are you doing here?"

"Are you kidding me?" She stepped out of the kitchen, spatula in hand and a scowl on her pretty face. "You went to work. You're supposed to be resting. You're lucky I didn't come down to the station and drag you back home by the ear."

"I did rest. For four days." He kissed her cheek and went to the stove and lifted the lid. "Smells good. Seriously Abby, I appreciate it, but you don't have to take care of me. I know you probably have better stuff to do than watch my ass."

"You almost died. Of course I'm going to take care of you. And it looks like you need taking care of. Sit. I'll get you some stew. How are your legs?"

"They're fine. I told you. I'm fine." He snagged a bottle of beer for himself and a soda for Abby and settled in at the kitchen table. "How was work?"

"Same old, same old. All the girls think you're a hero and wanted to come over and help take care of you. Jeez. It's creepy when your friends want to give your brother a sponge bath."

He choked on a sip of beer and chuckled. "Sorry. Can't help it if the ladies love me."

"Eww." She stuck out her tongue and shook her head.

Well, at least those girls were interested in him.

Marco picked at the label on his bottle and recalled the sight of Mistress Jasmina in all her glory as she broke that man down with her whip. It was one thing to imagine what exactly it meant to be a submissive, and another, more terrifying thing to see it with your own eyes. Hearing the crack of leather on flesh and skin slapping skin. To smell the salty, musky scent of sweat and sex. Watching and feeling the wave of lust as it consumed every person in that room until they writhed as one in sexual torment until the mistress released them all with power of one word. Absolutely mind blowing.

He hadn't been the only one to come in his pants at Jasmina's command. The couple who had been hot and heavy on the loveseat had fallen onto the floor and fucked like beasts along with several others who joined them. To his right several men had their cocks out, timing their strokes to match Jasmina's, all of them enthralled in her performance. If it hadn't been for Amaryllis' presence at his side, he might have forgotten who he was and joined them in their circle jerk. In a word, Jasmina had been magnificent.

And absolute hell on his libido. After she had walked off arm and arm with her sub, he ran out of there so fast, he barely said goodbye to Mrs. Kilsgaard. He jerked off twice the moment he walked through his front door, and again in the shower just that morning. Never had he been so hot for a woman that she infiltrated his every thought.

When he had reached for his dick for the fourth time in twelve hours, he said fuck it and went into work, even though his muscles were sore from venturing out the night before. His body wasn't bouncing back as quickly as it had when he was younger, and he felt the strain as if he'd climbed up Mt. Rainier. Nonetheless, there was no way he was going to spend the entire day jerking off to a fantasy, so he had hobbled into the office, only to be tormented by lingering arousal while in the midst of his coworkers instead of the privacy of his home.

There had to be a way to get Jasmina off his mind.

Abby set a thick manila envelope on the table. "This was on the porch when I arrived."

He righted the envelope to see his name and address scrawled in an elegant script across the front. In the corner was an address. No name, only a return address that he recognized.

The Cavern.

Immediately his dick began to harden and he jumped from his seat to race out of the room towards his office. "Be right back," he mumbled.

His hands shook as he practically mauled the fastener and withdrew a black folder. Purple feathers framed his name, which was written in gold ink in the same script as the envelope. Inside were what looked like legal documents, and his eyes were immediately drawn to the two names on top. Marco DeWinter and Mistress Jasmina.

"Hot damn," he groaned and fell into his chair behind his desk.

In the left pocket was a typewritten letter on heavy cream-colored stock. The purple feather image was stamped on the top in metallic ink. The paper fluttered as he withdrew it from the pocket and held it up to the light.

My dearest Captain,

You have been invited to join me in my dungeon at The Cavern to begin your introduction into the bondage, domination, sadist, maso-

chist lifestyle in which you recently expressed an interest. Under my tutelage you will receive the proper instruction and guidance on how to behave as a submissive and the skills for pleasing your Mistress. All of our interactions will be conducted with safety and respect as the utmost priority.

In this folder you will find the contract outlining the exact details of our arrangement. Read this document in its entirety and answer all questions honestly. Any false answers or hedging could lead to serious complications or dangerous situations, and could be grounds for immediate termination of the agreement.

The journey to accepting one's submissive nature is difficult and mentally taxing. You will experience highs and lows you have never imagined. This lifestyle is not for everyone, and I will understand if you decide not to accept my invitation. You will learn that in all things, you always have a choice.

Please text me your response to the number listed below. If you wish to continue, bring the completed contract to the bar at Tutala, Thursday evening at 8pm to discuss your answers and solidify our arrangement. If your work schedule does not allow for this time, please let me know of an alternative.

I look forward to your reply.

Mistress Jasmina's signature was scrawled across the bottom in purple ink along with a phone number.

"Wow." Marco blew out a breath and wiped his hand over the back of his neck. "Wow."

This chick was serious. If he hadn't seen her in action the night before, he might have thought she was acting way over the top with this entire dominatrix persona. If anything, this letter coupled with the of her cracking that whip, confirmed she was one hundred percent committed to her role. One miscalculation on her part and that sub could have been castrated on the spot.

And you want a piece of that?

Yeah. Maybe. Hell, he wasn't certain. After what he had witnessed along with that letter, it was crystal clear this was no game to Mistress Jasmina. If he was in, he had to be in one hundred percent. If not, then he needed to leave her the hell alone and stop tormenting himself with fantasies of what might have been.

He pulled out the contract and flipped through the pages. His balls drew up into his body and he felt his eyes bug out their sockets the more he read. Mistress Jasmina was certainly thorough. There was a section for his medical history, which was left for him to fill out, but under the instructions on how to obtain a blood test for any sexually transmitted diseases, she had marked "already fulfilled." His blood must have been tested when he was in the hospital.

"Whoa."

While it was comforting to know he wasn't carrying any STDs, he was horrified to realize he hadn't even thought about the consequences of engaging in this sort of activity. When she said safety was a priority, she was leaving no stone unturned.

After the section on the cancellation policy and communication protocols (sexting was allowed, photos were not) came the list of likes and dislikes.

"Oh. My. God," he groaned and dropped his head in his hands. "What the fuck is a Gates of Hell?"

Rope bondage. Prison scene. Shibari. He didn't know what two-thirds of the items were and the rest just fucking blew his mind. Whatever they were, his cock was so ready to try all of them out, it was practically bursting from his pants as if it wanted to read the list itself.

"Marco. Dinner's ready." The patter of Abby's footsteps drew near.

"Fuck." He slid the fancy folder under the ink blotter and

covered the contract with his arms. "I'll be right there."

Her cute little face appeared in the doorway. "Are you working?"

"Kinda of. Just some L&I paperwork."

Poor girl. She had no idea her brother was such a pervert.

"You need to take it easy. In fact, you don't look so well. Are you getting sick? Your forehead is all sweaty."

"Yes! No. I mean, I'm not sick-sick, just tired. I think I'll turn in early."

"Oh. Okay. I'll leave the stew in the crockpot in case you get hungry later."

"Thanks. Oh, and Abby? Thanks for everything. The cooking, cleaning. All of it. I really do appreciate it."

"You're welcome." She rocked back on her heels with a delighted smile.

He reached for his wallet and pulled out all the cash inside. "Here. Call your friends and go have some fun. Within reason. Enjoy being young while you can."

"Really? Wow. I think I like sick Marco." She took the money from his hand. "What about you? Are you ever going to have any fun while you're not yet ancient?"

The papers under his arms seemed to catch fire and burn his skin. "I'm working on that."

"Goodnight." She mussed the top of his hair. "Call me if you need anything."

"Will do."

He waited for the sound of the door closing behind her before reaching for his computer. As the fan whirled and the tower booted up, he dialed the number on the letter into his cellphone. His thumbs hovered over the keys as nerves and excitement played tag in his gut.

Abby's words rang in his ears. One word, really. Ancient.

Time was passing him by. His body wasn't springing back as it once had. All too soon he was going to wake up old and weary with nothing but memories of dark alleys, courtrooms and Coulter's wisecracks to warm his bones.

God, how depressing.

In his hands the phone vibrated with a text from his team. They had intel on Smithwick's return.

What the hell was he doing? He was weeks away from closing the biggest case of his life. Every second of his day should be devoted to nailing down details in Smithwick's takedown. Nothing else was supposed to matter but seeing that asshole's dynasty turn into ashes.

Contract. Phone. Contract. Phone. Back and forth his eyes danced. What to do? What to do?

"Fuck it," he bit out and typed out his response then hit "send." Never had such a tiny word affect him so greatly.

MARCO REACHED FOR the burnished gold handle on the door to Tutala only to drop his hand within millimeters of the shiny surface. Where was this unusual bout of indecisiveness coming from? He was the captain. He gave orders. He made life and death decisions all the time. He had made *this* decision. All he had to do was go inside.

And have his life change forever.

In the past, he had always trusted his instincts, and right then they were wide awake and flashing their red and blues. He had two choices, pull over or try to out run 'em. Did he have the guts to walk across that threshold?

A couple appeared on the opposite side of the glass door and stared at him with puzzled frowns. He flashed him a weak grin and opened the door to allow them to pass.

"Stop being a chicken-shit and get your ass inside," he muttered under his breath.

Once inside the entry, he paused and waited for lightning to strike or the blare of trumpets to herald the monumental accomplishment. Nope. Nothing but the soft strands of Mozart or some other dead composer, filtering through the sound system and the fresh-faced hostess standing at the ready with an armful of menus.

"Can I help you, sir?"

"No, thank you. I'm meeting someone in the bar."

She gestured in that direction with an open palm. "Then have a good evening."

"Thanks."

Tutala was one of the premier restaurants in the city, catering to both the uber-rich and upper-middle class set with its modern, clean décor and French-influenced menu. There was an air of sophistication one felt upon entering, a sense of style that inspired you to be on your best behavior. Quite opposite of The Cavern, which infused a person with the sense of letting loose. Since both establishments were owned by the Kilsgaards, he found the dichotomy amusing.

At this time of night, the bar was filled with the suit and tie crowd, schmoosing over the next big investment opportunity. Marco straightened the lapels of his black sport coat one more time and smoothed the front of his white dress shirt for good measure. Earlier when he had dressed and shaved, he felt as if he were getting ready for junior prom, only this time he was a thousand times more nervous. Back then he knew the night was going to end with a heavy make-out session and perhaps a chance at second base. After the research he did on the list Jasmina had sent him, he hadn't clue as to what this evening would bring.

A quartet of men who had been vacating their table parted, revealing Jasmina sitting at a corner table. The bolt of lightning he had expected when he entered struck and stopped him dead in his tracks. The room faded like in one of those cheesy chick-flicks and the din of clinking silverware and inane conversation faded away to a dull roar.

She sat like a queen with her shoulders back, hands in her lap and her head held high, delicately perched atop her slim neck. Her dark hair was in a low ponytail with the smooth ends sweeping along the pale column of her skin to curl against the curve of her breast. The sleeveless black cocktail dress she wore was cut in a deep v, exposing a generous amount of cleavage. Man, he couldn't wait to get his hands on that milky-white skin, or his mouth, or to bury his face between those soft mounds and fall into the scent of her flesh. God, he could almost taste her.

Damn, he mentally cursed as his cock kicked. He knew he should have taped the thing to his thigh. How was he supposed to concentrate with all the blood in his body pooling in his groin? All she had to do was be in the same room and he was ready to blow. What was going to happen when she finally touched him?

A grin tugged at his lips as he realized that soon, he was going to find out.

With one solid step after another, he made his way to her table, all the while reminding himself to be cool. He wasn't a hormonal teenager or a bumbling virgin. He was a man. A total badass. He could handle one petite woman.

As he drew near, she broke off her conversation with the pretty redhead who stood near her table and looked up at him with that look he dubbed the princess face. Her lips remained in a straight line, but her big brown eyes lit up with joy. She liked what she saw, but damn if she was going to let you know.

The redhead, who was the bar's manager, turned to follow Jasmine's line of sight and propped her hand on her hip when she saw him standing there.

"Marco," Ari said in that annoyed, you are my nemesis, way she always did when they crossed paths. She still hadn't completely forgiven him for tricking her into confirming that her boyfriend was the vigilante he had been tasked to hunt down. The girl could hold quite a grudge.

"Ariel," he replied, knowing how much she just loved her given name. "You look nice tonight. Lavender is your color."

"Always the charmer." She shook her head with a sigh. "Bale isn't here tonight."

"I'm not here to see Bale."

"Oh." Then she noticed how his eyes kept sliding to Jasmine and those incredible lips. Her eyes rounded and she gasped. "Oh!"

The giggle she hid behind her hand confirmed that she had an excellent idea of who Jasmine was and why he would be meeting with her. His face grew hot, but he refused to let embarrassment lower his head. Jasmine was watching and the last thing he wanted was to appear like a stammering fool.

Ari caught her breath and batted her lashes. "Can I get you anything, Marco?"

"Stella will be nice."

"Coming right up. Anything else?" She looked towards Jasmine.

"I'm fine, thank you."

"Then I'll bright back. And thanks for those links, Jasmine. I'll let you know how it goes."

"I'd love to hear it."

Marco waited for Ari to depart, then pulled out the chair to Jasmine's left. He moved to take a seat then paused. Was he "on" now? Was he supposed to wait until he was invited to sit? Or was he just standing there, looking like a big dork?

He decided to err on the side of caution and wait for her to make the first move. The longer he stood, the broader her smile grew until she nodded at the chair. "Relax, Captain. Please, have a seat."

He released a small sigh and sat down. "You look absolutely stunning."

"Thank you. You're looking quite handsome yourself. I like a man who makes an effort in his appearance. I've always found you to be a very good-looking man."

Appreciation warmed her gaze and she reached for her glass of wine. The plump pillows of her lips were painted a deep red, and when she pulled the glass away, a perfect imprint of her lips remained on the glass. Immediately he began to ache, desperate to see that color smeared on certain parts of his body.

"Captain, are you all right?"

"Truthfully, Doc, I don't know. Shit." He swiped a hand down his face. "I mean, ma'am, or Mistress. Hell, I don't even know what to call you."

"Jasmine is fine, for now."

A server appeared by their side and set a chalice of beer on a napkin before him. He murmured a thanks and before the liquid had a chance to settle in the glass, he snatched it up and took several healthy swallows. The brew was cold and burned a bit as it slid down his throat. Jasmine watched him with that princess look on her face, making him wish his chair were equipped with rocket packs to fly him out of there before he made a bigger ass of himself. God, why didn't he just turn in his man-card now?

Or he could stop being a pussy and come clean.

He set the glass on the table and leaned forward. "Jasmine, can I be honest here?"

"Please do. Lying or concealing your thoughts and feelings will not work in a relationship like this."

"Good. Good." His thumbs tapped a staccato beat on the tabletop. "The truth is, I have no idea what I'm doing here. I'm a very focused guy. My work is everything to me, and yet I can't stop thinking about you, about Mistress Jasmina. I'm the guy that gives orders, not takes them. In fact, I hate being told what to do. But for some reason, when I see you, I want to fall at your feet and do whatever you wish. I don't understand."

In an instant, the princess look was replaced with one of compassion and her posture softened. Mistress Jasmina disappeared and Dr. Jovanovich was there, sliding her chair closer and placing her hand over his.

The heat of her palm against the back of his hand made his breath catch at the same time his heart rate slowed behind his ribs. Magic was in her touch and he gripped her fingers to capture the calming sensation.

"What you're experiencing is perfectly normal. Even in this day and age, society tries to dictate what is considered a strength and what is weak. What is male and what is female, and the reality is that it's different for everyone. Being a submissive is not a sign of weakness. And being a submissive does not mean you are any less manly. Believe me, Captain. You are all man, and once I get my hands on you, you will never question just how much of a man you are."

Her fingers tightened around his and he felt his lips curl to match her smile. "I didn't really get what you meant when you said it wasn't about sex. Then I saw you with that whip and got more confused. I should have been horrified to see that guy humiliated that way."

"But you weren't."

"No. I don't know what I was, exactly, but I was..." Fascinated. Turned on. Shocked. All of the above and more. "I don't know how to explain it."

"You and I work in a similar field. People rely on our leadership, our ability to maintain in control during chaotic situations, to make life or death decisions every day. To live with that level of stress day in and day out takes a toll on the human spirit. No one can sustain that lifestyle forever. So, to compensate, a person will turn to different vices to find a balance. Some may choose exercise, or they may turn to alcohol or drugs or begin overeating. As I said, it's different for every person. In our case, I refocus my need for control in another direction, and your subconscious seeks to disengage altogether. I think you'll find that if you feed that need to give up your control, when it comes time to step back into that leadership role, you will be able to do so from a fresh perspective and with the knowledge that you will have a haven to step away from the madness. Sometimes that thought alone brings people great comfort."

What she said made so much sense, he felt the angst of the last few days dissipate. The sensation almost made him giddy and a chuckle burst from his lips. He sandwiched her hand between his. "So you're saying I'm not crazy?"

"Did you really think you were?"

"Sometimes. But I guess it would be a sign of craziness if I didn't question my reactions."

"I suppose so." Her lashes fluttered in that distinctly feminine way that was sexy without being cutesy.

"So what made you become Mistress Jasmina?"

She glanced away and her tongue flicked over her lips as she reached for her wine. The pace with which she lifted the glass and took a slow sip made him wonder if he already hit upon a delicate topic.

Just as he wondered if she was going to answer the question, she spoke, "I come from a very old school family. Eastern European. The men ruled the castle, women were—are— expected to stay home and raise the children. I fought against that tradition in the ways a young girl does. Staying out late, going to college, moving out on my own the moment I was old enough. But I never thought of myself as dominant. I had boyfriends, lovers, nothing really serious. And while the sex was never bad, it wasn't spectacular. The relationships just fizzled out and whenever the parting came, I was never crushed by it.

I was in my first year of residency, and a man came in with symptoms of cardiac arrest. We went to work on him immediately. He made it through surgery magnificently; all was looking well. But he died in recovery. No reason. No medical explanation. It was as if he had given up the will to live. And that made me angry. I did everything right to save his life, yet in the end, I really didn't have any control over the final outcome. When I got home that night, I took my frustration out on my then boyfriend. I wanted to forget. I wanted it rough. I wanted to take back control, and I used his pleasure, his responses to regain that control. It was the best orgasm of my life."

"And Mistress Jasmina was born," he said, enraptured by the way her eyes lost focus as she remembered the journey.

"Not quite." A bittersweet wistfulness flicked across her face. "I knew I had stumbled upon something, but I didn't know what it was. So I did some research. Secretly went to clubs to observe. And I found a Master who was willing to take me on as a protégé. Then Mistress Jasmina was born."

"And what of the boyfriend?"

"He went away. He wanted to be the one to wield the whip and didn't understand why that wasn't going to happen. I don't blame him since I was trying to make sense of everything as well. After that, I have come to realize full-time boyfriends and being a Mistress don't mix."

"What happened with your last sub. Army?"

Again she reached for the wine. "There were several things, but the most important was the realization that he was looking for more in a Mistress than I was willing to grant him."

A spark of curiosity jolted his senses. "Like what?"

She gazed off into the distance. Her eyes flashed and her brow furrowed, and he wondered if she was crafting an answer or figuring out a way to dodge the question.

A short, indrawn breath preceded her answer. "The Dom/sub relationship can take many forms. Some subs require twenty-four-hour guidance, some couples marry, while others are looking for a shorter-term commitment. Personally, I don't have the time or patience to care for a live-in submissive. It wouldn't be fair to him when I know a lot of time I will be called away. Army was much like you. A new sub who knew he had a submissive nature but didn't know how to feed it. I agreed to train him, and we worked well together. But he wants more. He needs more than the attention I can provide, and he deserves to find the Mistress who can feed that need. So I'm helping him with his quest."

Part of him was relieved to know the split was amicable, while a stab of disappointment poked him in the chest. Several times she mentioned the word training, as if her role was to break in new recruits and then send them out into the world. He didn't like the thought of her sending him on to another Mistress or having another sub take his place, although what was he expecting?

He liked what he saw in Jasmine. A lot. And he wasn't opposed to getting to know her on a more personal level. Well, more personal than just sex, anyway. But she was right. Neither of them had time for a serious relationship, and once he had a taste of this entire BDSM lifestyle, he might discover that it was not for him after all. Hell, even the contract stipulated a trial period for just such a situation.

He cleared his throat and reached for his own glass. "I said it once and I'll say it again. He's lucky to have a friend like you."

"Thank you, Captain." She sat back, straightened her shoulders and lifted her chin. Bam. Mistress Jasmina had returned. "Did you bring the contract with you?"

"I did." He withdrew the tri-folded pages from his inside jacket pocket and set them before her.

On the surface, Jasmine was like a serene lake. Quiet, tranquil, nary a ripple disturbing the placid scene. But as he sipped his beer and watched as she read over the pages, he saw the myriad emotions cross her features that were so slight, only his knowledge of micro-expressions caught the movements.

Her eyes narrowed ever so slightly in concentration. When she was pleased, she tilted her head to the left in a tiny nod. The briefest flicker of a brow, a tick near the corner of her mouth when she was amused, all her thoughts played out across her beautiful face.

Then she came to the page of the long list of acts he was willing to engage in. He sat up in his seat as she ran her finger down each checked box. Occasionally she would glance his way with a calculating eye, and he felt sweat began to gather on his upper lip. What had she read that made her look at him as if she already imagined him at her mercy?

She tapped at the paper. "You have no desire at all in a homoerotic encounter?"

At the mention of the word, his ass clenched tight and his heart skipped a beat. "Nope. Not in the slightest. Sorry, Doc."

A grin tugged at her lips and she sighed. "Pity."

There were a lot of things he marked as undecided, but

touching another dude in that way? Or have another dude touch him? Uh-uh. Not going there.

"Well, there is certainly enough here for me to work with." She set the contract down and skimmed her hands down her side. "Did you have any questions for me?"

"Yeah, what exactly is expected of me? I know in the contract we have a designated meeting time, but will I be at your beck and call?"

"Not at all. What I expect from you is your respect and courtesy. The moment you walk through The Cavern's door, your time belongs to me. I understand that your work schedule is unpredictable, as is mine, but when we're together, nothing else exists. When you are out and about your day, you are welcome to do as you wish. If a work situation arises, you will give me as much notice as possible. On occasion I may send you an instruction, but don't fret. I will never ask you to do anything that may cause an embarrassing situation."

"So no orders for me to wear a pink g-string under my work clothes?"

The husky notes of her laughter made his abs clench and his hands flinch, eager to gather her close to feel the vibrations against his skin.

"What you wear to work is entirely up to you."

"That's a relief." He slid the chalice back and forth on the tabletop and hoped he sounded nonchalant as he asked, "And we're to refrain from intimate relationships outside the, uh, dungeon, right?"

The question was more to confirm her stance than his. Between pining for Brett and the Smithwick case, a girlfriend never fit into his life, and he had grown tired of one-night stands years ago. And selfish as it might seem, considering she wasn't his girlfriend, he wanted Jasmine all to himself.

She chuckled again. "I have yet to meet a woman who allowed her significant other to visit a dominatrix. Although I guess there might be one or two in existence. So, yes. I will insist that we remain exclusive. I like to devote all of my attention to one man. However, I may bring in another on occasion to assist with a scene, for the most part it will be just you and I."

A hundred different scenarios of who those people might be and how they were going to assist flashed through his mind, one dirtier then the next, and he felt the buzz of anticipation raise the fine hairs on his neck and arms.

"Where do I sign?" he asked in a voice far raspier than he intended.

Jasmine reached for the clutch he hadn't noticed resting on the seat next to her as she flagged down Ari who stood by the bar.

As Ari drew near, Jasmine held up the contract. "Can you make me a photocopy, please?"

"Certainly," she replied with a curious shifting of the eyes between the two of them before she departed.

Marco groaned. "She's going to read that."

"Maybe." She sat back in her seat as if the idea didn't bother her, which it probably didn't. "She may be looking for ideas. You're not the only man who's interested in exploring their submissive sides."

It took a second for the implication to set is. "Wait a minute. Bale? Big guy, deep frown, biceps as big as my head, can rip a car apart with his bare hands. That Bale? Submissive?"

"Ah, so you've met."

Ari's return halted any further questioning. A red flush covered her face from hairline to neck and she set the papers down in front of Jasmine with a barely audible, "Here you go," before dashing away.

Yep. She had read them.

"Shall you do the honors, Captain?" She handed him the fountain pen.

The plastic held the warmth of her touch. His heart beat faster as the tip touched the paper and he scrolled his name across the page in what turned out to be purple ink. He smiled at the sight. Mental note: *Jasmine likes purple.*

He signed the duplicate contract and slid both over to Jasmine who signed her name with a flourish and surprisingly clean penmanship. Guess not all doctors had illegible handwriting.

"Shall we make a toast?" he asked when she had placed the pen and one of the contracts in her purse.

"Why not?" She lifted her glass. "To a new adventure."

"Sounds good to me." They clinked their glasses and from over the rim he saw her eyes narrow. The brown of her irises deepened and all he could think about was smoke and sin.

"So, Jasmine." He cleared his throat. "What now?"

"Well..." she trailed off in a way that immediately put him on high alert. Somehow in the last half-second a shift had occurred in the universe and he sensed he was about to be schooled. She crossed one leg over the other. Her skirt hiked up, exposing a long length of creamy thigh. "Now, you call me Mistress Jasmina, or Mistress. Do you understand?"

Holy shit. The game was on.

"Yes," he croaked and her brow rose. "Mistress. Jasmina," he added.

"Good. Scoot your chair back a bit and angle yourself toward me."

The slight scrape of the wood on tile sounded like a chainsaw in his ears. A quick glance to the left and right confirmed no one seemed to be looking their way; however that didn't lessen the tension rolling in his gut.

"Spread your legs apart. Wider," she commanded in a low, husky tone.

The fabric of his slacks pulled taut across his lap, outlining the thick line of his erection. He should have been embarrassed, but damn, the woman turned him on, and obviously she wanted to check out what she had signed up for. *By all means, baby, go ahead and look to your heart's content.*

A minute passed in silence as she ate him up with her intense stare. Her lips parted as she breathed in and out in slow, steady draws that drew his gaze to those luscious breasts while his fingers pressed into his thighs to fight the urge to fidget like a school boy in math class.

Mistress Jasmina flexed her foot, sending the black stiletto to the floor with a tiny clatter. Purple polish glittered on her toes as she stretched out her leg and rested the flat of her foot on the ridge of his cock, making him hiss with the contact. As her toes massaged his hard-on, he glanced around the room, convinced every eye in the bar was on them.

"Look at me," she commanded and dug her big toe into his scrotum with the most delightful pressure. "The only person you need to focus on is me."

A moan caught in his throat and he nodded.

"I meant what I said about your time outside of the club belonging to you. But as of the moment you signed that contract, your body belongs to me. You will take care of yourself and come to me in the same, if not better, condition as how I left you. As for your cock," his dick twitched beneath the sole of her foot, happy to be addressed, "you will not touch yourself in any way sexual without permission. Do you understand?"

"Yes." He swallowed hard. "Mistress."

"Good. Before our appointment tomorrow you will trim down all the hair around your cock. Do not go down to bare skin." She chuckled low in her chest. "You are not prepared for what will happen if you do."

What was that supposed to mean? Did she mean physically or the punishment she'd met out if he disobeyed?

"I can't wait to play with you," she said, and drew back her foot, leaving him a hair's breadth from coming in his pants, again. And he wasn't supposed to find relief? Oh God, the torture had already begun.

She slipped her shoe on and rose to a stand, gathering her purse. She pushed the fingers of her right hand into his hair and stroked his scalp down and around his ear. Her thumb brushed his parted lips, and on her face he saw a calculating hunger like a lioness lying in wait while the hapless gazelle grazed in the brush, unaware that at any moment she was going to bounce and tear it apart.

Lord help him, he couldn't wait.

"Until tomorrow, Captain." She dropped her hand and walked away.

Like a magnet to metal, his head whipped around to follow her progress. His tongue almost fell out of his mouth as he saw that the back of her dress was cut so low, the entire expanse of her spine was bared down to the dimples above her ass. Judging by the murmurs that erupted around him, he wasn't the only one enjoying the view of her swishing hips.

He wiped the back of his hand around his mouth and motioned to Ari. "Can I have another Stella and the check, please?" He needed something to cool his boiling blood.

"Sure. But don't worry about the bill. This is on Jasmine's tab."

"Really? Wow. I've never not paid before." He was the man. The man was always supposed to pay. "That's okay. I can still take care of it."

She popped her hand on her hip. "Sweetie, if what just happened here is what I think just happened here, you are now a kept man. What Jasmine says, goes. And she'll know that you paid."

Dare he risk displeasing his Mistress? Or just sit back and enjoy being, as Ari said, a kept man?

He sat back with a smile. Well, there was a first for everything.

CHAPTER SIX

MARCO SHOOK OUT his hands and arms like a swimmer preparing to dive into the deep end of the pool and let loose a nervous chuckle. Maybe he should do some stretches and warm ups too. Who knew what the evening was going to bring, and judging be the room's décor, he'd best be up for anything.

Frosted-glass wall sconces illuminated the room in a soft, candlelit glow. The effect was quite soothing. If only the racks of whips and floggers hanging against the caramel-colored suede walls, and the bars and pulleys suspended from the ceiling offered the same amount of comfort.

Was Mistress Jasmina going to break him in gently or tie him to one of the pieces of furniture in the room and have at him? Of the six pieces of leather-covered apparatuses, the only ones he recognized were a table and a chair.

"This is nuts, this is nuts, this is nuts," he muttered to the giant armoire that sat locked in the corner. He knew it was locked because he had tried to take a gander at what was inside. Of course, if he had really wanted to get a look at the contents, he could have picked the lock, but it wasn't a good idea to piss off his Mistress before they even begun.

The door opened without warning, and Mistress Jasmina stepped inside the room. Unsure of how to respond to her entrance, he reverted to his police academy days and snapped to attention where he stood. Hands to his side, chest up, he faced forward and stared at a spot on the wall just over her shoulder.

From his peripheral vision, he saw that she was, as his grandfather would say, dressed for bear. Black was still the predominant color of her outfit, but a red satin bustier replaced the see-through top, and the leather skirt was switched out for skin-tight pants that fed into thigh-high lace up boots. If the idea was to torture him with making him work all those laces free to get to her covered body, he wasn't going to last past the first boot.

Jasmina approached him in slow, crisscrossing steps. She had left her hair down so the ends curled around each breast, and her make-up was minimal except for that tantalizing red lipstick staining her lips. She circled him once before coming to a stop scant inches before him and regarded him with her princess expression in place.

"At ease, solider," she said.

Marco released a sigh and shifted his weight to both feet as he clasped his hands behind his back.

"From now on, when you enter this room, you will wait for me on your knees, sitting on your feet, palms down on your thighs and gazing to the floor. Unless you are instructed otherwise, this is the position you take at all times. Do you understand?"

"Yes, Mistress."

"You will also not speak unless instructed. The only sounds you are allowed to make without permission are sighs, moans, gasps, and any other sound of pleasure or distress. When we are in a scene and you have a reached a limit outside of your comfort zone, you will say the word 'stop'."

"Like a safe word?"

"In a way, except the only word you are allowed to use is

stop. If I have you bound too tight, or you are feeling ill effects, let me know and we will pause to assess the situation. Be warned that if you say stop more than once, the scene ends immediately."

"I understand," he said, then shouted when she reached out and twisted his nipple through his shirt.

"Ow. What was that for?"

"You had spoken without being asked. I didn't ask if you understood."

"I didn't know we were starting," he shot back.

All the muscles in her face went lax, and in her eyes he saw disappointment as she went completely still. Her immediate withdrawal was like a bucket of cold water over his head.

"I'm sorry, Mistress Jasmina."

She blinked once and reached to twist the other nipple.

He bit back a curse and was about to ask why, then realized he had spoken again without being asked. Message received. He'd have to figure out another way to ask for her forgiveness.

Since she hadn't given him permission to move or speak, the only option left to him was to hang his head in shame. With each second that passed with nothing but the faint sound of their breathing filling the room, the fear that he had already crossed the point of no return created a band around his chest that tightened by the second. He felt like the dog that pissed the carpet and their master was chewing them out.

Except Jasmina didn't shout. The icy silence closed in around him until he trembled with the need to drop to the floor, bury his head in her belly and beg for forgiveness. The urge was crazy. They had barely begun and already his emotions were all over the place.

The loss of control almost had him bolting for the door and then she moved. A slight shifting of her knees followed by her hand lifting to rest on the top of his bowed head. Her cheek brushed his as she whispered in his ear, "Take off your shoes and socks."

His knees buckled with relief and the breath shuttered from between his lips. He wasted no time slipping off his wingtips and socks while she took a seat on a low-slung chair. She crossed one leg over the other and settled her hands on the slanted arms.

"Shirt next followed by your pants. Fold them neatly and set them on that stool to your left."

The plastic buttons of his shirt felt like ice against his finger, and the cool air hitting his overheated skin was a welcome respite. He stripped off his undershirt and set that on top of his shirt. The belt came next. He worked the zipper of his slacks over his erection, then drew the material down his legs, revealing his deep purple boxer-briefs.

Jasmina gasped, and he saw a big grin curl her lips before she resumed her bored expression. That little crack in her cool as a cucumber demeanor released the weight of anxiety in his chest. He surprised her. He pleased her. If he did it once, he had the power to do it again.

He slid his thumbs under the waistband of his underwear then stopped. She hadn't mentioned anything beyond removing his slacks. He snuck a glance in her direction and saw the smile in her eyes.

"Take off those sexy briefs."

He bit back his own grin and took off his last stitch of clothing. When no further instruction came, he dropped to his knees and set his palms against his thighs and lowered his head. Free from its confines, his cock stiffened further and rose in the air. The night before he had done as she asked and trimmed the hair around his dick, surprised at how much larger his cock appeared. Why hadn't he been doing that his entire adult life?

From what he'd been told and had seen with his own eyes in the locker room, he possessed a decent-size cock. Not overly long, but it held a nice curve, and the ridge around the head was nice and thick, stroking all the best places once seated inside a tight pussy. Hey, he never had any complaints. However, Mistress Jasmina was a connoisseur of cocks and he hoped he impressed her with a good showing.

Like a panther rising from its resting place in the sun, she left the chair and walked toward him. She dug her fingers into his hair and stroked his scalp. God, his eyes closed, he could come from that touch alone.

"I understand this is new to you. You're just learning. But my expectations are high. Think of this time as the same as when you were a rookie in the police force. In fact, I think that's what I'll call you. Rookie. You see, here at The Cavern, you have to earn the use of your given name." She leaned forward and her bustier gapped, giving him an excellent view of the curve of her breasts. A few inches from his nose, a heavenly spice-scent rose from her warm skin and he swayed, ready to pitch forward into her cleavage. Her lips brushed his ear as she continued. "You have to earn the right to hear me scream your name when I come. Do you understand, Rookie?"

"Yes, Mistress," he answered with a puff of his warm breath against her bare shoulder.

"Good." She pressed her nose against his neck and breathed in deep. Her tongue flicked out to lick the pulsating vein before she straightened with a satisfied sigh. "Now stand and let me get a better look at my new toy."

He climbed to his feet and stood straight and tall. As she circled him, he sucked in his gut. He had gotten a little soft around the middle; otherwise he was proud of his build, and from the slight smile on her lips, she liked what she saw.

In her four-inch heels, she still only came up to his chin. He could easily overtake her physically, but the power she had over him with just a look made him weak in the knees.

She came to a stop behind him and placed her palms against the back of his neck. She smoothed a line down his back, her thumbs pressed deep along the channel on either side of his spine. When she reached his ass, she said, "Bend over. Keep your legs straight."

Great. He bit back a moan as he did as he was told. Dear Lord, please don't let him pull a hamstring. He knew he should have done some stretches when he arrived.

His fear for his hamstrings diminished when she gripped the cheeks of his ass and spread them apart. For a long while he felt the heat of her gaze on his ass and flames erupted across his face. Humiliation and desire waged a war in his mind with both sides putting up a hell of a fight.

Vulnerable didn't begin to describe how he felt with his cheeks held open wide and cool air kissing his puckered hole. Embarrassed? Yes. Exposed? Of course. Completely depraved and ready to fuck anything that held the slightest bit of resistance? Absolutely.

"You may straighten," Jasmina said with a pat on his butt and gestured to the padded table. "Lie down on your back."

Goosebumps erupted as his hot skin hit the cool leather. He didn't fail to notice the stirrups attached under the tabletop and the restraints at the sides and near his head. His imagination exploded with the possibilities of the wicked things she had planned.

Mistress stood at the head of the table and gazed down at him from above. Her hands lifted and she placed her thumbs on his forehead. Over and over she smoothed the line of his eyebrows and down under his neck. Man, he loved the way she massaged his scalp. His eyelids grew heavy, and he swore he was floating on a cloud. Her touch extended to his shoulders and the cap of his shoulders. He hadn't realized how tense his muscles were until she dug with her fingers into his sore spots.

She moved around the table and lifted his right hand. For a long time she studied his palm before pushing her thumb into the center. Oh so slowly, she brought his hand up to her face, nuzzling his palm with her nose before resting it against her cheek. His breath caught as he watched her eyes close on a sigh. She was so soft and delicate in his hold, her skin like silk against the light caress of his fingers as he cupped her face.

So sexy. So sensual. So... "Beautiful," he breathed out. "You are so beautiful."

She smiled against his hand. "Thank you."

Before he blinked, her hand shot out to twist his nipple. "Ow."

"That was for talking. And this," she twisted the other, "is for touching me. I did not tell you to curl your fingers."

Right. Damn it.

He sucked in his lips to refrain from any more outbursts and concentrated on studying his Mistress as she continued to work him over.

As she examined the almost-healed wound on his chest, her eyes narrowed and for half a second he saw her doctor expression as she turned her head to the right and left. When she caught his gaze, she nodded as if she had read his mind, "Looks good."

The tips of her fingers scored his ribs and he flinched. She did it again, and he squirmed, resisting the urge to laugh. She tugged on the fine hair across his belly and again, he bit his lip.

"Stop it." She latched on to his nipple and pinched it tight, pulling the bud higher away from his chest until his eyes watered. "You're holding back your responses. If it tickles, then laugh. If it feels good, by God I want to hear it. Understand?"

"Yes, Mistress," he panted.

"We shall see."

And with that, she dragged her fingernail in a deep groove from under his armpits down to his flanks. His hips bucked and he almost shot off the bed with a shout.

"Finally," she huffed and went to work on his thighs.

With her nails and fingertips, she scored, scratched and pinched his lower body. She pushed her knuckles into the bottoms of his feet, tickled the sensitive area behind his knees and ran the flat of her hand up the inside of his thighs as he bucked and moaned on the table. All the while she left his cock alone to bounce with his movements and trail a fine line of precum across his belly. He gripped the edge of the table until his fingers ached to keep from reaching for his dick and stroking himself to completion. This was by far the best and worst massage of his life.

By the time she stepped back, he was covered in sweat and heaving as if he had run after a felony suspect. Jasmina too was breathing heavily. Her hair was mussed and the tops of her breasts glistened with a fine sheen of perspiration. Excitement glittered in her gaze as she eyed his cock with hunger.

"Good boy," she cooed. She reached under the table and the hum of a motor kicked up. The side of the table his torso rested upon lifted until he reached a sitting position.

She knocked his legs apart to rest down on either side then pulled another chair up to the foot of the table. From the sidebar she collected a glass tumbler then rejoined him.

"Take your dick in your hand and stroke it."

He jerked as if she had poked him. What was it about her talking dirty that got him so hot?

A moan rolled up from his gut as he gripped his cock and began to move his hand up and down.

"That's right." Her breath ghosted across his shoulder as she whispered in his ear. "When I give the order, you will fill this glass with your cum."

She pressed the glass into his left hand, then sauntered over to the chair and took a seat.

Having her sitting there, watching him masturbate with rapt attention brought him to the edge much too quickly. He tried to pull back and make it last until she gave the order, but she kicked the end of the table with her foot. "Make it feel good, Rookie. I want you in tears."

Done and done. He held his breath and clenched his jaw, pumping his cock until his forearm ached. Mistress Jasmina watched his hand and studied his every stroke, her breasts rose and fell with bated breaths. Her lower lip fell open followed by the tip of her tongue peeking out to sweep the plump little pillow as if she could taste him on her palate.

"Ah, God," he gritted out. A tear slipped down his cheek and his body tightened to the point of breaking.

Jasmina's head tipped back and she moaned as if she inhaled his torture. Then she snapped forward and nailed him with a hot stare. "Come."

Fire erupted out his cock in great bursts of energy. He barely remembered to catch the milky fluid in the crystal glass before he shot all over his legs, and stuffed the head of his cock into the opening.

"Keep going." Jasmina jumped up and rushed to his side. Laying her hand over his, she continued to stroke his dick. "Every drop, Rookie. Every drop belongs to me."

On and on his orgasm went, leaving him too weak to do anything more than moan and lie there in his own sweat as more cum dribbled into the glass. Just as well, he still hadn't been given permission to speak.

When his cock had nothing left to give, Jasmina took the glass from his hand and held it up to the light. It shocked him to see how much fluid he had produced. Truthfully, he didn't think he had that much in him.

Way to go, you.

She tipped the glass, this way and that, even going so far as to sniff the rim. Holy hell, was she going to drain the glass? That would be as hot as fuck.

Instead she lowered the glass and dipped her finger into the cream. She rubbed the tips together as if testing the texture. She dipped again then proceeded to rub his cum onto her wrists and the base of her neck as if it were perfume.

Knowing that she was marked in his cum sent a primal surge of lust through his depleted body, and to his surprise arousal stirred anew. Dear God, she was going to kill him.

Yeah, but he'd have the biggest grin on his face when they laid him in his grave.

Once she was painted to her liking, she went to the bar and set the glass to the side. Through sleepy eyes he watched her take out several white towels from what looked like a crockpot then retrieve a bottle of water from the mini-fridge.

"Drink." She cracked the top open and handed it to him.

He guzzled the water so quickly, he suffered from brain freeze. "Ah."

"Easy there, Rookie." She wiped the sweat from his brow with the warm towel then continued to swab his chest and legs. Before the cloth had a chance to cool, she swapped it for another.

A monster orgasm and a sponge bath? He definitely could get use to this.

"Lift forward," she said and worked on his back. "How do you feel?"

"I don't know," he sighed. "I can't explain it."

"Try." He heard the grin in her command.

"I feel...alive."

Yeah. It could have been minutes or hours since he walked through that door. He felt as if he'd been dragged over hot coals, shot to the heavens, electrocuted, enveloped in a warm hug, torn apart at the seams and sewn back together all at the same time. Only once before had he experienced such an extreme range of emotions. The night he almost had Smithwick. But that night had ended in bitter disappointment. This euphoric feeling was completely unknown.

"I didn't know." He paused to wet his lips. "I didn't realize..."

"Letting go does that to a person. You did well, Rookie. I have hope for you yet."

Thank you, Mistress.

He wanted to tell her. He wanted to do a lot of things, like reach out and touch her arm. He wanted to remove the towel from her hand so that her bare palm was stroking his cock and not through the textured cotton. He wanted her kiss. He wanted to know what she tasted like, how her lips felt on his skin.

He wanted Jasmina.

The plastic bottle crinkled in his grip as he restrained the urge to sweep her up and take her to the floor. That wasn't their deal. She controlled him. And so far, he loved it. He hungered for it. And he was ready for more.

"Drink up." She guided the bottle back to his mouth. "I don't want you fading from dehydration."

He did as he was told and watched her walk to the phone attached to the wall and pick up the receiver. "You may enter," she said to whoever picked up on the other end.

What was his Mistress planning now? He jerked up from his seat and bit his tongue to keep from asking.

A moment later the lock to the door disengaged and a woman walked in. With a fuchsia-pink bobbed haircut and matching pink lace bodysuit, she looked like an x-rated version of a little girl's doll. From the way she stood with her spine straight and her gaze aimed at the floor, he figured her to be another sub. Who was curious about his cock if the way she snuck a peak at his lap was any indication.

"Don't you dare." Jasmina slapped at his hand as he moved to cover up. "Rookie, this is Pixie. Her master has loaned her to me for the moment. She will dress you and see that you can walk without falling over. You're still dealing with a huge rush of endorphins and I don't want you to crash on your way out."

His Mistress was leaving him? Alone with another woman?

Disappointment cooled his lust. Just a week ago the idea of being fondled by two women on the same night would have been an epic fantasy, but now the thought left him cold. Mistress Jasmina had branded him as hers, and her touch was the only one he craved.

Wow. He closed his eyes and drew in a breath to help clear his head. He had fallen. And fallen hard.

The brush of fingers on his cheek had his eyes flying open in alarm. When he realized it was Jasmina, he relaxed.

"Will I see you on Tuesday?" she asked.

"Absolutely."

"Good." She brushed the hair off his forehead and softly bade him goodnight.

The click of her heels on the floor as she walked out the door made his chest go tight, and that scared the hell out of him.

Not even his infatuation with Brett made him want to drop

to his knees and crawl after her to beg for one more touch. And to think, they had only had one session. A session when they really hadn't done anything all that kinky. Damn, emotionally he not only had jumped into the deep end of the pool, he'd done a frickin' cannonball and was drowning.

"If you are able to stand, I will dress you now."

With his Mistress out of the room, the girl looked him up and down with a hungry look that said she couldn't wait to get her hands on him.

"Pixie. Is that your real name or do you still have to earn it?"

"It's my sub name."

Right. "Look, Pixie, I am perfectly able to dress myself. You can turn around and it will be all good."

The ends of her pink hair flicked her cheeks as she shook her hair. "Mistress Jasmina said for me dress you."

"I understand. But with all due respect, I'd rather dress myself."

"If she finds out, she'll punish me and then my Master will punish me, and he hits hard." Her hand went to her backside and rubbed up and down.

"How about a compromise? I'll put on my pants and you can help with my shirt. That way, we're both happy and no one has to know the truth."

She popped her hip out and shot him a grin. "You're brand new, aren't you? The truth always comes out."

"That's why we're going to keep our mouths shut. Or else I'll tell Mistress Jasmina you tried to do more than just dress me."

Her mouth formed an "o" and she sucked in a breath. "Are you a switch?"

"A switch?"

"Yeah. Both Dom and sub? 'Cause let me tell you, you just

got me hot and subs don't do that to me."

Well that wasn't something he had thought about. He shrugged. "Maybe."

"Well don't be. Mistress Jasmina is in no way a submissive. If you want to keep her happy, I'd squash that instinct."

"I think I'll do just fine being myself. So are you turning around or not?"

"Not. I'll let you put on your underwear. But I get to watch."

Hey, if all she wanted was to have a peek, he'd take the concession.

He turned to the side to keep her in his peripheral vision while he reached for his clothes and slipped on his boxers. Pixie beat him to the rest of his garments and knelt on the floor, holding open his pants. She took too much pleasure drawing them up his legs and pulling the tag over his cock.

"Nice undies," she cooed.

"Just get on with it or I'll dress myself," he bit out.

"I'm working on it." She winked then worked his t-shirt over his head and smoothed the cotton over his chest with swirling motions of her palms. His white button-down was treated with the same extra attention.

"She mentioned nothing of the shoes," he said and took his loafers from her hand. "I got it from here."

"Ooo, you are a feisty one. I hope our Masters put us together in a scene sometime soon."

His heart stopped. "Does Mistress Jasmina share her subs a lot?"

"Rarely. But it's been known to happen."

Then he was going to have to do his damnedest to make sure she wanted him all to herself, for Mistress Jasmina belonged to him and no one else.

CHAPTER SEVEN

J ASMINE NODDED AT the doorman and swept through the entrance to the sanctuary of Amaryllis' private suite. In actuality the inner lair wasn't all that private. There was always someone doing something to someone within the penthouse loft, and most of the time the persons involved weren't Amaryllis. Ever since she married Lucian, she spent more time in their apartment, and Jasmine didn't blame her for wanting to keep such a tasty morsel all to herself.

Tonight was ladies' night in the suite, with Mistresses enjoying the peace and quiet away from the noise of the dance floor or party rooms. Some had their subs at their feet or chained to an apparatus while others, like herself, were solo.

She spotted Madeline resting on a couch, using her sub as an ottoman while watching a Mistress draw a tic-tac-toe with a riding crop across the back of a man suspended from the ceiling. On her way to join them, Jasmine stopped by the bar and asked for a bottle of water and a ginger ale, which she received with a smile from the cute bartender.

At last count there were about twenty Masters and Mistresses who utilized The Cavern's facilities, but only a few were considered permanent residents, and she was lucky enough to be counted as one of them. The title granted her the use of her own playroom and the ability to come and go as she pleased. Invaluable freedoms in her opinion.

She loved it here. Within these walls she was not alone in her desires. She was respected and admired. There was always new knowledge to be gained and interesting people to talk to. She could lose herself in the sway of the crowded dance floor or find clarity when focused on one person. Sure, the club was dark, and at times the stench of sweat and sex was overwhelming. But that's what she liked best. The teaming mass of humanity who said, "fuck it all" and lived for the moment. In a word, The Cavern was heaven.

"Well..." Madeline said as Jasmine sat down next to her. "How did it go with the new sub?"

"Good." She took a sip of her soda and turned her attention to the floor show.

"Good? That's all?"

"Yep."

"Liar. I can smell your pussy from here." She reached between Jasmine's legs and copped a feel. "And your pants are soaked through. Honey, that is more than just good."

"Keep your hands to yourself, missy." She slapped at Madeline's arm with a chuckle. "Okay. It was really good."

"Spill it. I want to hear all of the juicy details."

"You know I don't tell."

"Come on. Give me something. Cock size? Any special talent? Did he at least make you come hard?"

"I didn't let him make me come."

Madeline's eyes boggled. "Are you serious? Why not?"

"Because the anticipation is just as sweet for me as it is for him."

"That's insane. I can't go one day without coming. Keep your head down, Megabyte. Mommy is talking." She used the sole of her boot to push the sub's head down. "So. Is he a keeper?"

Million dollar question. "I don't know. He responded beautifully, but I didn't push him that hard. He's new. Really new. Time will tell."

"Hmmm. But you want him. You want him bad. I can see it in your eyes. You act all calm and untouchable, but you want to ride that man into the ground."

Jasmine couldn't help but smile at Madeline's words. The woman was incorrigible.

Of course she wanted to ride the captain's cock. It was quite lovely, and the way his body rolled with the sensations she inflicted upon him was absolutely delicious. That's why she had worn pants, to remind herself that the evening was about seeing to his needs and not hers.

"As I said, he's new. The moment I really drag him over the coals he may balk and become a complete disappointment."

Madeline nodded. "Like what happened to Elizabetta earlier."

"What happened to Lizzie?"

"You didn't hear? Her new sub tried to Dom her and turned into a big bully when she wouldn't play his game."

"Is she all right?"

"Physically, oh yeah. She had him on his knees real quick when he tried to tackle her. She's been taking those self-defense classes from Bale, you know. And Lucian and Jax were there right away. But mentally, I don't think she's taking it too well. She really liked this guy."

"Son of a bitch," Jasmine muttered and twisted the cap off the bottle of water as if it were the asshole's head.

Why did men think they had to physically assault someone to show their strength? Elizabetta wasn't the first one to have a male sub try to prove his manhood by taking it out on his Mistress, and unfortunately she wouldn't be the last. As long as man questioned their sexuality, there was going to be some dumbass who turned violent when faced with the truth.

Lizzie was a good Mistress, just starry-eyed and young. She liked them big and muscle-bound. Alphas begging to be mastered. Except she doubted her abilities and suffered from low self-esteem. Jasmine saw she did her best to hide her insecurities, but when a sub who wasn't fully invested in the relationship sensed a weakness, more often than not, they exploited it. She had potential. She only had to believe in it.

"Where is she now?"

Madeline shrugged. "I saw her leave with Amaryllis."

"Poor kid. At least Amaryllis has a way of making things better."

"True that. Now I'm depressed. I hate that. Megabyte." She nudged him with her heel. "I'm horny. Crawl over here and lick my pussy."

And that was her cue to leave. "I'm outta here. See you later."

"Are you going to find a man to satisfy that itch? Or better yet, a woman?"

"No." Madeline was all about instant gratification and never appreciated the torture of holding out. "I'll be heading out soon, but first I have a pixie to interrogate."

MARCO SNAPPED HIS gum and tried to instill a sense of calm into his twitchy muscles. This meeting was dragging on for what felt like forever and it was obvious to all of them working-grunts that nothing constructive was going to be resolved.

Ever since the state decided to legalize marijuana, the department had had monthly meetings as to what was considered legal and illegal when complying with federal law.

In other words, government officials didn't know whether to shit or get off the pot and refused to make a decision that might damage them in the polls.

To make it look as if they were making an effort, the commander tasked them with these monthly sessions. It was all bullshit and Marco found them tedious on a good day.

But tonight was a Mistress Jasmina night. In two short hours he'd be submerged in her world. All day long his skin tingled with anticipation, and he was anxious to feel her hands on his flesh. All day long, his eyes kept skipping to every clock and timepiece in the vicinity. The only time he felt the least bit calm was while working on details of the Smithwick case.

They were homing in on his capture and the minute that rat-bastard stepped back on city soil, his ass was grass.

But Smithwick was not in the city. And all of Marco's daily work was caught up. Funny how the prospect of mind-blowing sex motivated a man. The only thing standing in his way was Commander Asswipe and his long-winded speeches.

The commander lifted is eyes from the stack of papers on the podium and heaved a sigh. "Are there any questions?"

If any of you shitheads makes a sound, I'll kick your ass into next week.

Marco held his breath and counted to ten. A quick glance around confirmed that almost every man in that room was just as tense as he.

Asante sighed again. "You're dismissed."

Hot damn.

Marco was the first one to the door and halfway down the hall when Cassidy caught up to him. "Good lord. I thought he'd never shut up."

"You and me both, kid."

He stopped by his desk to do a quick scan to ensure everything was locked, off and put away. Of course anything of real importance was hidden where snoopy bosses couldn't find it.

"Spectacles, testicles, wallet, watch," he mumbled as he slapped those areas. He was good to go. "See ya, Coulter."

"Wait, wait, wait. What's the rush? Trent's poker game doesn't start until eight."

"I told Trent I'm not going to make it. You guys have fun."

"What do you mean? You're always there." He followed Marco to the elevator. "What's more interesting than Samuel's melt-your-face-off chicken wings?"

Marco paused with his hand over the down button. "I can think of a thousand things more interesting."

Coulter shrugged. "I can only think of one. Women. Oh, hey. Are you meeting a woman?"

"On a Tuesday? No." He felt his face heat with the lie and pressed the button several times in rapid succession.

"Holy shit. You're blushing. It must be a woman. Who is she?"

The doors swooshed open. About damn time. "Goodnight, Coulter."

Cassidy slapped the doors back open. "Come on, Cap. A name, description, something."

"Move your hand."

"A name."

"Look." Marco pointed over Coulter's shoulder. "Boobs."

The man fell for it and turned. "What?"

Marco knocked Coulter's hand away so the doors could close then sagged against the wall with a sigh. Coulter was going to be worse than the paparazzi on the trail of a juicy scandal. An annoyance for certain, but for Mistress Jasmina, completely worth it.

The heavy rush-hour traffic had his hand reaching for his

flashing light, but he left it in its holder. She already had enough power over him as it was. No need to prove how desperate he was for more of her attention.

The gate for the private parking garage under The Cavern lifted with the swipe of his entry card and reminded him of the parting of the red curtain before the feature presentation. The card was a perk of being Mistress Jasmina's submissive. Private parking and backdoor access to the club.

He breezed past the doorman at the entrance without making eye contact and headed straight for the dungeon. The guy knew what he was there for and didn't need to know any more.

To his surprise, Mistress Jasmina was already seated in her chair when he opened the door.

She was dressed in his favorite mesh halter top and a skirt that was so short, it appeared as if she wore nothing from the waist down.

He shut the door behind him and dropped to his knees before her as he had been instructed. As much as he wanted to follow the long line of her bare legs with his gaze, he kept his head down and waited and waited. And waited.

"Rise and undress," she said without the slightest inflection to give away her mood. He rose and reached for the top button of his shirt. "Like last time."

The act was like last time, but there was a different, tense vibe in the air that made his mouth go dry. At any moment he expected the proverbial other shoe to drop, and he didn't mean his wingtip or the stiletto balanced on the end of her foot.

Once bared, he knelt on the floor and waited for further instructions. Jasmina crossed then re-crossed her legs and watched him in silence for several long minutes. Her intense gaze on his naked body felt as strong as if her hands actually touching his flesh.

After a slow blink of her eyelids, she rose to her feet and stood above him like an Amazon warrior. She crossed to the wet-bar and poured a glass of yellow liquid into a crystal tumbler.

"Have a drink, Rookie. You're going to need the calories tonight." She handed him the glass with a daring smirk. "Don't worry. It's only pineapple juice."

He took the offered cup and brought it to his lips. As discreetly as possible, he took an exploratory sniff for good measure and breathed a slight sigh of relief at the familiar but unexpected sent of pineapple. Liquor made sense, but why pineapple juice?

When the glass was drained, she took it from his grasp and licked her lips while tapping a steady rhythm on the crystal with her short fingernails.

"Last week when I left you, I had given you specific instructions. Did you follow them? And I suggest you think carefully before you answer, Rookie." Her softly spoken question cracked in the air as effectively as a whip.

Shit. The pixie squealed. Panic beat in his chest, and a thousand excuses flew to his lips. But Mistress did not suffer excuses. If he dared to utter them, there was nothing stopping her from walking out that door.

He swallowed down his nerves and answered, "Not exactly."

"Explain."

"I helped Pixie to dress me."

"I see," she sighed with disappointment. "It appears as if you require another method of training for you to understand that my word is to be obeyed. Forehead to the floor, hands by your head. I want that delicious ass pointed to the sky."

Marco bent over as a new wave of panic washed over him. There was no doubt in his mind that this time she was going to punish him with more than a pinched nipple.

The click of her heels against the floor sent shivers down his spine. The creak of the wardrobe cabinet doors opening and the clunk of unseen items as she sorted through her equipment made his gut clench with anticipation.

"I knew you hadn't followed my orders the moment I looked at Pixie's face. The way she held her breath told me she had something to hide. Plus, if she had gotten her hands your body, she'd would have been wet and ready to fuck. I'm sorry it must come to this, but you have to learn. Now, what should I choose? Ah. A good old-fashioned wooden spoon will do nicely."

Oh my God, she's really going to spank my ass.

He gulped and tried to relax. The last time he'd been spanked with a wooden spoon was when his mom caught him dumping food coloring into his sister's bottle of hairspray. He doubted this experience was going to be the same.

"Count each one out loud and say thank you."

Crack.

Her swing landed as her words registered. He wasn't sure what shocked him more, the blast of pain across his butt cheek or the order to thank her.

"Ah, one," he stammered. "Thank you."

"Louder." *Thwack.*

"Two. Thank you, Mistress."

Jasmina peppered his ass in steady smacks from the fleshiest part of his cheeks to the backs of his thighs. The sharp stings settled into a fiery ache that pulled him into another dimension in a gentle suction like the tide pulling back from the shore. God, yes. This was what he needed. Nothing else existed but the burn encompassing his body and the way he felt as light as a feather, rolling along on the current of Jasmina's ocean. Not his job, not his family, nothing but what Jasmina granted him to feel.

The smacks stopped at twenty-five, yet he swayed backward, reaching for the next swat.

"Good boy," Jasmina cooed and placed a kiss on the curve of his hot skin. "You may sit up."

As he sat upright, the room swayed then cleared in sharp relief the moment his tender backside hit his legs. Damn. He might not be able to sit properly for a week.

"Do we have an understanding now, Rookie?" she asked as she secured the cabinet.

"Yes, Mistress."

"Part of me wishes you disobey again just so I can redden your fine ass some more, but I think you may have enjoyed it too much. Perhaps I'll spank you again for a reward some other time."

With that his cock jerked in agreement. God, he really was a perverted bastard.

"I must say, watching you fall into the rhythm of the spanking made my pussy ache." She reached for the zipper on the side of her hip and tugged down the tag. The skirt fell to the floor without a sound to pool at her feet.

With her sheer top clinging to her torso, she was just as good as naked. Maybe even better. Her breasts were still a mystery but from the waist down she was all lush curves with full hips and thick thighs that looked as soft as velvet and strong enough to grip him tight around the waist while he fucked her hard.

And hard he would take her when finally granted the opportunity. Mistress was not a delicate flower, and he suspected a timid lover would disappoint her.

"You like to talk a good game, Rookie. Let's see how talented your mouth is." She sat in her chair and hooked a leg over each arm. Her thighs parted giving him the perfect view of the bare lips of her pussy that were already slick with her arousal and made him hunger for a taste. "Crawl to me."

With pleasure.

He felt like a feral jungle cat with his shoulder blades rolling and the heavy weight of his cock bobbing between his thighs as he stalked across the floor, only she wasn't prey. Even spread out in a vulnerable position, Jasmina held all the power.

"Use your mouth and your hands to make my pussy feel good," she ordered.

It took a great deal of effort not to fall upon her like a starving beast. The silky skin of her inner thighs felt cool against his hot palms as he skimmed them up her legs to part the petals of her labia. In the past, oral sex had been something he had performed more to pleasure his partner than because he enjoyed the act, but now he craved the feel of her clit on his tongue and her flavor on his palate.

He touched the tip of his tongue to the pink bud and held still, waiting until her hips shift to before rolling his tongue in slow circles and plunging both thumbs into her sheath.

In anticipation of when he'd be asked to please his Mistress in this manner, he was not ashamed to admit he did some online research by watching a lot videos. By the way she squirmed in her seat, the effort had been well worth it.

"Ah!" she gasped with a startled jump and tunneled the fingers of her hand into his hair as she melted against his tongue. "Hmm. That's nice. Slow down. I don't want you to tire before I'm ready. That's it. More pressure. Umm."

With her direction, Marco brought his Mistress to the brink over and over again, learning what pleased her most. He discovered she loved to walk the razor's edge, relishing the anticipation of being pushed off the cliff into the sea of oblivion.

He replaced his thumbs with two fingers and worked them deep inside her. Just as her sheath quivered with orgasm, she would tug at his hair for him to back off and build her up again.

As he fucked her with his hand, he watched from beneath his lashes the way she clenched her teeth together to hold back her moans, how her dark eyes glittered with lust and the pink flush graced her round cheeks. Her breasts heaved beneath her top, and with her free hand, she pulled the material across her nipples for more stimulation. Even so close to orgasm, she was in complete control.

Desperate to see her come undone, he crooked his fingers and began massaging the inner walls of her pussy, learning where she was smooth, and where she was rough and experimenting with his touch from glancing caresses to solid taps on her flesh.

When he hit a sensitive area, she cursed and pressed his face tighter against her snatch. "Right there. Don't stop. Yes. Yes. God. Don't stop. I swear if you stop, I'll hang you by your dick."

For some reason that thought turned him on and he moaned around her clit, making her sheath tighten in return.

"Yes." She worked her hips harder. "That's it. I'm going to come. Yes. Yes."

A deep groan eased out from her lips as the walls of her pussy rippled and her cream flooded his mouth. Damn, he felt like a god as he hovered over her and watched as she writhed against his hand.

It was at that moment when he realized the truth of their arrangement. They might have signed a document that stated for the next three months she owned him, but he now saw how he owned her as well. As he worked her down from her high and her body jerked with residual spasms, she belonged to him. A fact that was confirmed when she raised her sex-drugged eyes to his and he saw the surrender in her gaze.

For a brief second he felt the earth move and the planets align in that heart-stopping sappy way that signified a significant life change. It was as if a neon sign in the shape of an arrow was pointing right at her saying "She's the one. This is your woman. She's yours for the taking."

And she knew it too. Her eyes widened and he heard her breath catch before the princess look returned and Mistress Jasmina was back in charge.

She gripped his wrist and brought his wet fingers to her mouth. With the flat of her tongue she licked her cream from his skin, sucking the tips into her mouth with gentle pulls. Once she was finished, she placed his hand on the arm of the chair. "You've pleased me, my pet. For that you shall be rewarded. Place your other hand on this arm. Keep your hands in place."

With his arms caging her to the chair, it might have appeared as if she were in the submissive position, but the second she gripped the base of his cock, he was completely powerless in her hold. She swiped at the tip of his damp cock with her thumb then guided it down to strum her clit.

"You've made me so wet and slippery. I want to feel you glide against my clit. Pump your hips. That's it, fuck the lips of my pussy."

He closed his eyes on a groan and plowed the length of his cock between the swollen folds of her sex. The woman was diabolical to tease him with such a promise. All he had to do was pull back an inch and in a heartbeat he could be buried balls deep inside her and hammering home until she screamed his name, his real name, to the sky. Just a tiny a fraction of an inch and he'd be in heaven. Or absolute hell.

What pleasures would Jasmina withhold if he got greedy? What worse forms of torture would she subject him to if he took what he desperately craved?

His fingers dug like claws into the leather and his jaw ached from clenching his teeth together. She hadn't given him permission to come and he was ready to fire off like an AK-47 with a hair-trigger.

"That's it, my pet." She scored her nails down his chest and arms. "Keep this up and you'll make me come again."

Sweat burned his eyes and his nostrils flared with his harsh breathing as he watched her fingers tug at the collar of her shirt. The plump pillows of her breasts spilled out to lie like perfect mounds of whipped cream upon her chest. She pinched each rosy nipple until they stood to attention like gumdrops.

"I know how much you like my tits. Would you like a taste?"

"God, yes," he thought he said. The words probably came out more like a grunt than anything intelligible.

"Put your mouth on me. Suck my nipples and make me come."

He bent his head and drew one dusky peak deep into his mouth, lashing at the tip like he had her clitoris not minutes before. The harder he sucked, the more labored her breathing grew and the harder she ground her pussy against his shaft.

"Yes. Yes," she panted and pulled his hair. "I'm coming. I'm coming. Come with me. Come with me. Now."

The force of his orgasm made his eyes cross and back arch as hot cum erupted out the swollen head of his dick, coating his Mistress in five days' worth of milky fluid. Over and over he spurted until his limbs gave out and he fell back on his heels in a sweaty, heaving mess.

"No, no, no. Come back here."

Somehow he found the strength to crawl back between her splayed thighs. She reached down and stroked his shaft, drawing forth another dribble of cum and a deep groan.

"Well done." She smiled up at him like a pagan goddess of

sex and sin with her breasts marked with his teeth, and her legs splayed wide open revealing her skin glistening with his seed. There wasn't anything he wouldn't do for her at that moment.

"Now, lick me clean."

What?

Was she suggesting what he thought she was suggesting?

"Mistress?"

"You heard me. Lick me clean. I allowed you to spray your cum all over me. Now lick it up. Every drop. I think you even got some on the chair. All of it must be cleaned up."

Lick his own cum? Was she insane?

Judging by her fierce stare and the firm set of her jaw, the answer was no.

"Are you disobeying my orders, Rookie?"

"No, Mistress." He swallowed hard. Holy hell. Was he really going to do this?

Think about something else. Imagine it's jam.

He lowered his head and laid the flat of his tongue against the curve of her breast near the smallest droplet.

At first he tasted nothing but the salt of her skin.

This is good. I can do this.

He followed the trail down her sternum to the pool around her navel. He held his breath and dove in.

The sweet aftertaste that lingered on his tongue was unexpected. Almost citrusy like…pineapple.

The little minx. She had this planned the entire time. At least she made the effort to make the experience enjoyable. With his apprehension over the taste and texture of his own semen alleviated, he lapped at her skin with renewed enthusiasm. And God almighty, did he come a lot.

It was so depraved, so debauched. He should be awash with humiliation, burn with the shame of engaging in such a perverse act, but instead he felt such a sense of freedom, he was light-headed with the high.

"Good boy." Jasmina wrapped her arms and legs around him and held him tight. "You're coming along just fine."

CHAPTER EIGHT

"**G**OOD MORNING, GENTLEMEN." Marco strolled into the war room and set the tray of coffees on the center of the table. "Italian roast and doughnuts for your morning's pleasure."

Coulter's pen fell from his hand. "Who are you and where's my captain?"

"Stuff it, Coulter," Marquez said and reached for a cup. "He brought the good stuff and it's free. Thanks, Cap."

The rest of his team murmured their thanks as Marco took his seat near the head of the table.

"That must have been some date last night."

"Date?" Peters asked around a mouthful of maple bar. "Are you getting some action, Cap? My wife will want to know all about her."

Santiago raised his hand. "Does she have a single friend?"

"Can't a guy bring in coffee because he likes the people he works with? If you're going to be dicks about it, I'm not gonna do it again, so drink up. Santiago, what have we got?"

"Two of the contacts on Konkle's phone are brothers, Alfonso and Hector Tabateri." He licked the sugar off his fingers before typing in the commands to bring up a copy of their driver's licenses on his laptop to display from the projector shining against the white wall. "They've been linked to several massage parlors that were suspected fronts for prostitution.

Lately they've been specializing in mobile services where the girls come to you."

"Who are the girls?" Marco asked, making notes for future questions.

"According to L&I reports, there are eight employees. All women with middle-American, Anglo sounding names. Yet the permanent establishments employ predominantly Asian women, many of whom are not legal. Services can only be booked for the mobile services via their website. Peters has more details about the website."

Peters wiped a napkin across his lips and took over the keyboard. "It appears as if the brothers are tracking IP addresses of those who search the site and request bookings. If we try to book an appointment with one of our computers, they'll say no one is available. In fact one website completely shut down after we clicked on some of the links. If we want to set up a sting, we can't use department resources or those suspected to be department resources."

"Marquez, get on obtaining outside tech," Marco directed. "What else?"

As Santiago recited the details of the next contact on Konkle's phone, Marco's cell vibrated near his elbow. He glanced at the screen then sucked in a breath. A text from Jasmina. After a quick glance around the room, he pulled up the message.

Drink a glass of pineapple juice before our next meeting. I'm hungry.

Hot damn. Was she planning on sucking his cock until he came down her throat? Sweet Jesus, he sure hoped so.

If he had his way, he'd be the one in the chair with Jasmina kneeling between his legs. Her lips would be painted a dark red and stretched around his dick as she slurped to her heart's delight. Or maybe she'd tie him to the table again, working him over and over until he sprayed like a geyser all over his belly and she was the one to lick him clean. Man, that would be awesome.

"Captain."

Or maybe she'd be the one sitting in the chair and she'd have him stand before her, his knees quaking as she tormented him with the edges of her teeth. His Mistress was quite clever with ways to make him shake.

"Captain."

What if she—

"Marco!"

"What?" He started and saw his men staring at them with identical frowns on their faces. "Was there a question?"

Coulter looked to the phone in Marco's hand and then down at the bulge straining his zipper. "Not anymore."

The rest of the men snickered around their doughnuts.

"Continue," Marco ordered with a rasp in his voice and waved at Santiago.

"Are you sure? I can wait if there's a…pressing situation. I don't want to make things *harder* on you."

"Continue," he said again, this time through clenched teeth. "Please."

Santiago snorted back more laughter and jiggled the pointer that was on a photo of a man displayed on the screen. "As I was saying, this man, Rosetti, did you hear what I said about him?"

Not a word. "Yeah, yeah."

"He's a dealer that was released on probation two weeks ago and hasn't checked in yet. He's been known to stay in dive motels in Dunlap and Cedar. The casino out there was his territory."

"Are drugs his game or does—damn it." The phone he forgot he was still holding vibrated in his hand and about made him jump out of his skin when it vibrated. This time it wasn't a sexy text from his Mistress but an incoming call from Dispatch. He picked it up immediately, snapping his fingers to alert the others a call to action may be imminent. "DeWinter."

Yep. A routine traffic stop had turned into a drug seizure. As he took notes he gestured to his men to pack it in and standby for assignments.

"We're on our way." He stood and slipped the phone into his pocket. "Unexpected drug seizure. Coulter and I will check it out. Marquez, get on securing a plant for the massage parlors. Santiago, alert Briggs out in Cedar that she may have a freshly paroled dealer in her neighborhood. Let's plan on meeting back around two."

The trip down to the parking garage was made in silence as Marco created a mental checklist of things to be aware of when they arrived on the scene. Smithwick wasn't the only distributor in town and he knew it was foolish to be too quick to add this incident to the list of the man's crimes and miss identifying a new player.

The second the car door shut them inside the SUV, Coulter started in on him. "Who is she? And don't pretend you don't know who I'm talking about. You're seeing a woman. Or a guy. Is that it? You're gay and never told me?"

"What?" Jesus. Talk about going from zero to sixty in a nanosecond. "I'm not gay. I am…seeing someone, but it's new and none of your business."

"I disagree. If she's causing you to lose focus, then it does affect me and the team."

"Get your panties outta your ass, Coulter. I'm completely focused on my work and you of all people know that."

"Do I? We've been working our asses off for the last three years and then right when we're on the cusp of closing this case, you've got a new girlfriend. One you won't say a thing about, and you've never been this tight-lipped before. Don't you think that's a little suspicious? How do you know this girl isn't one of Smithwick's operatives to get you off his trail?"

The idea made him snort so hard with laughter he hurt his sinuses. "Believe me, she's not an operative. Look, I have never been more determined to see Smithwick caught than I am now. And I am not distracted. I have my reasons for keeping quiet, so let it be. We have job to do now, so let's go."

Coulter snapped forward in his seat and gunned the engine. "Yes, sir."

Damn it all to hell. Despite their status within the department, Coulter was the closest person Marco had to a friend. All of his men were tight, but Coulter was like a little brother. And his lieutenant was right. Never had Marco withheld information about a lady friend. While he wasn't the kind to fuck and tell, he also never deliberately refused to share the tiniest tidbit about a woman who managed to turn his head away from his badge for any length of time.

Was that wrong that he was so secretive? Sure, men didn't share details of their lives like women did with each other, but there was always locker room banter. Only the nature of his relationship with Jasmina prevented him from engaging in such talk. It wasn't because he didn't think Coulter wouldn't understand. Of all people Coulter would probably be the only one to not blink an eye at the arrangement he had with Mistress Jasmina.

Well, he'd probably quirk an eyebrow, but Coulter had been to The Cavern. He knew what went on within those walls. Whether he was a Dom or a sub Marco wasn't certain, but at least the man had an idea that there was more to sex than the missionary position.

Marco glanced at the younger man to his side and felt the urge to spill the truth tickle his lips. What would he say? "I've met this amazing woman who's smart, sexy and can make me come like a rocket. But it's more or less a business arrangement. I've signed a contract that she can do whatever she wants to me for the next three months. After that, who knows?"

And there was the rub. What they had *was* more or less a business arrangement. Jasmina wasn't his girlfriend. And he didn't want it to be business. At least he didn't think he did. He wanted to talk to her like a man and not a submissive. He wanted to talk about her to his friends and not think twice about if that was appropriate. He wanted to be with her out in the sun and see if her hair was really as dark as it appeared. He wanted to wake up next to her in the morning and kiss her awake.

He wanted to kiss her. Period.

On the lips. Mouth to mouth, tongue to tongue. He wanted to hold her to his chest and feel her melt against him.

Maybe Coulter was right and he was allowing his arrangement with Jasmina to distract him, but he wasn't going to quit her. No way. She was making good on all her promises and he'd never felt physically better or more relaxed in his life.

A shift in strategy was in order. A realignment in priorities. Smithwick was first, followed by family. His time with Jasmina was beginning to rank right up there. When the three months were over and Smithwick was firmly behind bars, perhaps it would be time to take his relationship with Jasmina to the next level.

He bit back a smile as he imagined how she would react when he asked her out for dinner and a movie.

JASMINE ADJUSTED THE plum-colored bodice of her corset and blew out a slow stream of air from her pursed lips. The dressing room she shared with the other Dominatrixes at the club was empty, leaving her alone with her thoughts and the sexy tunes of Paolo Nutini playing on the sound system. The feel of the satin against her palms made her nipples tight and her pussy wet, well that and the knowledge that she was going to fuck her handsome captain that night. She was so hyped up that the simple act of applying lipstick had her ready to orgasm.

Why was that? Marco wasn't the most submissive or outrageous lover she ever had. He wasn't the most vanilla either. And she did love his expressions when he was presented with the new and unusual. His Adam's apple was so cute as it bobbed in his throat, and the way his eyes danced as he worked out whether to comply with her orders always made her want to smile.

When she had demanded he lick his cum from her skin, she thought he'd bail. Most men assumed that the biggest tests their Masters made them face were ones of pain and physical endurance when actuality it was those of the mind that were the most difficult to pass. Those invisible lines men didn't know they drew in the sand until made to cross them fascinated her. One second they dared you to come at them with a paddle but then turned into total prudes the moment you ask them to taste their own cum.

Not Marco. After a moment of hesitation, he took to the task with great enthusiasm and drive. There was no doubt he had intended to give her the best orgasm of her life. And he had succeeded.

"Get your head out of the clouds, Jaz," she told her reflection. "The be all and end all of men is not Marco DeWinter."

She wasn't a teenager with dreams of happily ever after. Happy for now was more her speed. Success at her job, a man to play with, that was all she needed. To want for anything more was just being greedy, not to mention exhausting.

With a last look at her backside to ensure the lines of her skirt fell to her liking, she left the dressing room and made her way to the common areas of The Cavern. The place was like a second home to her, actually more like her first home. She didn't have to hide her naughty side, or pretend she was an asexual or submissive creature like she did in all other areas of her life.

The other patrons she passed in the hall nodded in greeting or murmured hellos. Here she was respected for just being herself, and the freedom was a natural high.

The door to her dungeon was closed, but she knew Marco waited on the other side. Jax reported his arrival fifteen minutes before their scheduled appointment. Either the captain was eager or he wanted more time to explore her lair to gain knowledge. She suspected the answer was both.

Marco was naked and waiting on his knees as she entered. So far he was responding well with his training and turning into an excellent sub. Again she wondered what it was about him that made her temperature spike and her fingers curl in anticipation of sinking her claws into his flesh. Sure, he was handsome, but if one went purely by physical attributes, Army carried more muscle and pretty-boy charm than Marco.

No, Marco's appeal was that he was a wild card. Devil-may-care on the outside, brooding and intense on the inside. He had the ability to distract you with a charming smile or anecdote while rifling through your personal history at the same time. Good thing he was one of the good guys.

"Good evening, Rookie," she greeted and circled his kneeling form a few times to enjoy him at several angles. She dug her fingers into his thick hair and tugged. She was fond of his salt-and-pepper locks. Too many men were losing their hair or shaving down to the skull. What was she supposed to hold on to when a man ate her pussy?

She hugged him from behind, draping herself against his back to whisper in his ear, "Did you miss me?"

"Yes, Mistress."

"Hmmm," she hummed and scored light-pink lines across his chest with her nails. "I missed your cock. I think it's time we get better acquainted. Stand up and lie on the table."

As he rose, she saw him try to suppress a smile. He liked the idea very much; too bad he had no idea what she had planned.

Once he was laid out, she secured his arms by his sides, placing a kiss onto the center of each palm before wrapping the cuff around his wrist and tightening it into place.

Just because she could, she ran her hands over his body, enjoying the varying textures and the play of his muscles and body hair under her palms. His contented sighs made her skin tingle and when he closed his eyes, she let loose with a wicked grin. He was so putty in her hands.

For almost an hour she took her time squeezing and rubbing his flesh, alternating with her hands or a favorite tool. It was amazing the level of naughtiness a simple kitchen implement could create. The smack of a spatula against a thigh was so delightful, and a fondant cutter created the cutest indentations in the skin.

With each pass of her hand or arm near his erection, Marco would try to angle his hips for contact which she would deftly avoid. The little game continued until he was near tears with anticipation and to be honest, she was too. There was only so much temptation she could withstand and she had reached her limit.

From inside the drawer under the table she withdrew a condom and ripped open the top. The wrapper fluttered to the floor as she rolled the latex down his throbbing length with a long, firm squeeze.

"Thank God," Marco gritted out and bucked his hips.

Next she took out a leather and metal contraption that had his eyes widening in surprise.

"Wha—" he bit back the question with a grimace. The man was learning to hold his tongue.

She slipped the metal ring down the shaft of his cock until it fit snugly around the base. Around each thigh she wrapped the straps then circled around to cinch his balls into a nice, tight package. As he twitched on the table, she removed her skirt. Dressed in only her corset and thigh-high boots, she climbed onto the table and sat astride him like a rider on a bucking bronco.

Sweet heavens, she couldn't hold back any longer.

She grabbed his cock and aimed the tip at the entrance to her body. With Marco's gaze fixed at her juncture, she began the slow descent down his shaft, her greedy pussy gobbled up every inch until she hit bottom. Oh, the stretch burned so good. This first time was going to be quick.

She rolled her hips to the right and left, back and forth, searching for the perfect fit, and when she found it, her breath caught and her fingers dug into his sides. It was times like these when she wished she could grow her nails out longer. The style was not productive in the medical field, but oh how she'd love to draw blood as she rode her toy hard.

And he was her toy, he belonged to her. Marco was nothing but a beautiful instrument of pleasure. Built to serve her in whatever manner she wished. As she rose and fell, getting closer and closer to the edge, she reveled in his torture. The muscles in his arms bulged, straining against his bindings. His head thrashed against the table and his hips jerked beneath her, trying to plow his cock further inside.

"Do not come," she barked and worked her hand between

them to rub at her clit. "Do not come."

The direction ended on a moan as the rush of electricity swept up her body and set her ablaze. She slammed her hips down, trapping the throbbing length of his erection in her pulsating sheath. Blood rushed in her ears and her vision swam, but underneath it all was the unrelenting hunger for more.

"Yes, more," she said out loud and began the rise and fall on his cock.

"Oh God. God," Marco began to chant and shake, his sweat-slicked body slid between her thighs with sporadic jerks.

She dug her fingers into his flanks and bent over to take one of his sensitive nipples into her mouth, taking care not to rip him to shreds. His cries made her feral, ravenous, almost violent as she licked and bit his flesh, leaving streaks of red lipstick to mark her territory.

The delicious curve of his cock filled her again and again, the head stroking her g-spot and hurtling her to another orgasm with break-neck speed. His name flirted with her lips as she caught fire but she held it back. It was too soon to use his name, no matter how much she wanted to scream it to the sky.

Spots floated in her vision and her lungs burned as she crashed to his chest. Little jolts of energy twitched in her muscles and her pussy continued to suckle his cock that was still as hard as marble in her soft sheath.

Above her came the sounds of Marco muttering. Only a few words were understandable, such as sodium, chlorine, and iridium.

Was he reciting the periodic table? She lifted her head and saw his eyes were tightly shut and his teeth clenched together as he rattled off element after element.

Now this was new, and unexpected. Using sports statistics as a distraction from coming was not unknown. This scientific method was most certainly intriguing.

"Rookie. Look at me," she demanded with a twist to his nipples. "Are you ignoring me?"

"No—no, Mistress," he gritted out. His face was shiny and flushed, the skin of his cheekbones drawn tight as he fought to remain in control. "Please. Please…"

Oh, they were so pretty when they begged.

She climbed down and waited for her legs to steady before crossing to the foot of the table. She made a great show of pulling the stirrups into position. The loud click of the metal snapping into place made his body jerk. After she placed his feet in the holders and tied them down, she lowered the end of the table and stepped between his spread legs.

At his groin, his cock pulsed hot and heavy. He was so thick and red it was almost obscene in appearance, and she did love obscene. She ran the tip of her finger up the seam of his sac and smiled as he whimpered.

From her drawer of tools she withdrew a small anal plug and a tube of lubricant. When he saw the appliance in her hand, he began to struggle in his bonds. The restraints creaked and the skin around his wrist turned bright red, but she knew he was in no pain.

She teased his puckered hole, round and around then inserted the gel-slickened plug in a slow glide. For a man who protested so much, the thin phallus went in with ease. She flipped the switch on the bottom of the plug and grabbed the base of his cock and squeezed hard.

"Are you ready to come, Rookie?" she asked and worked him with her hand.

"Fuck yes."

"Where do you want it?"

His feverish stare nailed her in the eyes. His nostrils flared and the tendons of his neck stood out in stark relief as he snarled, "Down your throat. Every drop."

If it was possible to orgasm by words alone, she did so as he raged at her like a raving beast. There was no doubt in her mind that if he were free, he'd be on her in an instant, tearing her apart as he fed his lust.

And sweet heaven above, she wanted him to. She wanted him to hold her down and pillage her body for his relief.

But not today. Today she was in charge and she would take from him what she wanted.

Her hands shook as she released the straps and slipped off the cock ring and condom.

Precum oozed from the tip. "Watch me and come," she said and swallowed his cock until he hit the back of her throat.

His hips lifted off the table as the first stream shot out so hard, she didn't even taste it. The second and third were just as fierce but spread across her tongue with a sweet aftertaste.

She used both hands and a firm suction to milk him of every drop, just as he wanted. The plug in his ass kept his orgasm going for several long seconds and added another level of ecstasy she could see turn him inside out.

The power she held over him was like a drug heightening the senses. Her vision was sharper, her skin more sensitive. She couldn't get enough of his texture, his taste, the sounds he made as he continued to jerk in his bonds. The dichotomy was amusing. She, a mere woman turned this big, strong man turn into a sobbing heap and made him love it.

Whether he realized it or not, she had just made him her slave. Only she had the power to make him feel that good, that elated, that treasured. Who wouldn't kill for an opportunity to feel that way again?

But as Spider-Man often said, with great power came great

responsibility. Riding a high of endorphins made him a danger to not only himself but to her as well. One brief loss of focus on her part could result in an injury to them both.

As if she was in any shape to take care of either of them. Her legs shook as she walked to the bar to retrieve a set of warm, wet towels. The weakness made her smile in victory. What better indicator of success than feeling as if her quadriceps were on fire?

Aftercare was one of her favorite moments of playtime. Seeing the results of her work, demonstrating to her sub that he meant more to her than a plaything, even though she may have treated him as such not moments before. But she truly cared for her subs, and this was her preferred method of showing them her affection.

"I'm going to step away to call a steward to carry you to the bed," she said after she released him from his bonds and removed the last bit of her lipstick off his skin.

"No." He latched on to her wrist with surprising strength. "I can make it."

"And fall to the floor the second you try to stand."

"I can make it." He dark gaze sought hers. "If you'll lie beside me. I can make it. Even if I have to crawl."

Her breath caught and a shiver stole across her bare skin. The plea in his gaze turned her inside-out. "This time," she conceded and stepped away from the table.

At least he took his time in sitting up and waited with a few shallow breaths before trying to stand. He wobbled the few steps to the bed but made it under his own power before collapsing onto the mattress.

She stifled a chuckle and crawled in beside him then drew the covers over their bodies.

"That's nice," he murmured and drew her close. Sleep

tugged at his eyelids and she expected him to pass out at any second.

Only he didn't fall asleep. He lay quiet in her arms as she traced the lines of his muscles in his chest and shoulders with the tips of her fingers, yet his lips quivered and his brow furrowed as if he had something on his mind but didn't know how to ask.

"How are you feeling?" she asked and brushed his hair off his forehead.

"Amazing. Light." He let go with a dry chuckle. "Humble. I had no idea... I guess I should turn in my man card."

"Why? Because I penetrated your ass?"

He laughed. "No. Because I bawled like a kid and felt completely helpless."

"And you liked it."

He looked into her eyes. "I loved it. I just didn't realize I was so weak."

"Being submissive is not a sign of weakness, remember?" She reached out and twisted his nipple. "A weak man would have run, not reveled in the pleasure."

"Right, right. I guess I never considered how...intense this whole experience would be."

"And we've only begun."

"I won't survive," he moaned, but his smile suggested he wouldn't mind, then the smile faltered. "Am I performing as you expected?"

Ah, man-speak for "do you like me?"

"Yes. You are."

"Better than expected?"

"No."

"No?" His brows shot up. "What do you mean no?"

"I expected perfection."

"Oh," he breathed out on sigh, then his eyes widened as he understood her meaning and a smug grin spread across his lips. "Good. That's good." He melted deeper in to the mattress. "Can I ask you a question?"

"You may."

The smile turned into a smirk at the subtle correction of his grammar. "How was your day?"

"How was my day?"

"Yeah."

How was your day?

Each word on its own she understood. Even with those words combined into a query, she was able to comprehend, yet at the moment it was as if he were speaking a foreign language.

"How was my day?" she repeated with a pause between each word.

"Yeah."

"I don't understand."

"It's a simple question. Did you work today? Did you run errands or meet with friends? Was it good, or did you have one of those days when you want to bitch at the world, or did something neat catch your eye that made you glad to be alive?"

"My day was…fine," she answered slowly, still uncertain as to the motivation behind the question. "Why do you ask?"

"You go to great lengths in taking care of me and I wonder who takes care of you?"

She drew back in surprise. "I do."

"Then where is your release? When are you able to step away and relax?"

"Being with you like this is my release."

"And afterwards? Who bathes the sweat from your body? Who tucks you into bed? Who is there for you to lean on and make sure you're getting what you need?"

"I, um…I—" Her throat closed up and suddenly it felt as if the blankets wrapped around her chest tightened to steal her breath away.

The relationship Marco was describing was what "normal" people had. It was coexisting, long-term, intimate on a level far greater than what the two of them shared, yet far more superficial as well.

There was only so much time she a had to devote to another person. It wasn't fair to pretend to offer more than the brief moments she painstakingly carved out for her submissives as she did now. Did she ever long for more? On occasion. And then she'd see one of her colleagues at the hospital embroiled in a spat with their significant other, and the longing died.

However, lounging besides Marco's warm body, with his sexy half-smile just inches away from her as they shared the same pillow made her question her "Cavern only" policy.

Foolish thoughts. She swallowed against the lump in her throat and shrugged as if the idea amused her. "You want to give me a bath? That can be arranged."

"I mean it. Who takes care of you, Jasmine? I mean, Mistress."

The use of her name was deliberate and they both knew it. His gaze fell to her lips, which softened in response. With a slight tilt of her head, her lips would be on his. Touching, rubbing, tasting him in a way she had yet to do.

Tears welled in her eyes and that panicky feeling returned to take flight in her chest like the flutter of hummingbird wings. To kiss him right then would not be as a Dom with her sub, but as a woman kissing a man. Neither one in charge. No one steering the ship. Chaos created on a whisper.

Marco shifted a scant millimeter closer. His hand on her arm tightened, subtly pulling her closer toward him although they lay breast to chest. As the puff of his breath kissed her cheek, the lights flickered.

"What was that?" he asked.

A timely reprieve.

She drew back with a small sigh of relief. And the captain thought a little anal play was intense.

"Someone's at the door. A flashing light is less obtrusive than a knock or doorbell. Come in," she said in the door's direction in a raised voice.

When Jax entered the room, she immediately sat up. The bouncer would never interrupt her unless it was an emergency, and the clench of his jaw only added to her concern.

"Sorry, Jasmine," he said from the door. "Madeline's sub is having chest pains. Apparently the dumbass took a blue pill and he's on heart medication."

Men. Son of a bitch.

She looked back to Marco and mentally cursed again. He looked so cute and rumpled lying against the bedding. She wanted to stay by his side, but duty called.

"Rookie, I'm sorry."

"Don't be. Go." He settled deeper into the pillows. "I'm fine right here. Take as long as you need."

"Your adrenaline is still crashing."

"I'll keep an eye on him," Jax offered.

"No offense, but I can look out for myself," he huffed.

"No offense," she responded for the bouncer. "I don't want you falling to the floor. Be good." She ran her hand down his chest before climbing off the bed to dress. "Besides, I don't want anyone else to stumble upon you and think you're ripe for the taking. And Jax will wait outside and come in only if he hears the thud of your body hitting the hardwood."

"I'll try not to be so irresistible," he said with a smug grin.

"Rest." She pulled the covers up over his chest and dropped a kiss on his forehead. Oh why did he have to be so adorable?

The moment she stepped out into the hall she asked Jax, "Has 9-1-1 been called?"

"Of course. He's in the clinic now. I'll fill you in on the way then come back for your man."

The clinic was the name of the onsite medical room they used for any emergency situation. When one combined alcohol, sex and people in one location, it was inevitable a crisis would erupt, and Amaryllis liked to be prepared to take care of the people under her roof. All the bouncers were trained in first aid, but Jasmine was often asked to assist in the more serious situations until medics arrived.

"He's sweating like a pig and breathing hard, trying to make it seem as if he's fine, but you can tell he's hurting."

"Understood."

"So..." he said in a way that put her instantly on edge. "I didn't take the cop for a screamer."

"Don't you know, Jax? I turn them all into screamers."

"I know." He chuckled. "But I have to admit, Jaz, I was getting turned on hearing you work him over. When's his contract up? I may have to petition you to take his place."

The thought of Marco no longer being her sub made her steps falter.

"Are you okay?" Jax asked.

"I'm fine. It's the shoes," she lied with ease and continued on as a heavy weight settled in her chest. So far Marco gave no indication that he wanted their time to end. But they were in the honeymoon stage. When the three months were up, would he want to move on? Or would he want more?

While his earlier line of questioning wasn't entirely out of place, it did suggest he was interested in her life outside of the club. Any other woman might be happy to have a man like Marco interested in her for more than the hour or two of pleasure, but the idea of how a relationship like theirs would work outside of the club exhausted her just thinking about it.

Marco was not the type of man who'd enjoy being treated like a dirty secret, and if she began to think of him as more than a twice weekly appointment, sooner or later her family would find out and start asking questions, maybe even want to meet him.

Nope, nope, nope. Not going to happen. One night with her family would undermine all the authority she worked hard to establish.

She and Marco could not exist outside of The Cavern, and if he pushed, well, she'd be happy to find him a new Mistress.

Sure you will.

"What do you say, Jaz?" Jax's question interrupted the verbal smack-down her subconscious was about to lay down. "Do you wanna to Dom me?"

She glanced his way with a noncommittal shrug and took a page from Amaryllis. "I'll keep you in mind. For now."

CHAPTER NINE

MARCO WALKED ACROSS the threshold of the emergency room at Schuster-Siegel Memorial Hospital and took careful note of who, what and where as he made his way to the nurse's station. At the moment the lobby was quiet, with only a few people occupying the seats. The calm was deceptive. In the span of a heartbeat a barrage of crazy could barrel through the door in a blaze of sirens and flashing lights.

The hospital was one of those rare places where nothing and everything happened in a nanosecond. One second the halls were filled with the elation that came with a new life beginning on Earth then swung to the opposite side of the pendulum to the crushing grief of a loved one passing. A glut of emotions occurred under one roof and sometimes within feet of each other. It was almost as if the plain white walls and cold, minimalist furniture were a blank canvas for the day's events to be written upon. No one part of its design intended to sway the outcome or emotions of the individuals who entered its domain. Calm, yet unsettled all at the same time.

It took a special type of person to handle the extremes. An unique individual who could juggle the calm and the crazy. Someone like Jasmine. Her need to have an environment entirely under her control made so much more sense to him after being witness to her everyday world.

He wished the reason for his visit to the emergency room

was his beautiful Mistress, but alas, duty had called. A woman had been found in a Dumpster behind a motel. To everyone's surprise the brutalized girl was still alive and now was awake and conscious enough to answer questions.

"Good morning, Jenna," Marco greeted the young nurse behind the counter. "Happy Friday to you."

"If it was my Friday. You're looking much better than the last time we saw you, Marco. Way better." She turned her gaze to the man at his side and tossed her blonde ponytail over her shoulder as she batted her lashes. "Hi, Cassidy."

"Morning." Coulter set the white paper bag they had brought with them on the desk by her keyboard. "Some sweet macaroons for the sweet ladies who we all know truly run this hospital."

"Oh, you two are too much. Hey, girls. Our favorite police officers are here," she called out toward the back office behind her.

Yes, he and his men understood the importance of sweet talk. These nurses were overworked, underappreciated and loyal to each other and their patients. A little kindness shown to the right people went a long way in speeding along their investigation.

"We're here to see the girl from the motel. I heard she's awake," Marco said.

"She's up," Jenna replied. "Doc Jo is with her now. Follow me and I'll take you down and see if she's ready for visitors."

"Doc Jo? You mean Jovanovich?" Excitement and dread raced through him at the thought of seeing Jasmine.

Of course he was happy to see her, but this was the first time their paths had crossed outside of the nightclub, and it was almost impossible to be near her without sporting some sort of an erection. Not the best of appearances when conducting an investigation.

"Yeah. I'm sure she'll be glad to see how well you're doing since your accident." The nurse smiled.

Coulter snorted as he followed. "Watching you fall from that roof was about the scariest moment of my life, Cap. But now I can't stop laughing when I think about it."

"Glad to be a source of amusement for you."

Nurse Jenna stopped them outside a closed doorway. "Wait right here."

She took a moment to knock and announce her arrival then poked her head inside the room.

"Dr. Jo will be with you in a few minutes," she said as she stepped back out into the hall. "Can I get you fellas coffee or water?"

"We're fine," Marco answered for the both of them. "You don't have to wait with us."

"Believe me, Officer, I don't mind." She giggled and tossed a come-hither glance at Coulter.

The door opened and Jasmine emerged. It struck Marco dumb at how similar yet completely opposite Jasmine's personas were.

She was still beautiful, almost regal in her posture and the confident tilt of her head. There was a strength evident in her bearing that radiated like a thousand-watt light bulb. However, with her hair in a braid and the rumpled scrubs and lab coat, she appeared almost innocent, unassuming, steady. All good solid attributes for a person to be described as, but they lacked the sparkle of how he knew her to be.

"Hey," he greeted in maybe too friendly a fashion, for her eyes widened in surprise. For half a second he wondered if he should have dropped to his knees as if there were in her dungeon.

"Hello," she replied with as much formality as one could fit into a two-syllable word. "You're looking well, Captain. Good morning, Lieutenant."

"Right." Marco shook off the ill effects of her rather imper-sonal greeting and focused on the purpose of his visit. "How's the patient?"

Jasmine hugged a clipboard to her chest and answered in a quiet tone as if she didn't want to be overheard, "Awake. Cognizant. Broken for now, but she's a fighter."

"What are the extent of her injuries?"

"Her right forearm is fractured, her ribs cracked on the left side. Several lacerations to the face and body and a good amount of swelling that is starting to go down. The little I was able to find out suggests someone beat her and tied a pillowcase over her head in an attempt to suffocate her before leaving her body in a Dumpster."

"What else do you know about what happened to her?"

"Not much. When the medics brought her in, they said a hotel guest heard loud noises, bangs and grunts, coming from behind the building and spotted her trying to climb out. She hasn't elaborated about her ordeal."

"Was she…you know, raped?" Coulter swallowed hard mid-sentence. For an officer on his team, the man was quite squeamish when it came to delicate matters.

Jasmine sighed with a slight frown. "There is evidence of intercourse, but whether that was before or during the attack, she won't say. We administered a rape kit just to cover all bases."

"Good. Good." Marco nodded, disturbed by the conversa-tion in ways he never expected.

How many times in the past had he had similar discussions with Dr. Jovanovich regarding the status of victims he'd come to question? In both of their lines of work, they'd seen the ugly and tragedy that befalls humankind. This part of their lives was "normal", every day, and that reality burned in his throat like acid.

Dr. Jovanovich was no longer just a consultant. She was a flesh and blood woman. Female. Delicate, although she'd probably take a belt to his backside if she heard him describe her in such a way, but that was how he felt. He cared about her. He cared for her. It was his job to protect those he cared about from the horrors of the world. However it wasn't his place to protect Jasmine. And that detail burned him most of all.

He swallowed hard against the bitter pill of truth. "We'll do our best to make our visit short. We don't want to cause her any more discomfort than she's already in."

"I know you won't." She offered him a polite smile that too rubbed him the wrong way. He wasn't a stranger. Couldn't she offer him a little personal consideration?

She knocked on the door as she said, "I'll introduce you," then turned the knob.

Across from the doorway a young girl stood before the window, frantically trying to squeeze her body through the tiny opening allowed by the safety hinge.

The clap of Jasmine's clipboard hitting the floor covered his curse as they both raced to the girl.

There wasn't time to consider her comfort as he wrapped his arms around her torso and hauled her away from the window as she kicked and flailed with pain-filled shrieks.

"Coulter, grab her legs," Marco instructed as he dodged her fist. The girl reached back and pulled his hair so hard, tears sprang to his eyes.

Together the two men wrestled her back onto the bed as Jasmine withdrew a set of straps from under the bedframe and began to bind them to the girl's ankles.

"They'll kill me. They'll kill me," the girl kept shrieking. "They'll find me and kill me."

"If you keep screaming this way, whomever it is you're afraid of will find you for certain," said Jasmine in a tone Marco recognized as her no-nonsense dominatrix voice. "Stop this right now. You'll hurt yourself further and that I will not allow. I will sedate you if necessary."

"I wouldn't test her," Marco warned. "Doc isn't one to make idle threats. Calm down and all will be fine. No one will hurt you here."

The wails fell into gut-wrenching sobs that had to hurt her broken ribs. "They'll find me and finish what they started."

"Not on my watch." Jasmine tightened the last strap around the girl's free wrist. "Lieutenant, will you please close the door and dissuade anyone who may be coming to assist us? I don't want to cause a greater disturbance than we already have."

"Right." Coulter ran to the door and Marco could hear him intercept an orderly out in the hallway.

Jasmine ran her hand down the girl's hair in a soothing motion before reinserting the I.V. needle into her arm. "Jenny, I promise you, as long as you're under my care, no one will harm you."

"They're too powerful," she choked out in stuttering breaths.

"I'm not without my own set of skills. Now, do I have to you sedate you, or will you behave? With either choice, you will respect these men and me."

"Don't drug me. Please." Her head rolled against the pillows and her legs shifted as best they could in her bound state. "I don't want to go to sleep."

"Then calm yourself. I won't put you to sleep, but I am going to give you something to dull the pain. I'm going to ensure you didn't do more damage to your ribs while you answer these men's questions. This is Captain DeWinter and his partner Lieutenant Coulter. They are good men and I trust them. You can trust them too."

"And I trust the Doc." Marco spoke up as he pulled a chair over to the bed. "She saved my life a few weeks ago." In more ways than one. "You're lucky to be in her care. Now, Jenny, it is Jenny, right? All we want to do is find the people who hurt you and make sure they don't hurt anyone again. Understand?"

Her bloodshot blue eyes appeared doubtful, but she nodded anyway. Now that she was sedentary Marco was better able to take in the girl's condition. She didn't appear to be older than fifteen, but the shape of her face was difficult for him to make out from the bruising on her cheek, jaw and forehead. Rope burns wound around her throat, and the skin above the cast on her arm was mottled with purple splotches and adorned with criss-cross hatch marks that matched the set on her other arm. Whoever had harmed her was one sadistic bastard.

"We'll start real simple," he said when Coulter returned to take down the interview. "How old are you?"

"Seventeen," she replied in a small voice.

"Where are your parents?"

She shrugged with a wince.

"Where are you from?"

"Spokane."

"What brought you out to the big city?"

"Ran away."

Ah... An idea of how she might have come under attack began to form and he saw where her story was heading. "Why?"

She sighed. "My parents aren't good. They suck. They drink and yell and drink some more. Everything sucked."

"How long ago did you leave?"

"A few months ago."

"And where have you been staying?"

"I don't know," she said with her eyes cast down.

What did that mean? "Can you explain?"

"I was staying at a motel until my money ran out, which was really fast. And nobody wanted to hire a kid," she sneered and began to pick at the threads of the sheet covering her belly. "I was sleeping on the street when a man came up to me and said he could get me work as a dancer. I know I'm from the sticks, but I'm not stupid. I knew what he meant. But I had nothing. Less than nothing..." she trailed off as a sob worked its way up her throat.

"It's okay, honey." He lifted his hand to pat her on the leg then immediately let it fall and looked to Jasmine. With a nod and an eyebrow wag, he silently asked her to be the one to offer comfort. Jenny had the most trust in Jasmine, and he was a male. Odds were good it was a man who hurt her. "Where did this man take you?"

"He took me to a massage place."

"Massage?"

Behind him, Coulter sucked in a breath and his own spine straightened with a snap. A thousand questions stung his lips like an upset colony of bees but he forced them back. Jumping to conclusions did nobody any good, but his radar was pinging so loudly, he knew Coulter sensed it as well.

"Do you remember where this massage business is?" He hoped he was able to keep the excitement out of his voice.

Her brow furrowed. "Downtown. Near the phó place."

"Which one?" There were easily six on one street alone.

"Not far from the x-rated theater. I thought that was where he was taking me."

Fuck yeah. That was a former location of one of the Tabateri brothers' prostitution hubs. Was it possible the boys never officially closed shop? By the frantic scribbling of Coulter's pencil across the paper, that question was going to be thoroughly investigated soon.

"What happened when you went inside?"

"As soon as we walked through the front door, he put a bag over my head, tied my hands and dragged me through the shop and out the back."

"How did you know it was the back if there was a bag over your head?"

"They put me in a van, or something without backseats, and I could smell trash through the fabric. There weren't any Dumpsters where we entered from the front."

"What happened next?"

"We drove for a while. I don't know how long. When we stopped, they pulled me out and took me up some stairs and into a building. We walked for a while and when we stopped, they took off my hood. I was in a big room with some other women. But I don't know where exactly I was."

"Was it a house or an office building?"

"A house. A big house with a huge yard and a fence. We weren't allowed outside, but there were windows and I could see. They were locked, but I could still see."

"Who were these women you were with? And how many?"

She tried to shrug again and winced. "Girls. From all over. Only a few of us spoke English. Most were from somewhere in Asia. I think all over because some of them didn't want to talk to the others. I don't know how many of us there were. New ones would arrive and old ones would be taken away. Anywhere from ten to fifteen at any given time."

"So you were with these girls. In a house. For a few months. All of the time?"

"Most of the time." Her voice grew small again and she

swallowed hard. "Every few days I was tied up and taken to places. Motel rooms. With men. To-to—" Whatever it was she wanted to say couldn't seem to break past her lips.

"Would it be a good guess if I said you were forced to have sex with these men?"

"Yeah," she said on a shaky exhale.

Mentally Marco gave a little fist pump and held back a victory snarl. The situation she described sounded just like a Smithwick operation. He had a thousand more questions for the girl, but by the droop in her eyes, he saw she was fading fast. Any further investigation about the house and the girls had to wait.

"Tell me about what happened last night."

"I was taken to another motel to do my thing. This guy was twisted. Really kinky. Cut lines on my skin with a pocket knife. Gagged me the entire time so my screams couldn't be heard. Then afterward the man told my john that he'd take me and five more. They were talking about how much we'd cost and stuff about transport and places with the name "stan" in them, and I realized they wanted to take us out of the country. I freaked and made a run for the door. Both of them tackled me and I fought. Fought hard and screamed as loud as I could hoping someone would hear me. No one came. But they beat me and choked me until I passed out."

"And then you woke up in the Dumpster."

"Yeah." She finally raised her eyes to meet his gaze. The blue in her irises looked electrified against the red rims. "If they find out I'm alive, they'll kill me. I saw them kill another girl who fought. That's why I never did, but I knew that if that man took me away, I'd be as good as dead anyway. If they know, they'll find me. They're powerful and scary."

This time Marco went with the need to comfort her and laid

his hand on her arm. "They won't find you, Jenny. I promise. I just have one more question for you. Does the name Smithwick sound familiar?"

"Yeah. I think he's the boss."

"Fuck yeah," Coulter bit out before he caught himself. "Sorry."

Marco shot his lieutenant a scowl and a wink. He wanted to react the same way. He turned back to Jenny. "What Coulter so eloquently means is we know who you're dealing with. And you're right, he is dangerous. That's why we're getting you out of here pronto."

"Excuse me, Captain," Jasmine piped up. "Are you crazy? You're forgetting that she's injured and still requires medical attention."

"I know, but the longer she stays here, the more she's in danger. And I've got a plan." He leaned forward in his seat. "Believe me, Jenny. Smithwick will have to get to me before he gets to you. I'll keep you safe. Dr. Jovanovich, is there a private place we can talk?"

She crossed her arms and for several seconds regarded him with that deep stare with a slight tilt of her head. She wanted to argue with him about the girl's care, he saw the words in her eyes, but she nodded and gestured with her hand to the door. "I know a place."

"Good." He stood and reached for the call button by the bed and pressed it into Jenny's hand. "Hang tight, little girl. If anyone comes in here you don't recognize, you press this button and scream as loud as you can. I don't care if they say they work her or not. Understand?"

She nodded, staring up at him with wide eyes. She hugged the call button to her chest and for the first time in his presence, relaxed into the bed.

"Show us the way, Doc."

Jasmine led them down the hall to a small room furnished with a loveseat, coffee table and two chairs. There was a sliding door in the wall that she slid shut for more privacy. By the copious amounts of tissue boxes and leaflets on grief lining the countertop, he realized this was the room the doctors used to deliver bad news to family members.

She turned toward them with the princess look on her face. "How much danger is she in, really?"

"A lot. Do you remember about a year ago, when the police were in a shootout with a drug dealer and the girl he had kidnapped and had a bomb strapped to her neck?"

Her brow furrowed. "Yes."

"Same guy. His name's Smithwick. He's moving into human trafficking and we've been on his trail for years. Jenny may be our only witness to the inner workings of his organization. If he knows she's alive, he will have her killed."

Jasmine drew in a breath and nodded. "What do you need me to do?"

"Yes. That's my girl." Before he realized he moved, he swept her up in a hug and dropped a kiss to her cheek. "First thing is we need protection. Coulter, call Santiago and tell him to drop everything and get here, but don't make it look too obvious. Until he gets here, I want you to stand guard. I only want our team around her from now on."

"Right, Cap," he said with a bemused smirk on his face.

"Oh, sorry," Marco murmured to Jasmine who looked at him with eyes wide with shock. He realized he still held her in his arms and stepped back. "Anyway, Coulter, gather all of the photos of Smithwick's associates the Chameleon compiled. Once Jenny's settled, we'll see if she recognizes anyone. Now go."

"I'm on it." Coulter turned to leave but there were still questions in his eyes as he left them alone.

"Where are you planning on taking her?" Jasmine asked, smoothing down the sides of her coat.

Marco chuckled, already anticipating her reaction. "The Cavern."

She didn't disappoint. "Excuse me?" she exclaimed and looked at him as if he were crazy.

Crazy like a fox maybe. "Think about it. You'll have access to medical supplies, the Kilsgaards have plenty of space, no one will think to look for her there, and with Lucian and Bale nearby, no one will get to her. Those two have mad skills when it comes to protecting people. In a situation like this, I'd trust no one else."

"Why do you think Lucian will agree?"

"He's a smart man with powerful friends and a familial grudge against Smithwick. He'll agree. And another thing, Jenny reminds me a bit of Bale's girlfriend, Ari. New to town with nothing but the clothes on her back and a hope and a prayer. Can you think of a better person to mother Jenny than Amaryllis?"

The idea elicited a small grin. "I concede it's a sound plan, *if* he agrees."

"He will."

Her raised eyebrow said that remained to be seen. "I'll prepare her for transport with as much discretion as possible. It won't be easy, but I'll do my best."

"I have the utmost confidence in your skills." He reached out and drew her back into the circle of his arms. This was it. Smithwick's capture was so close, he could practically smell the man's expensive cologne. "I wish I could share more with you, but this is good. This is great. Soon, we'll have an asshole behind bars and protect more girls like Jenny. Once she's settled, we should celebrate, just a little. Nothing fancy. How about dinner? When are you free?"

"Dinner?" She stiffened further in his arms. "You want to have dinner? Together?"

"Yeah. And don't pretend that you don't have dinner. You eat. We all do. When are you off work?"

"I, uh—" she cleared her throat and brushed away his hold. "I don't—can't have dinner."

"Why not?"

"Because it sounds like a date."

"It is a date."

"Right. Remember? I don't date."

"Then think of it as dinner with a friend. We are friends, right?"

"No."

Frustration burned in his chest and he restrained the urge to pull out his hair. Damn it. The woman was determined to cut him off at the knees. Or the balls. "What are you saying?"

She closed her eyes for a second and sucked in a hurried breath before she lifted her chin to say, "Look, Captain, I thought I had been perfectly clear when we entered our arrangement. I am your Dom. You are my sub. Out in the real world we do not socialize. Only at The Cavern do we exist as a couple. I'm sorry if you've come to believe otherwise, but that's how things are."

"Are they?" He stalked toward her. Whether she realized it or not, she had issued a challenge he was more than ready to accept. "And what if I want more? Hell, what am I saying? I do want more."

She gasped and stumbled backward as he crept closer. For the first time he saw her look anything but in control. "Well you can't have more."

"Why not?" He stopped within millimeters of her heaving chest as she hit the wall. "I want you, *Jasmine*. I like you. You're smart, sexy, have a wicked sense of humor and can make me hard with a blink of your lashes. I want to spend time with you. Is that so hard to believe?"

"You can't have more."

"Why not?"

"Because I don't have more to give," she shouted and pushed against his chest. "Don't you understand? I'm at work seventy-plus hours a week. The only time I can spare are the few hours I manage to have at the club. That's all. And that's what you agreed to. Damn it." She squeezed her eyes tight. "I don't even have time for this conversation. Let me know if Lucian agrees. In the meantime, I'll get Jenny ready for transport."

She stormed out with the ends of her coat flapping behind her like the tail of a kite in a windstorm.

Yeah, he was pissed she shot him down, but the woman did have a point, much as he hated to admit it. She had never agreed to a relationship outside of The Cavern. And at the time he signed the contract, he hadn't thought she'd be so obstinate about the mere idea of seeing him as more than her sub. Added to all of that, they were both busy professionals. Seriously, what was he doing thinking he could try to have a relationship anywhere close to normal when the biggest break in his case fell into his lap? Jasmine was right.

He hated that she was right.

There had to be a way to make it work between them. He was tired of leaving her at the end of the night. Hell, he hated not being able to kiss her when he wanted or even hold her close. Simple things that men and women did to show affection when not tearing it up between the sheets. Was it too much to ask to have a girlfriend?

From his jacket pocket his phone vibrated. A glance at the screen confirmed that Santiago was on his way. Duty called.

Apparently he was asking too much.

With his right hand he pressed the buttons to call Lucian while his left dug into his pocket for his pack of gum. Maybe he should take up smoking.

Convincing Lucian to offer his facilities to harbor a witness took little effort, just as he suspected. If there was one thing Marco could always count on was the men in the Kilsgaard family and their willingness to protect those who need it.

There was a knock on the door before Coulter entered the room. "Santiago's here."

"Thanks, Cass." He returned to his conversation with Lucian. "I'd appreciate it if you didn't tell Amaryllis right away. Let's get Jenny settled before your wife goes all Daddy Warbucks on her."

"I'll do my best, Captain." Lucian laughed. "Your witness will be in good hands."

"See you soon." He ended the call. "Let's find the doc and get our girl out of here."

Coulter stood in front of the door with his arms crossed. "What's going on?"

"Where have you been? An angel has risen from a Dumpster and granted us a boon."

"I mean with you and the doctor. There's this weird energy between you two I don't remember being there before. Are you—are you two dating?"

Aye, the rub. He snorted. "Believe me, we're not dating."

"It's okay if you were. She's cute in that sexy librarian sort of way. I mean, if she wore her hair down and you thought of her by her first name and not Doc. What is her name again?" he scratched his head. "Jasmine? Yeah. That's hot. Jasmine…wait a minute."

Marco held his breath as he saw Coulter put the pieces together. With his hand to God, he swore he saw sparks fly from Coulter's hair when the man hit the answer.

"Holy shit! Dr. Jovanovich is Mistress Jasmina. Why have I never put it together?"

Suddenly Marco turned into Vinny Barbarino from that old show *Welcome Back Cotter* he used to watch on Nick at Night, sputtering and laughing as if Coulter were crazy. "Are you insane? You think Dr. Jo is a dominatrix? Are you high?"

"No, I'm right because I never said the word dominatrix and you know who Mistress Jasmina is."

Fuck.

"And if you know who Mistress Jasmina is, then…oh…" His jaw fell open and eyes boggled. He then emitted a series of ohs, all with varying pitches and lengths, but Marco heard each statement as if Coulter actually said the words.

Oh, you're not dating Dr. Jovanovich.

Oh, because you're seeing Mistress Jasmina.

Oh, which means you're her submissive.

Oh, so I guess you like to be spanked and taken up the ass.

Marco sighed. "You're going to catch flies with that open trap, Coulter."

He blinked several times and shook his head. "Sorry, I just— I didn't think you swung that way, Cap. Wow. My mind has been thoroughly blown. In a million years, I'd never have guessed you're all for being tied up and slapped around by a woman. I'm trying to picture it and I gotta tell you, I'm totally shocked."

"Shut up, Coulter."

"Hold up, boss." Coulter side-stepped to block the exit. "You can't drop a bomb like that and leave."

"I didn't say anything. You're the one jumping to conclusions."

Coulter drew imaginary circles in the air. "Your face said it all. Come on. I need details. What's it like? I heard Mistress Jasmina is amazing. Does she make you wear leather? Has she made you lick her boots?"

"My God, you're an idiot," he groaned and smacked his gum. "Drop it and let's go. It's not important."

"You're wrong." He widened his stance and popped his neck back and forth as if he were preparing for a throw down. "From what I can gather, you started seeing her after your accident, which means she's the reason you've been mentally checking out recently. And now we've had a huge break in our case that she is directly involved with. I need to know if you can keep your head on the case or is it in her pants?"

His fingers curled into fists and he felt sweat gather along his forehead. "You're asking to get your ass kicked, Lieutenant."

"I'm being a good cop who's worried about a member of my team. You'd ask the same questions if the situation were reversed and you know it."

Fuck it all to hell.

Marco sucked in growl and turned away from Coulter's knowing smirk to pace the four feet to the wall and back. Why was it that all of a sudden he'd gone from being the undisputed alpha to a complete and utter dumbass?

"God dammit," he snarled.

Coulter looked at him with puppy dog eyes. "I'm here for you, Captain, if you need to talk." He threw up his hands in defense as Marco feinted like he was going to deck him. "I'm kidding. I mean, I'm willing to listen, but geez, you're wound tighter than a tube-top on a sumo wrestler. What's going on?"

"Nothing. In the grand scheme of life, it's nothing." He dug the heel of his hand into his eye and let out long breath. "I'm seeing Mistress—Jaz—Doc—her. I've been seeing her for a few weeks to help with stress."

"Is that what you call it?"

"I swear to God, Coulter."

"I can't help it." He chortled. "I'm curious and intrigued and jealous as hell. I know a lot of people who were disappointed when Mistress Jasmina picked a new sub. I didn't know it was you, and I didn't realize she was Dr. Jovanovich. The lights and atmosphere, the few times I've seen her have been from a distance, I didn't piece it together. Man, what's it like?"

"How do you know so much about her?"

"I'm no stranger to The Cavern, as you well know. I have friends there. I keep my ear to the ground. Now what's it like? You're killing me."

"It's…freeing. I don't have to think about anything but her, and I don't have to guess about what to do or how she's thinking because she tells me. For a little bit of time, I can just let go."

"Has she whipped you?"

"I'm not answering that. No specifics."

"Man, you're no fun." He rubbed at his jaw. "So what happened after I left you two that pissed her off?"

"What makes you think she was pissed?"

He drew another circle around his face. "That woman was spitting nails."

"Fuck." How had things blown up so badly? "I asked her out."

"Out?" His brow crinkled. "Like out out?"

"Yeah."

"Like on a date?"

"Yes."

The crease across the forehead deepened. "I heard Mistress Jasmina doesn't date."

"She doesn't and neither does Dr. Jovanovich. Apparently I've broken an unspoken rule and dared to ask her to spend time with me outside of the club."

"Oh," Cassidy drew in a long breath. "I see. Huh. That is a quandary. I'm sorry, Cap. Does that mean your arrangement is over?"

Ah. The magic question and he greatest fear. "I don't know. I hope not."

"You like her."

"Of course I do."

"No. You *really* like her."

He stared at his friend for a long while before he nodded. "Yeah. A lot."

Coulter smiled. "I wish you the best, man. Now the truth. Is the sex good?"

Marco stepped around him to slide open the door. "What goes on in the dungeon is not about sex."

"But if it was?"

His smile stretched so far his cheeks stung.

"I knew it," Coulter crowed.

"Come on. We have a girl relying on us to keep her alive."

Together they walked to the nurses' station. Before they could ask about Dr. Jovanovich's whereabouts, she stepped out from a nearby office with a sheaf of papers and walked in their direction.

Coulter sputtered with laughter before he sucked in a chuckle and Jasmine's eyes narrowed. If it were physically possible, he knew they'd be two daggers lodged in his chest.

"Sorry, Cap," Coulter whispered.

All he could do was grunt in reply. Nothing left to do but

hope Jasmine didn't take her anger out on his hide.

Actually, if she didn't, he'd know for certain their relationship as he once knew it was over.

CHAPTER TEN

J ASMINE PULLED THE blanket over the sleeping girl's chest before crossing to the window and checking the lock one last time.

Jenny had yet to attempt another dash out the window, but it didn't hurt to be extra cautious. So far she had rested peacefully in her new quarters on the top floor of Amaryllis and Lucian's penthouse; however once her strength returned, who was to say fear wouldn't propel her back into danger.

She left the bedroom door open a crack and walked down the long staircase to join Amaryllis in her living room.

"Her color's looking good, but her blood sugar is high. Quit giving her soda and sweets."

"It's my house and you can't tell me what to do." Amaryllis held up a pair of pink open-toed heels. "Which do you like best with that dress on the chair? These fuschia shoes or the white flats?"

She gestured to all the shopping bags and clothes. "What's all of this?"

"Jenny's new wardrobe."

"Ah. Of course. Well, fairy godmother, let her sleep before playing fashion show. I'll be back day after tomorrow to check on her condition. Call me if she doesn't seem to be managing her pain. Do not give her any medication without asking me."

"Right, good doctor." She saluted. "Are you off to meet with the handsome Captain DeWinter?"

"I am," she answered slowly. If he showed up.

In the two days since he had asked her out, all communication between them had been solely about Jenny and her needs. He didn't give any indication that he wanted to cancel his appointment, but he had fallen into what she called "Icemanmode." Direct, emotionless. Not a single warm glance or passion-filled word.

Which was how it should be when they were out in public.

An itch started over her right eye in response to the lie she kept telling herself. If she kept repeating it enough, maybe she would convince herself it was the truth.

"Again, don't rush her, Amaryllis. She's not one of your projects."

She smiled sweetly. "For now."

"Oh, God." She rolled her eyes. Why did she every teach Amaryllis how to use that phrase to her benefit? "Then I'll be back *tomorrow.*"

Amaryllis stuck out her tongue. "Go on and tame that delicious hunk of policeman. Do dirty deeds and show him who he needs to worship."

"Good night, Amaryllis." She waved and left the giggling woman to her profusion of fabric and footwear.

The Dominatrixes' dressing room was empty and silent, which was why she loved coming to the club on off nights; however the silence was too much for her taste that night. She turned up the speakers that piped in the tracks from the dance floor. Usually the constant thump-thump-thump of the bass annoyed her, but she needed the noise to cover the whispers running through her head that made her doubt her stance with the captain.

She had no reason to feel bad about turning down his request for dinner. She never lied or led him to believe their relationship extended beyond the walls of the club. Quiet opposite in fact.

He had to understand her refusal wasn't because she didn't like him. She did. Very much so. She liked how he could make her smile with a simple quirk of his brow and the way his eyes sparked when he was happy. And the way he treated Jenny most definitely caused her heart to flutter. He was so kind, so compassionate. Ready to slay the young girl's demons at a moment's notice. All very swoon worthy qualities.

Gah! She shook her head and attacked her hair with extra vigorous strokes of the hair brush. What was wrong with her? She didn't have time to rearrange her life. And his job just hit a major turning point. The next few hours were all she had to offer. It was time to remind them both of their place.

For the evening's attire, she chose a wrap-around dress in deep-purple silk. Underneath the sumptuous fabric she wore a lacy half-bra and matching boy-shorts for an added layer of texture. She went without her shoes, and if Marco had been paying any attention, that clue alone should be a warning as to her current frame of mind.

As she neared the door of her dungeon, she ignored the beads of sweat that trickled along her hairline. She refused to believe the captain would not show because she turned down his offer of a date. The man wasn't that petty. She hoped.

She paused with her hand on the doorknob and released a long breath then opened the door partway to peek around the edge. The sight of his bare feet made her heartbeat slow and her nerves settle. Thank the lord he was able to push past her refusal. Of course his pride had probably been stung, but truthfully, their relationship worked best within The Cavern's walls. All she had to do was reinforce that truth.

This was her dungeon, her sub, her rules. The control was in her hands.

The captain sat naked, on his knees, palms on his thighs, and awaiting her instructions like a good boy. However his eyes slid in her direction and he watched her as she crossed the room to stand before him. That bold gaze looked its fill, burning through the fabric of her dress to touch her with a firm caress. His tongue swept over his lips and she saw his thumbs stroke the insides of his thighs, the tips grazing his erection.

Did the captain want to play a game? Oh, it was on.

"Let's take a field trip," she said and walked over to the wardrobe. From inside the cabinet she withdrew a pair of black cotton pants and a satin mask. She handed him the pants then stepped behind him to tie the mask around his head. "In case we run into anyone you know."

He made a wicked looking Zorro with the black fabric hiding the top half of his face and hair and nothing else covering his body. The slightest smirk tipped the corner of his lips and his eyes blazed from the open slits as he silently confirmed his intent to be ornery. Oh, yeah. The game was so on.

She held out the pants and ordered him to dress. He wasn't going to reap the benefit of having her touch him yet. As a final accessory, she added a studded collar, complete with a leash, around his neck.

"Come along, boy." She tugged on the leash and led him out of the room.

The main playroom was congested as a crowd gathered for the scheduled floor show. Madeline caught her eye and waved her over, gesturing for her to share her loveseat in the front row.

"Hello, handsome," she greeted the captain as they neared. "Are you going to share your toy today, Jasmina?"

"Perhaps." She sat and directed the captain to sit between

them. The fit was tight and Madeline made sure to squeeze in extra close by pushing her lace-covered breasts into his sides. "No sub tonight, Mad?"

"Nope. I had to let Megabyte go and Ponyboy had to work, so I'm solo. What are your plans for the evening?"

"That depends." She leaned in to whisper in his ear. "Would I be correct in saying Lieutenant Coulter is aware of our arrangement?"

"Yes, Mistress," he replied and his earlier confidence seemed to falter as his gaze fell to the floor.

"Did you two have a good laugh?"

"Absolutely not." And his jaw clenched as if the idea were ludicrous.

She looked back to Madeline. "My plans are still in the works."

"Come on, Jaz, let me touch him." She stuck her nose under his chin and inhaled deep. "He smells so good. Please, please, please."

"Begging does not become you. You can touch his right leg only. He's been a bad boy."

"Yay!" She clapped her hands then dug her fingernails into his quadriceps.

Marco grunted and flashed her a glare. Jasmine responded by offering a sweet smile and scored her own marks into the cotton covering his muscular thigh, except instead of flinching, his lashes fluttered and he sighed her name.

The lights dimmed and a spotlight highlighted Jorges, the club's designer and sometime Master of Ceremonies, standing on the platform.

"Watch the show," she said to Marco but kept caressing his thigh.

"I'd rather watch you," he murmured in a voice so low, she

could have imagined he said the words.

"Welcome, everyone," Jorges greeted. "We have a real treat in store for you tonight. Joining us from the shores of the Baltic Sea, please welcome Vitaly and Katarina."

He swept his hand toward stage right and a couple emerged from the shadows. Black spandex with splashes of red and blue glitter adhered to their bodies like a second skin from their necks down to their ankles. At their groins and Katarina's breasts, the fabric was cut away, exposing their more interesting parts to the audience.

"My God," Madeline muttered. "You can walk the plank on that erection. Yummy."

Her observation wasn't that far from the truth. The moment the music began, Vitaly lifted Katarina into the air. She placed her left hand on his head and stretched one foot behind her as her left foot perched upon his cock. Once she was settled, Vitaly let go and spread his arms wide. They held the pose for several seconds then moved on to the next strength move to a round of applause.

Over the notes of the gently swelling Gregorian chants, the couple lifted and twined around each other in a series of poses that appeared impossible for a human to attempt, let alone accomplish. One of the more impressive moves was a vertical sixty-nine position with Katarina hanging upside-down, legs in the air while holding on to her lover's waist and Vitaly's hands were up over his head. He then grasped her by the waist and with a flinch of muscle, he tossed her into the air and caught her by the hips. She notched his cock against her sheath and slowly impaled herself on his length. Once he was seated, they both leaned away from each other until they formed a tabletop supported only by Vitaly's strong feet and core strength.

The duo was impressive and Jasmine would have been enthralled by their physicality but her attention was diverted by the man to her right who moaned in her ear as she massaged his thigh and belly. The texture of the hair covering his abdomen and the heat of his skin felt so nice against her palm. With the tight fit of the three of them on the couch, he had draped his arms across the back. His hand cupped her shoulders and his fingers dug into her skin as she alternated between light scratches and firm caresses.

"Please touch my cock," he moaned in a whisper. "Please. Please."

She lifted her gaze and saw him watching her with lust in his eyes. "Watch the show."

"Please, Mistress."

"Watch them. Not me." She tugged at the hair around his navel.

"I'm so hard for you." He thrust his hips. The strength of his erection threatened the integrity of the fabric trapping his cock.

"Watch them," she bit out and twisted his nipple.

Instead of flinching, he sucked in a breath and groaned, "Oh, yeah, baby."

"You're testing my patience, Rookie."

"Why? Because I enjoy your touch and your touch alone?"

"Because you are being a brat and that's unacceptable. Madeline, stop touching him. He doesn't deserve such pleasure."

Madeline ran her fingertip across his cheek. "Don't play with the queen bee, Rookie, or you'll get stung."

"I like her sting," he said with a laugh.

Jasmine cupped his jaw in a firm grip and drew him close until they were nose to nose. "Stop acting like a child. You are being disrespectful to our guests. Be quiet and watch the show."

The smirk faded. "Yes, Mistress."

It wasn't unusual for a submissive to test their master's authority, but she never imagined the captain would resort to such childish behavior. The sulking was not in the lease bit attractive.

So far she had gone easy on the captain, breaking him in slowly into the lifestyle. Apparently he needed the more direct approach.

Behind his back, she stared hard at Madeline until the other woman turned her head and met her gaze. Jasmine lowered her lashes in a slow blink and Madeline's smile curled with wicked intent. Her friend might not know the details, but she was aware that the hammer was about to be brought down hard.

Vitaly and Katarina ended their routine with a flurry of twists and stage dives as the music reached a crescendo and the audience burst into applause. Jasmine took that as her cue and stood. She walked toward the now empty stage and the crowd sucked in a collective breath. She hadn't planned on putting on a performance and she usually kept her public play contained in Amaryllis' private room unless asked to specifically perform in the main area. This impromptu exhibition was an anomaly the club's regulars were quick to relay to any newcomers in attendance.

She crooked her finger at Madeline. "Bring him here."

"This is going to be good." Madeline laughed and tugged on the captain's leash. She pulled him onto the stage as Jasmine walked over to the controls on the wall and lowered a three-foot long bar from the ceiling.

Jorges sidled up to her with a frown on his brow. "What's up, Jasmine? I don't like the look in your eyes."

"Bring me my whip. The short one."

"Jaz…"

"Jorges…I have a willful submissive that needs to be punished. Will you bring me my whip or do I send someone else?"

He let out a low whistle but nodded. "We're not done with this conversation."

"There's nothing to discuss. My whip, please, or I start to improvise."

"Coming right up, Mistress."

Jorges was right. Something was up, and she couldn't put her finger on it. The captain's blatant disrespect made her mad enough to draw blood and see him grovel on his knees for forgiveness. Her present state of mind was probably not the best for wielding the whip, but she was still in control and if any part of their arrangement was salvageable, her show of dominance had to be big.

She joined the pair back on the stage and positioned the captain under the bar. "The one thing I will never tolerate is your disrespect. I have been kind to you and my kindness ends now. Grab onto the bar."

The captain's eyes widened and he swallowed hard, but he grabbed the bar without a word of protest.

She stepped behind him and said to Madeline, "Strip him. And take your time."

"Yes ma'am." Madeline giggled and ran her hands down his chest before grabbing the sides of his pants and lowering them to the floor in a long glide.

Jasmine focused on securing the straps around his wrists and not on the sight of Madeline's hands on his skin. The two had participated together in play before, but seeing her friend score her nails down the captain's naked backside made her throat burn and a pool of jealously swirl in her stomach.

The reaction was crazy. He wasn't hers. Not in that sense. He was an object to find pleasure with and bring pleasure to. He was hers to do with as she wished, and if she wanted him to fuck every woman in the club, that was her prerogative. Right? Right?

"Your whip, Mistress." Jorges appeared at her side with whip in hand.

"Thank you."

The captain jerked his head around and looked at her in disbelief. He opened his mouth to speak then snapped it shut and turned back around. The muscles in his back bunched and rolled and his breathing quickened.

That's right, pretty boy. Time to put up or shut up. "Stand back, Madeline. Let's see just how much he likes my sting."

Madeline backed up and sat on her knees. "He's sweating already, Jasmina."

"Good."

Crack. Crack. A red 'x' covered his entire back in razor-thin lines.

He gasped and jerked. His grip on the bar tightened as it swung back and forth with his movements.

"Don't turn around," she said as he turned his head to look back at her. "I wouldn't want to mark that handsome face of yours."

She let the whip fly three times in rapid succession. After counting to ten, she struck each butt cheek then again across his back.

"Hey, Maddie. Rookie here is a breast man. Show him how pretty your tits are."

"With pleasure." She pulled down the zipper on the front of her corset and parted the sides as if she were a flasher on a dark street corner. "Get a load of these babies."

Jasmine went back to work, adding more strips of red to his skin. With each lash he let out moan and swayed on his feet. In the room of fifty-plus people, all were silent except for the players on the stage. Jasmine and the crack of her whip, the captain with his gasps of pleasure/pain and Madeline who cooed as she watched him absorb each stroke.

"God, you should see his face, Jaz. And his cock. He's so hard and tasty looking. I want to suck him so bad."

No!

The tip of the whip caught him over the shoulder harder than she intended.

Fuck.

Her hand went slack with shock. The whip hit the floor with a thud as she struggled to catch her breath.

Get your shit together, Jasmine.

She left the whip where it lay and pressed her front along his sweaty back. His skin felt as if it were on fire and burned her through the silk and lace.

"How about it, Rookie? Would you like that?" she taunted even as the very thought made her stomach roll. "Do you want Madeline's mouth on you?"

"No," he panted. "Only yours."

"You don't get to choose." She stepped to his side to reach around and grabbed his cock at the base in a rough grip. "You do as I say and I say you come. Now. I want you to come all over Maddie's breasts."

"No." He turned his feverish eyes toward her. His hot breath washed over her lips as his cock kicked in her hand, but still he resisted. "I want you. Only you. You're the only one who gets my cum."

"Come on her now," she snarled.

"Only you," he growled back.

She brushed her lips against his ear and moaned, "Come for me. Marco."

Marco.

For the first time, she called him by name, and the reaction was just what she intended. The pupils of his eyes expanded before they rolled back and his cock jerked, spraying cum all over Madeline's heaving breasts. Jasmine gritted her teeth and worked his cock, milking his erection for every drop as he shuddered in her arms.

"You bitch," he mumbled. "Well played, Mistress. Well played."

Instead of the euphoria of satisfaction singing through her veins, it felt as if sand filled her body. Gritty, hot, itchy sand that made her limbs heavy with regret.

What the hell just happened? Where was her control?

There was no need to look any further than this moment as an example of how not to treat a submissive. She was unhappy. The captain was unhappy. The only person who had derived any pleasure was Madeline who was enthusiastically rubbing his cum into her nipples.

Tears blurred her vision as she realized the awful truth. She had failed her submissive.

"Jaz, I'm right behind you," Jorges said as he steadied both her and the captain while a steward worked on freeing his wrists.

"My room. Now." She brushed his hands away. "Help him. I can walk."

"I don't think so, Jaz. You're not looking so hot."

"I'll run ahead and prepare the room." She bent to retrieve her whip and leapt off the stage without another glance behind. She raced from the room with murmurs of confused patrons filling her ears.

The captain's needs. That was her only concern. Everything else, every thought that had nothing to do with the captain's welfare didn't, couldn't, exist. Focusing on that one task kept the jitters out of her hands and the tears from falling while she prepared the bed for his arrival.

The men were only a few minutes behind her with the captain grumbling his displeasure over being carried by Jorges and the steward. "I can walk."

Jorges chuckled. "Not this time, Rookie. Trust me."

"Please, Marco. Relax. Lie on your belly," she pleaded in a soft voice.

His lashes fluttered and he stared at her for several seconds before nodding and following the directive without a sound. Jorges fell just as silent as they both sensed trouble on the horizon yet didn't know from where the danger lay.

"Call me, if you need anything," he said and motioned for the steward to follow.

She grabbed the steward's wrist as he turned to leave them and whispered, "Wait outside by the door please."

His eyes flicked back at the captain before he nodded.

"Thank you," she said and climbed onto the bed to kneel by Marco's side.

After he settled, she placed her hand on the small of his back and reached for a cool compress. Creating a secure environment was crucial at this stage and the constant physical contact helped establish that security.

"Rest. Don't move, don't speak," she said and layered rows of damp cloth over his red back. "Your body needs time to readjust."

At the top of his shoulder was the spot her whip struck the hardest and the bitter tang of regret filled her mouth. Fortunately, the cut was shallow and did not require stitches but forevermore he would carry the mark of her carelessness.

"I'm sorry," she said in a voice thick with shame and applied antibiotic ointment on the cut. "I know better than to strike out in such a way. I didn't mean for it to go that far."

He chuckled into the pillow. "I kind of liked it. Showed me you didn't like the thought of Mistress Madeline touching me. I knew you cared."

"Don't be silly. Of course I care about your wellbeing," she said, deliberately avoiding the meaning of his statement. "Now rest."

"I'm not sleepy. Besides, I love your sponge baths."

"Really. Then why are your eyes closed?"

"The better to feel you with, my dear."

"Uh-huh." She pushed her fingers into his thick hair and rubbed his scalp.

"Damn, woman," he sighed while she mentally began counting. By the time she reached twenty-two, the sound of his soft snores reached her ears.

Aside from the laceration, any other marks on his body were superficial and already started to fade. Relief that she hadn't done any other permanent damage was short-lived. Deeper issues had raised their hands for attention and to not acknowledge them was only going to make things worse.

Just like anyone else, she hated confrontations, but she never ran from them either. The best course of action was to be as mentally and physically prepared as possible, and being dressed in a silk robe appearing as if ready for a dirty fuck wasn't going to cut it.

Marco settled deeper into the mattress as she covered him with a blanket and brushed the hair off his forehead one last time. She crept to the door and eased out into the hall.

"I'm going to change clothes and be back in a minute," she informed the steward. "He's sleeping now, but let me know if he tries to leave. I should be back before he wakes."

"Yes, Mistress. Do you want me to make him stay if he tries to leave?"

"Ask him to stay, but he may leave if he wishes. I'll make it quick so it doesn't become an issue."

The steward nodded and she all but ran back to the dressing area. In her experience, he should be out for a while after the scene they just experienced, but Marco had proven time and again he wasn't a normal man.

To her dismay the dressing room was occupied when she arrived, and by none other than Madeline and two other Mistresses.

"That was quite the show, Jaz," Madeline said as she leaned forward toward the mirror and adjusted her breasts in her corset. "I love to watch you bend them to your will."

Jasmine accepted the praise with a polite smile as she changed into a rather sedate, black knee-length skirt and emerald green blouse. The only concession to the club scene were the thigh high boots she tugged over her knees. Nothing about her behavior of the evening felt praise-worthy, but she didn't have time to banter with the other women, or contradict them. All her energy was need for the near future.

She wished the women a hasty goodnight then raced back to her dungeon.

The steward stepped away from the door as she neared. "All's quiet."

"Thank you." She opened the door and peeked inside. Marco was awake and sitting up with the white sheet draped across his lap.

He looked so sexy and tousled as he rubbed his eyes with the heel of his hands and his hair stuck up in all directions. So warm and manly. She wanted to crawl beside him, tug him back down and sleep the rest of the night away.

For a heartbeat, one long solitary heartbeat, she considered doing just that. Then she drew in a breath and her gaze landed on the neatly stacked pile of his clothes on the stool to her right. The outline of his handcuffs were visible through the pocket of his pants. A reminder of their outside lives that cut off the irrational train of thought before it split and divided into a cancer that grew out of control.

"Hey," he said and scratched at his chest with a yawn. "I didn't mean to crash like that."

"I'm surprised you're not still asleep." She crossed to the mini-refrigerator and withdrew a bottle. "Here, drink this."

"Thanks." He took the bottle of water and chugged half of it down in three large gulps. "I didn't realize how much energy is expended when being whipped."

His wink didn't make her feel any better. "Captain—"

"I love those boots on you," he interrupted. "But I don't like the frown on your face."

She smoothed her hands over her hips and straightened her spine. "Captain, this evening has proved to me that we are not looking for the same things from this relationship. I am letting you out of your contract. If you still wish to continue your exploration of your submissive side, I can—" God, she could barely speak the words—"arrange for you to be with another Mistress."

"What the fuck?" He sprang from the bed in all his naked glory. "Jasmine, what's this about?"

"That. That right there. Your disrespect for protocol is what this is about. For your safety I must remain in control. I cannot have you deliberately provoking me. It's too dangerous."

He sighed and rubbed at his neck. "Okay. I'm sorry, I was being an ass. But that doesn't mean that we have to stop."

"Yes, it does."

"Says who?"

"Says me."

"Well you're wrong. Is this—is this because I asked you out?"

She shifted on her feet. "There are several factors that went into my decision."

"Oh my God. It does." He shook his head and stalked closer. "What is so wrong about wanting to spend more time with you?"

"I already told you, I don't have the time to give. Look, I'm not going to rehash an old argument. It's best to end things now."

"Best for who? Dammit." He pinched the bridge of his nose, his lips tightened over his teeth as his body shuddered. "I don't know what has you pushing me away, but let's talk this out."

"There is nothing else to talk about. I'm sure in the morning you will see that I'm not what you're looking for and realize that there is someone else more suited for your needs."

"Right now all I see is a woman who is running from an imaginary problem. This isn't like you. You're the great Mistress Jasmina." He stalked closer and she inched away from the flames of anger and disbelief that burned in his eyes. "You make men like me fall on their knees begging to please you. You're not afraid of anything, yet now you're acting like a coward. Why?"

She didn't know, she wanted to shout as panic seized her by the throat. It wasn't that he was bigger or she feared for her safety as he loomed over her, but the urge to run burned down her legs. The crazy thing was she didn't know if it was to run into his arms or bolt out of the room.

That indecision forced her closer to the door and away from Marco. His overwhelming presence muddled her thinking and tempted her to forget all the rules that made the different parts of her life function as a cohesive unit. Was it a cowardly move to make a break for it? Maybe. But he would see, in time, she was doing him a favor.

"Good luck, Captain. I wish you well."

"Stop. Just stop." He snagged her by the arm and settled his hands on her shoulder. "I'm not going to let you walk away without a fight. Just tell me what's wrong, sweetheart. I'll fix it."

"Sweetheart?" She knocked his hands away. Was he insane? What made him think she'd tolerate being addressed as something so childish? Where had she gone wrong with him? "Did you just call me sweetheart? What in our history together made you believe you can address me in such a manner? I am not your girlfriend or your child, and there is nothing for you to fix. We are but two people who might have been able to share a mutual desire, but it's obvious we are not what each other needs. I don't have the time for games and I'm not going to waste your time. Goodbye, Captain."

"You're misinterpreting my intentions and not making any sense. Jasmine. Jasmine," he shouted as she turned to leave. "Don't walk out that door."

The rest of what he said was muffled behind two inches of wood as she closed the door in his face.

"Sweetheart," she muttered. "Of all the nerve."

Admit it. You liked it.

"It's degrading."

But you still liked it. And you are being a coward.

"He's not ready and neither am I."

The more you say it, the more you'll believe it. But know this, you probably walked out on the best man you'll ever have.

"Probably is the operative word."

Sure, the captain was possibly the perfect man for her. But inside she knew the painful truth. She was not the best woman for him.

CHAPTER ELEVEN

"CAPTAIN. COME ON, Cap, go home. You're gonna drool all over the evidence."

"Huh—what?" Marco jerked upright and swiped his palm down his face. "I'm up. I'm up."

Coulter reached toward him and peeled away the notecard stuck to his hair, then took the seat across from the desk. "Sure you are. It's six am. Have you been here all night?"

"Well, when you've been scooping up criminals at the rate we've been lately, a lot of paperwork accumulates."

"I take it she's still not returning your calls."

Marco didn't acknowledge the statement. He wrenched open the drawer by his side and rifled through the contents in search of a protein bar or anything to fill the hunger in his belly. The next time he stopped by his house he'd have to remember to throw some munchies into a bag to bring back to the station. Over the last week and a half he'd eaten his way through the buffet in the vending machine and his wallet was depleted of ones. Not to mention all of that junk food was giving him gas and the sodium was making his left arm tingle. An apple was more likely not to kill him.

"Do you want to talk about it?" Coulter offered.

"There's nothing to talk about."

"She hasn't replaced you."

He paused mid-bite and met Coulter's gaze for a second

before letting it fall and biting off a good-sized chunk of chocolate and nuts. "I don't know what you're talking about," he mumbled with his mouth full.

"Bullshit. You've been sulking and going non-stop since after the night she whipped you. I know you two parted ways."

The candy stuck in his throat as he sputtered. "How do you know she whipped me?"

Coulter smiled. "I was there. You were too distracted to notice me in the room. I recognized Jasmina before I recognized you."

"Do you think anyone else knew it was me?"

"I don't think so. Unless they know what your dick looks like." He smiled. "Your face was covered pretty well. So...what happened?"

If only he knew. One minute he was floating on a cloud of endorphins, then plunged into an icy pool of what-the-fuck when she broke their contract. In his gut he knew the fear he saw in her dark eyes was not caused by him but stemmed from something deep inside her. For days he tried to find out what had made her run but the damn woman was like a ghost. She wouldn't answer her phone or return his calls. No one saw her at the club and she was never at work when he stopped by. He tracked down her address, but all of his drive-bys came up empty.

He had hoped all she needed was some time alone. But it had been over two weeks and his patience was wearing thin. He wasn't going to wait forever. Didn't she miss him at least a little bit?

Marco shook his head and rearranged the paperwork on his desk. The only good thing that had come from his break with Jasmine was that his team was putting the royal smackdown on Smithwick's crew. Jenny's intel was platinum, putting names with faces and their roles in the organization. Add that valuable intelligence to his frustration with Jasmine and he'd become the Elliot Ness of the drug world. Now all he wanted was to put Smithwick down so he'd have more time to work on whatever demons Jasmine carried that prevented her from at least trying to engage in a "normal" relationship.

God. Wasn't that jacked up? His intentions should be to take a major criminal off the streets for the good of the people, not because he had woman issues. Perhaps he wasn't ready for anything more than a weekly fuck.

"Jeez, Cap. I've never seen you look so sad." Coulter laid his hand over his chest. "You're breaking my heart."

"Shut up, Coulter." He crumpled up a piece of paper and pitched it at the younger man. "The truth is I don't know what happened. I asked to spend more time with her and she spooked."

"Ahhh." Coulter leaned back in his chair and steepled his fingers in front of his nose. "It all becomes clear. She likes you."

"She has a shitty way of showing it."

"Hear me out. Mistress Jasmina is notorious for not dating anyone. You ask to get closer. She pushes you away and goes offline. She hasn't been seen at the club in weeks. Scuttlebutt at the club has all of the Doms wondering where she went. She hasn't spoken to anyone. Even Jorges is worried, and he's usually a cool customer. You got to her. I think she likes you but doesn't know how to handle it."

He frowned at his lieutenant. "How *do* you know so much information? And how have I not noticed you in the club?"

"If I had tits like hers two inches from my nose, I wouldn't notice anyone, even if they were on fire."

"True that."

Marco sighed and pinched the bridge of his nose. Having

Coulter share the same theory he had was a comfort, but it didn't make the situation easier to bear. Only the increased workload kept his hands off his phone and his mind occupied. Most of the time.

"I haven't given up on her yet," he said. "Once we wrap up this Smithwick case, I'll be at her door, on the phone, hell, I'll even throw myself off another building until she speaks to me."

Coulter chuckled. "I hope it doesn't come to that. Good thing we're close to shutting him down."

"We're damn close." He leaned forward and lowered his voice. "Peters is out getting all of our warrants in order. I think we'll be ready launch sooner rather than later." He tapped his finger on the calendar on his desk. Two more days and Smithwick's ass was his.

"Awesome." Coulter clapped his hands. "I need a vacation. But first, I need a cup of coffee. I don't know how you're even upright. Can I get you anything?"

"Where are you going?"

"Sit for a Spell. The stuff here will burn a hole in my stomach."

"Get me a large and a blueberry muffin." His stomach gurgled. "Two muffins."

"Will do."

Marco stood and lifted his hands over his head, stretching his neck to the left and right. The *pop-pop-pop* of his vertebrae aligning made him wince, but the resulting sensation was totally worth it. He needed to get Smithwick in a cage now, if only so he'd have the opportunity to sleep in his own bed for the entire night.

Or Jasmine's bed. And he'd make damn sure he wasn't the only one tied down.

"Hey, Cap." Coulter's shout preceded his reappearance at

Marco's cubicle.

"That was fast."

"You have to see this." Coulter handed him his cellphone. "This was on my Facebook feed."

The worried look in the man's eye made his jaw tighten with dread. He looked at the screen and groaned. "What the fuck is this?"

"It's going viral."

"Of course it is because no one has anything better to do. Dammit. Coulter—"

He was already waving him away. "Go. Find her. I'll let you know when Peters is ready."

"Thanks, man." He gave Coulter back his phone and reached for his car keys.

As he ran to the elevator, he tried not to give in to the panic that made his stomach lurch. The photos lighting up the internet could be nothing more than a harmless prank. Unfortunately, he had a suspicion as to who was behind them and the message they were sending.

Smithwick wanted him off his tail, and like with Fiona Corrione and her relationship with the Chameleon, Jasmine was now in the crosshairs.

JASMINE MELTED INTO the man's embrace and squeezed him tight around his middle. Funny how she only felt a brotherly affection for him when she had once delighted in making him scream in orgasm.

"I've missed you, Mitch." She laid her palm against his smooth cheek. "You're looking good."

He made a face, then pulled out a chair for her to sit. "I still hate hearing you saying my name."

"In here," she touched her heart. "you will always be my Army."

"Thanks." He took his seat across the bistro table. "You're still as beautiful as ever, but something's bothering you."

She readjusted her sunglasses and took a sip of coffee. "You're sweet but full of shit."

Even if the sun wasn't shining bright in the sky, she'd still have worn the dark lenses. Nights of punching the pillow and a full workload made the circles beneath her eyes look as if she had been hit in the face with two baseballs.

"I hope you haven't thought I'd abandoned you, but I did find you the perfect Mistress."

"I hope she's willing to wait three months. I've been called back into the reserves. They're shipping me out in three days."

"What?" She straightened in alarm. "Mitch. No."

"It'll be all right, Mistress. The time away will actually give me time to think, you know, about what I want from a Mistress."

His casual shrug didn't fool her. He was worried.

"Where are you going?"

He looked out into the distance and brushed a stray cherry blossom petal off the tabletop. "My guess, Pakistan, but the way the world seems to have fallen into a shit-storm lately, anyplace is possible."

"But you'll come back." She grasped his hand. "Promise."

"Of course I will." He flashed his Hollywood smile and she swore she heard the women sitting two tables over have an orgasm. "I want to meet this Mistress you've found me."

"I'll be severely pissed if you come back in a coffin."

"I love you, too." He kissed the back of her hand. "Now, tell me why you dropped Rookie."

She snatched her hand away and wrapped her fingers around

her cup. "It's complicated."

"Try me."

"It's really nothing you should be bothered with."

"Jasmine." The forcefulness in his tone shocked her. He had never raised his voice to her before. "You are my friend. Always. And I can tell there's something eating at you. I'm here to listen. What happened?"

She stalled for time by taking another long sip of her lukewarm Irish cream latte while Mitch stared her down until her heart pounded. She wasn't sure she liked this newly revealed dominance from him. She liked when he never questioned her reasoning.

The thought made her wince and the coffee congeal in her throat. Was it even possible to sound more shallow? Why would anyone want a friend or lover who thought their opinion was the only one that mattered?

"The captain asked me out," she finally eeked out.

"No!" Mitch gasped and clutched at his chest. "What was he thinking?"

"Knock it off." She kicked him under the table and felt the flames of embarrassment lick up her neck. "You know I don't date."

"I've heard you say that many times, but why not?"

"I don't have the time to invest in a relationship."

"Bullshit. You invested in me. You invested in him."

"Two days a week. And those were scheduled visits. If a cancellation had to be made, no harm, no foul."

"Ah..." He leaned back in his seat with and nodded. "So we're talking emotional investment. What's so wrong about wanting to spend time with someone you care about that doesn't involve leather straps and lubricant?"

She wanted to laugh, she did, but the truth wasn't that funny.

"When lines are blurred between inside the club and outside the club, expectations begin to form. Roles become cloudy." She licked her lips and voiced her greatest fear. "Reality intrudes and the magic disappears. I can't be in control twenty-four/seven, even if I wanted to be. And how can you maintain your authority over someone when they know your bathroom habits or whether you stack the dishes in the sink or put them away? Everyday life isn't sexy. Over time, the excitement you once felt in the dungeon will fade and all you'll be left with is discussions about who's gonna take out the trash or fold the laundry. It's all so…so bland."

"You. Are. Insane." He shook his head. "Jasmine, you're the type of woman who grabs life by the balls and laughs as you twist them harder. You'll never be in a relationship like you described. Sure, it won't be night after night of extreme play, but if you're with the right person, even the boring times will be fun." His grin turned rueful. "You know, when you ended our arrangement, I panicked. I didn't know if I would find a person to fill that need I have to be submissive. But by being on my own, I realized that you were right. I want a dominant woman in my life full time. And I know that's not you. I'll find her, just like you'll find the sub who can you not be the Dom when you need it." His eyes narrowed as he lowered his head and frowned. "But you won't find him if you keep pushing men away. If you want it all, Mistress, you'll have to risk it all."

She huffed and folded her arms. "I hate it that you sound logical, and I come across as nothing but a brat."

"You hate being vulnerable, and Rookie backed you into a corner. I'm not surprised you came out hissing." He shrugged and took a drink of his coffee as if doling out relationship advice were an everyday occurrence.

Amazing. She started to laugh and shook her head. "You

paid that much attention to me?"

"You were my world." The certainty in his voice made her breath catch. "You were the only one who showed me what I was searching for even though I hadn't a clue."

Jasmine smiled at him as her eyes watered and insecurities frothed in her stomach like sea foam caused by a massive wave. The words were barely audible as she admitted out loud, "I'm scared."

"Who isn't when their heart is on the line? It looks to me like you're living the alternative now. How is that going?"

"It sucks." She snorted and squeezed his hand. "Thanks for the perspective."

"Any time." He saluted with his cup.

They chatted until it was time for her to leave for her morning shift. As they parted, she made sure she hugged him so tight, he would still be able to feel her embrace wherever in the world the military sent him. With a promise to write, she walked the five blocks to the hospital with his words running through her mind like a song on constant replay.

Maybe she had overreacted some to Marco's desire for more. Wasn't it supposed to be a good thing when someone you liked wanted to spend more time with you? Shouldn't that make you burst with happiness and immediately run to change your social media status to "in a relationship?" God, it had been so long since she went out on anything resembling a date, how did Doms date their subs?

Lord, this was going to take a lot of thought.

"Good morning, Helen," she greeted a passing nurse as she entered the sliding doors of the emergency room.

Helen dropped her clipboard and stared as if shocked by her appearance.

"Are you all right?" Jasmine asked.

"Fine," Helen stammered and her cheeks turned dark pink. "I just—I. You. I didn't know you were coming in today."

"I'm on the schedule, right?"

"Yes, but I didn't think we'd be seeing you." Her eyes flew wide open. "I don't mean seeing-seeing you, just, oh—never mind."

"What in the hell was that about?" she muttered as the woman all but ran down the hall.

The oddities continued as she reached the nurses' station. The two women behind the counter looked at her with the same wild-eyed expression as Helen. Even the medics waiting at the counter looked her up and down as if trying to see beneath her clothes.

"Looking good, Dr. Jo," Dr. Rawlings smirked as he passed her. "I miss the purple, though."

"What?"

"Dr. Jovanovich." Dr. Reid's melodic baritone echoed down the hall from where he stood by the elevator door. "May I see you please?"

Jasmine knew the question was a command not a request. She ignored the twitters and chuckles from the peanut gallery and walked toward the chief of staff feeling as if she was being called into the principal's office.

The ride to the seventh floor was painfully silent as she kept her gaze on the doors and ignored the sidelong glance the older man directed her way. Dr. Reid was neither a friend nor ally to anyone in the hospital, which made him a great boss. His opinion of you was based solely on merit, which was an anomaly in the politics-heavy medical field. Whatever thoughts were going through his head had to be real doozies to have his forehead crinkle in such a manner as it was at that moment.

She followed him to his office and perched on the offered

seat across from his desk. He took his chair and eyed her over the hands he clenched in front of his nose.

After several seconds, he quirked a dark eyebrow. "What do you have to say for yourself, Doctor?"

"I'm sorry, sir. I don't know what you mean." What was going on?

"The photos, Doctor."

"I still don't follow."

Good heavens, was the man blushing? Dr. Reid? The man who during her second year of residency calmly and without a twitch of an eyelash removed a man's stuck penis from a flower vase filled with Jell-O? Who removed a chunk of cucumber out of a woman's vagina after her boyfriend got a little overzealous with a vegetable and acted as if it was no big deal?

She felt her eyes dry out as she watched unblinkingly as he picked up the papers on his desk and handed them to her face down. Did she want to turn them over and see what had him looking as if he'd rather be anywhere else but in the room?

Her hands trembled ever so slightly as she picked up the papers.

Mother fucker. She bit back the curse as she saw the photos that appeared to be screenshots from the internet.

Wow. Mistress Jasmina did cut quite a figure when she was dressed in all her dominatrix glory and tossing the whip. What kind of camera had the photographer used, an HD lens? The picture was laser sharp, capturing the slightest details, from the creases in her dress to the beads of sweat dotting her skin.

The photos were from her last night with Marco. In one she was lashing him with the whip, in the other she was pressed along his side. Although there was a blurred-out circle on the print, there was no doubt she had her hand wrapped around his cock. Even if she hadn't been, the censoring of the photo sure made it look like she did.

"Now do you understand?" asked Dr. Reid.

"I see...wow. I see—" Hey. She realized the screen shots were blown up to fill the page of paper and not the actual size from the internet. Instead of calling him out on the fact an enlargement of the photos was not necessary, she asked, "Where did these come from?"

"The photos themselves you would know better than I. Someone posted them on the front page of the hospital's website."

"What?" For everyone to see? Who would do such a thing? "Are they still there?"

"Heavens no. They were taken down as soon as they were discovered, but we're not the only website they were posted. Apparently they're everywhere. Even my son called from college, asking about the Dom doctor. His fraternity brothers want to meet you, but that is neither here nor there. We have other issues to discuss, namely what is the meaning of these photos?"

Jasmine kept flipping through the pictures, completely flabbergasted that someone had gone to such an effort to out her. Who could it be? "I'm still not understanding. Obviously I have interests outside of the hospital. But who posted these on the website?"

"That we do not know. It appears the hospital's hosting site was compromised and another user uploaded them."

"And IT can't tell who it was?"

"Our IT can barely keep our network running, let alone trace a hacker."

"Well what about—" she was about to say contacting the police, but what good would that do? Posting a photo was not really against the law. Right now the only harm was her embarrassment, if she allowed it. Ah, now the strange looks she received when she arrived all made sense. "I take it most of the staff have seen these?"

"And the board, and the news and many of our patients. I've been fielding calls all day about the slutty doctor."

She winced. "That's not fair. What I do on my own time is my business. I've kept my private life and my work life separate for years."

"Until now."

"I've not broken any rules."

"Technically, no." He adjusted his tie. "First and foremost we are a hospital. Our patients and their care come first. With all of the fuss stirred up by these pictures, it's been difficult to maintain that focus."

"I can't control that, Dr. Reid."

"I understand. My hope is this will all blow over soon, which is why I want you to take the day off. Actually take the next three. Perhaps by the time you return, the calls and visitors will have stopped."

Disbelief had her head feeling as if it were floating away. "I'm being suspended, sir?"

"Administrative leave."

"Are you kidding me?" Anger over the situation made her leap from her chair. "I'm being punished for a childish prank that is out of my control?"

"The ER is enough of a circus as it is, and my God, if I have to break up another group of doctors who are spending time away from their patients to ogle your...well..." He nodded his head as his eyes fell to her breasts, which at that moment were heaving behind her modestly cut blouse. "It's only for a few days. As long as you behave, I'm certain this will be nothing but a bad nightmare for everyone involved."

"As long as I behave," she repeated. Message received. She

was not to engage in any behavior that might appear the least bit unseemly. Great. Just great. She straightened and looked down her nose, giving her boss the expression she used when a sub had displeased her. "Is that all, Dr. Reid?"

He swallowed hard and nodded. He had to clear his throat to say, "Yes, Dr. Jovanovich."

Without another word, she turned on her heel and marched out of the office with her best dominatrix swagger. She had done nothing wrong, and there was no way she was going to let anyone make her feel any sort of embarrassment.

The elevator doors slid open and she stepped into the thankfully empty car. As they slid shut a voice shouted, "Wait up."

A white lab coat-covered arm thrust between the doors, prompting them to reopen. Dr. Goldwyn strode into the car and pushed the button for the lobby. Once they were enclosed, the young heart surgeon turned a car salesman's smile in her direction. "Jasmine, Jasmine, Jasmine."

Oh, God.

"Aren't you full of surprises. I have to tell you, I like what I've seen."

She refused to budge as he crept into her personal space, coming to within an inch of her arm as she clutched her bag as if it were a shield. She wasn't going to give the creep the satisfaction of knowing he bothered her.

"If I'd known you liked it kinky, I would have asked you out long ago."

She choked back a snort. As if he ever had a chance with her. Sure, he was pretty, but he was also conceited and a snob. The only respect she held for him was for his ability in the operating room.

"Seeing you in those picture, girl, hmm…there are so many things I want to do to you."

"You need your eyes checked, Goldwyn. If you looked closer, you'd have seen that I don't take it, I give it out."

"You just haven't met the right man. I can make you beg."

From the corner of her eye, she saw him lift his hand then felt the slide of his palm down her back.

Bam. Her bag hit the floor as she knocked his hand away and jabbed him in the solar plexus with her right fist. "Do not touch me."

"Hey. Hey. Sorry. I'm sorry." He coward in the corner. "I thought—"

"You thought wrong. And you can tell everyone of your misogynistic friends in cardiology, and anywhere else, that you'll only have me in your dreams."

She left Goldwyn huddled in the elevator and strode down the hall. All talking stopped as she passed the nurses' station and crowded lobby, looking neither right nor left as she kept her head held high and a swing to her step. The entire drive home was a blur as all her thoughts were centered on one question.

Who?

Who disliked her so much that they had gone to the trouble of taking her picture and posting it all over the internet, going so far as to hack their way into the hospital's website? She always took care to be polite and cordial whenever possible, and she kept a rather low profile, even for a dominatrix. The only person who could potentially have a reason to be vindictive was Marco, and posting photos was not his style. Besides, he was in the photos too, even if his face was covered by the mask. None of it made sense.

She parked her car in the garage under her condominium complex. Usually she would step out of the vehicle and enter the elevator to her unit without another thought, but as she opened the door, she scanned the area, peering into every corner and shadow in search of a possible stalker. Was the photographer perhaps someone from the club who felt she had scorned them somehow? At this point anything was possible.

The garage was quiet and the elevator empty as she stepped inside. The lift came to a stop on her floor, and the doors opened on a whisper.

"Jasmine. Thank God."

Marco was in the hall standing outside her door. He ran to her and engulfed her in a huge bear-hug, smashing her nose into his chest as he ran his hands over her body.

"I've been searching for you everywhere. You didn't answer your phone, you weren't home and the hospital said you weren't there when I called. I've been scared to death."

It was difficult to imagine Marco afraid of anything, but the trembles that shook him as he hugged her close were real enough. After the morning she had, his embrace was welcome, and she burrowed closer, inhaling the scent of his spicy aftershave, and sank into the comfort of his arms.

"I'm sorry," he said and ran his hands over her hair again and again. "I'm so sorry. I never meant for you to be dragged into any of this. I should have known better, dammit."

"I don't understand," she mumbled into his jacket.

"Let's get inside and out of the open." He stepped back enough to allow her to unlock the door and let them into her condo, but he kept within touching distance.

"Does your visit have something to do with the photos of us on the internet?"

"Unfortunately, yes." He paused in the entryway and surveyed the open area of her condo.

It had been years since she'd had a lover inside her personal domain. Her condo was more of a place to store her things and sleep than what one would call a "real" home. Her dungeon at

The Cavern was more her style and where she chose to display her true personality.

The living room furniture looked as if it had come straight from the showroom floor, which it had, courtesy of her mother's insistence that she move on from the college days of assembly-required pieces. The room was pretty but cold, and as she imagined what the impersonal space must look like through his eyes, all her confidence vanished. The encounters at the hospital left her feeling more vulnerable than she expected, and now Marco was the only person to have seen her in all aspects of her life. The illusion of Mistress Jasmina was officially broken.

She cleared her throat, eager to get to the heart of the matter and be done with it. There was a bottle of wine with her name on it in the kitchen. "What's going on, Captain?"

The worry that had darkened his eyes deepened to sorrow as the muscles in his jaw flinched. "Jesus, Jasmine, why can't you call me Marco?"

"Is it that important to you?" she asked past a dry mouth.

"Yes." He stepped closer. "Because you're that important to me, and I want to mean more to you than just another sub. Look, I know that we are two busy people and at the moment there is a royal clusterfuck going on, but I still don't see why it's so unreasonable for me to care about you and want to spend more time together. Am I really that bad to be around when you don't have me naked and trussed up?"

"No." A smile broke through her awkwardness and she gazed up at him through her lashes and laid her hand on his chest. "I've come to realize that the issue is all about me. Plain ol' Jasmine is not as exciting as Mistress Jasmina. To open this side of myself to anyone is not something I've been prepared to do. It's scary."

"What can I do to prove you can trust me with your heart?"

His question made her smile widen. The fact that he asked instead of stating that he was already trustworthy went a long way in soothing her fears.

"You can be patient with me," she said. "And honest. You can start by telling me what you know about those photos of us."

"Smithwick," he practically spat.

"Smithwick? The man you've been after? The one whose men tried to kill Jenny?"

He pulled her into his arms and rested his forehead against hers. "I'm getting too close and he's using you as leverage to get me to back away. I'm so sorry to have you caught in the middle, Jasmine."

"I know you didn't mean to."

"I should have known better," he growled. "I saw what he did to Fiona Corrione. Why did I think you'd be spared?"

"Fiona? Do you mean Lucian's cousin's wife, Fiona?" He nodded. "What happened to her?"

His lips tightened and he looked away. "Long and complicated story, but she was the one from a year ago who had been kidnapped and almost killed by that bomb. When she was kidnapped and brought to the city, I was called in to help with her rescue."

"I never put it together that they were one and the same. I've met her once. She looked fine and healthy."

"She is now. She was injured but survived. She's also why I knew Lucian would help us with Jenny. That night was the closest I've come to arresting Smithwick, until now. I wouldn't put it past him to use anyone close to me as leverage."

All the talk about kidnapping and threatening made goose bumps erupt over her skin and a shiver run down her spine as fear, true fear tightened around her chest. "How certain are you that this was him and not someone from the club who thinks I've slighted them?"

"I had one of my men contact Lucian and pull video from that night. Of course there wasn't anything from the room itself, but my man recognized one of Smithwick's associates from the footage we did have access to. He was there that night. I don't think it was a coincidence."

"Do you think he was after Jenny?"

"No. No one tried to get into the private residence. They were there for me."

"Well, I guess it's a good thing I was suspended then. I won't have to worry about watching my back at the hospital."

He reared back as if she had slapped him. "You were suspended? For what?"

"The C.O.S. thought it would be best that I lie low for a few days until the storm blew over. Apparently he's been inundated with phone calls all morning about Doctor Dominatrix. I say it's a suspension, but he's calling it an administrative leave. Either way, I have a few unexpected days off."

"I am so sorry, Jasmine."

"I know it's not your fault." She lifted on her toes and brushed her lips against the corner of his mouth. When his breath hitched in surprise, she froze in confusion then she realized what she had done.

After all they had shared physically, a kiss had never been a part of their play. Actually, she couldn't remember the last man she had kissed on the lips, but she knew she wanted that intimacy with Marco, and to move her mouth the scant millimeters over to press against his lips felt natural, as if she'd done so a million times before.

His arms tightened around her waist as he tilted his head and took what she offered with a deep sigh she felt all the way down to her toes. How strange to feel as if she were sinking in warm honey and floating in the sky all at the same time. Marco's kisses were just as she expected. Strong, thorough and with a hint of playfulness as his tongue swept into her mouth for a deeper taste. With his kiss he replenished her, satisfied the weariness of being on her own, and she in turn gave him comfort, a port of call, another piece of her heart.

She broke away on a gasp. "That was nice."

"Nice? Sweetheart, that was a lot more than just nice. If I had the time, I'd make you eat your words, but we've got to move. I need to get you someplace safe, at least for the near future."

"Safe? Safe where?"

"Don't know yet, but I'm getting Coulter on it now. I thought you might be safe with the Kilsgaards, but I want you by my side, otherwise I won't be able to concentrate."

"For how long?"

"A few days. We're moving on Smithwick as soon as we nail down the specifics. Could be as soon as tomorrow." He cupped her cheek. "Please come with me."

Staring into his dark eyes, she saw his worry and exhaustion. Lines bracketed his mouth and his cheeks carried several days' worth of stubble. "When was the last time you slept?"

"What day is today?"

"Wednesday."

"Two days ago."

Her poor man. Even if she couldn't offer tactical assistance, she could grant him the simple request of standing by his side. She brushed his lips with another kiss. "I'll go with you."

He wilted against her and sighed. "Thank you. Go pack a bag and I'll call Coulter."

"All right. If you need a drink or anything, help yourself in the kitchen."

At the door to her room, she turned to watch him over her shoulder as he sat heavily on the couch and dialed his lieutenant. Marco might want to be underway immediately, but that wasn't what he needed. With a smile she made her way to the bathroom and the sunken tub in the corner. This was her favorite feature in the entire condo and the main reason she had bought the overpriced piece of real estate. She turned on the taps and poured a fine layer of Epsom salts into the steamy water, then gathered the toiletries she'd need while they were away.

She didn't like the idea that she needed to hide from anyone, but her knowledge of this Smithwick character was practically nonexistent, and if it helped Marco to keep his focus and get the job done, remaining within sight distance was not an inconvenience. It wasn't as if she didn't have the time. Besides, what an opportunity to see Marco in his element, taking charge and displaying his command. She might just become tempted to let him Dom her. "Might" being the operative word.

"Running a bath is not the same as packing a bag."

She turned to where he stood at the doorway and sent him a wink. "In my mind it is. What's the word?"

"Coulter is securing a safe house for the team and will let me know in an hour."

"Perfect. That's plenty of time." She strode up to him and snagged his bottom lip between her teeth then laved the pinch with her tongue. "Strip."

"Excuse me?"

"Take off your clothes. Otherwise I will cut them off myself. I would hate to have you show up at the safe house buck naked."

His eyes narrowed. "And you'd do it too."

"Damn straight." She smiled.

While Marco removed his jacket and shoes, she splashed the hot water up the side of the tub to remove the chill from the fiberglass.

"Climb in," she directed once he was gloriously nude. "Is the water too hot?"

"Just a little." He sucked in breath and sat down. "I like it. Oh, I like that too," he said and tilted his head forward as she massaged his shoulders. "Okay. Maybe this was a good idea."

"When was the last time you took a proper bath?"

"Thirty-one years ago."

"That is too too long. I'll have to make this one extra special."

"Yes, please." He sank deeper into the steaming water and watched her with a lazy smile as she slowly pulled her blouse over her head. Bit by bit she removed her clothing, dropping each item on the floor before moving on to the next until nothing but steam cloaked her skin. From the vanity drawer she retrieved a hair clip and bundled her tresses up and away, then settled between Marco's knees.

"Your hand please." She took a soft crimson-colored cloth and scrubbed at the skin of his wrist before moving up his arm to his shoulder and chest. She made certain she was very thorough in her ministrations, rubbing and touching her man until he reclined against the tub with drowsy satisfaction.

"You're so beautiful," he murmured. "Come here. I want you in my arms."

"Like this?" She turned and settled against his chest. Her lower spine cradled the hard length of his cock as his arms came around her middle.

"Yeah. Now that's the ticket, baby. I could seriously get use to this."

She reached behind her and twisted his nipple. "Don't call

me baby. It's degrading."

"I can't help it. Mistress is too formal and I think of you as mine. Someone to cuddle and kiss. You're mine."

"I'm a grown woman. When we are in a scene, I am Mistress. When we are alone, you may call me my queen, your highness or my goddess, if Jasmine is too much for you to say. Never baby or sweetheart."

"I'll try, my goddess."

She lifted her chin for his kiss and melted into his hold as he supped from her lips in long draws and soft sighs. His hands roamed over her torso before cupping her breasts and massaging the mounds with strong fingers.

"Spread your legs," he ordered against her mouth. "Open up for me. That's it. Just like that."

"Marco," she gasped and grabbed his wrist as he plunged two hot fingers into her sheath.

"I love the sound of my name on your lips. I'm going to make you feel so good, you'll never think of sending me away again."

And with that promise, he raked his teeth along her shoulder and hooked two fingers inside her fluttering channel, stroking and massaging the responsive nerves while she writhed in his embrace.

She loved the flex of muscles in his arms as he played her body with a master's touch. The longing in his voice as he told her over and over how beautiful she was, how much he had missed her and how he loved making her come apart, pushed her toward the edge.

She had been willing to walk away from this? Why? Her stupid pride? Fear? Could she be any more dumb? She didn't deserve Marco's affection, but she was going to gobble it up until he realized he could do much better than her.

"You're getting tight, sweetheart, I mean—my goddess," he moaned against her neck. "So tight. Come for me. Give me your mouth and come for me."

She all but inhaled him as she screamed into his mouth and shattered like a glass balloon left too long in the kiln. All around her, the warm water lapped at her sensitive skin while inside waves of effervescent heat rolled from her pussy to her head and back down again where Marco rolled her clit between his fingertips. Her nails dug into his forearms, making him moan with her as he drew out her orgasm until another wave washed over her, drowning her with its heat and sucking her under.

"No more. No more, please," she begged past lips swollen from his kiss. His handsome face blurred in and out as her sex-drugged eyes tried to focus. "It hurts so good. But I want you. I'm hungry. For you."

Against her back, his erection burned like a molten pipe, throbbing and twitching as she wiggled and writhed. She knocked his hands away from her sex and turned in his arms. "Sit on the edge of the tub. Now."

Marco swallowed hard and jumped to attention. Water cascaded down his body like an erotic waterfall as he stood and took his seat.

"Oh, that's cold," he hissed when his back hit the tile wall behind him.

"I'll warm you up." She pushed his knees apart and scored pink lines up the insides of his thighs with her nails. She grabbed his cock around the base with both hands then leaned forward to suck the pearly drop of cum out of the little hole as if he were a straw.

"Fuck, yeah. Oh, my God," he groaned and his eyes rolled back.

"Hands to the side. Do not touch me. Your cock is mine."

"Yes, Mistress—Fuck!" he shouted as she opened her mouth and sucked him to the back of her throat. His hands fluttered on her head for a second before he remembered his place and dropped them to the tub's edge.

She hollowed her cheeks on the journey up then went back for another mouthful.

Ding dong.

What the hell?

Ding dong.

She jerked up right and swung her gaze in the direction of the front door.

"Who knows you're home?" Marco whispered.

"Anyone from the hospital, maybe," she replied just as quietly. "Coulter?"

Marco shook his head. "He'd call."

Ding dong.

Goose bumps burst across her skin as she stood and climbed out of the tub.

"Don't go out there," he hissed.

"I'm not going to answer the door." She whisked most of the moisture away with a towel then wrapped it around her body. "Just look through the peephole."

"Jasmine. Damn it." He climbed after her, but she was already tip-toeing through the living room toward the front door.

Ding dong.

Damn, they were persistent. She held her breath and looked through the little glass eye then pulled back with a gasp, "Shit."

"Jasmine Elianna Jovanovich, I know you're home. Open the door," the shrill voice pierced the wood and made her cringe.

"Fuck."

"Who is it?"

Marco stood behind her, dressed but still wet. His shirt clung to his torso and his trousers weren't quite pulled up to his waist. His lips were deliciously red and his eyes still held the fire from a moment before. Without looking into a mirror, she knew her own appearance was the same, which made the visitor's timing all the more hellacious.

"Jasmine?" he asked again.

She closed her eyes with a sigh. "It's my mother."

CHAPTER TWELVE

"J ASMINE, OPEN THIS door." Her mother's demand was accompanied by several firm knocks that rattled the door. "I saw your car in the lot and know you are home."

A multitude of dirty, nasty swear words sprang to her lips as she ran toward her bedroom. "Just a minute," she shouted.

Yes, her mother had been known to drop by unannounced in the past, but by the shrillness of her tone it was obvious something had crawled up her mother's butt, and Jasmine had a terrible idea of what that could be.

"What do you want me to do?" Marco asked.

"Stand back. Whatever it is she's come to say is going to be loud and nasty. Of all the times…" she muttered and pulled on a pair of yoga pants and a t-shirt. There wasn't enough time for a bra so a hoodie zipped halfway up was going to have to disguise the tell-tale jiggle. "And she won't be alone. She hates to drive. Please don't let it be Bruno."

Marco followed her back into the living room. "Who's Bruno?"

She opened the door then inwardly cringed as she died a thousand deaths at the sight of the tableau waiting in the hallway.

By the way her parents were dressed, it was if they were on their way to a funeral. A black cotton scarf covered her mother's hair, making her red-rimmed eyes appear ghostly against her pale face. She clutched a handkerchief in one hand and a bundle of papers in the other, both of which were clasped to her chest. Bruno looked no less somber in his dark suit and grim expression. When he met Jasmine's gaze, he muttered something under his burly mustache and looked at the floor as his cheeks turned pink.

"Mother. Bruno. What a surprise. What brings you by?" she barely managed to ask in a pleasant tone.

"What is the meaning of this?" her mother screeched and held up the fist full of paper. "This is not the daughter I raised."

Holy hell. She gestured for them to enter. Why bother to deny she knew the purpose of their visit? Playing dumb was only going to make the situation more painful. "Come on in."

"Your father, may he rest in peace, is weeping in his grave right now, saying 'Why Jasmine? Why have you brought shame to this family? Why do you stab your mother in the heart?'" she wailed then drew up short when she spotted Marco standing in the living room. The poor man looked as if he couldn't decide whether to be scared or amused. "Who is this man?"

"Marco, this is my mother and step-father, Bruno and Katarina Brodsky. Mother, this is Police Captain Marco DeWinter."

"A policeman?" Her eyebrows rose so high they disappeared under the scarf. "Have you come to arrest my daughter for indecency?"

"Katarina," Bruno muttered in a gruff tone and took a seat on the couch. "I don't think he is here as cop. He is barefoot. I think he is, what is the word? Boytoy?"

Marco's eyes widened in surprise while Jasmine rolled hers. If this situation had happened to any of her Dom friends, she'd be on the floor howling with laughter. At the moment all she wanted was to melt into the floor and be absorbed into the earth.

Lord grant her strength.

"Marco is my boyfriend," she answered.

"Boyfriend?" The way her mother said the word made it sound as if it were a disease. "You have a boyfriend? Since when? You have not brought him home. You have not allowed us to meet him and approve of the relationship."

Oh no she didn't. Really? Really.

"I don't need you to approve anything. I'm an adult who can make my own choices."

"Obviously not when you parade around dressed as a whore. I did not raise a whore!"

Jasmine felt the skin around her mouth tighten further. Her face was going to become permanently pinched the longer she tried to hold back what she really wanted to say. She crossed to Marco's side and placed her hand on his chest, drawing his attention away from the sobbing woman and onto her. "Marco, my suitcases are in my closet. Can you pack me some clothes you think will be appropriate for the next few days? My bag of toiletries is on the bathroom counter."

"If you need anything, call for me." He pressed a kiss into the center of her palm then looked toward her parents and nodded. "Ma'am. Sir."

The hard line of his mouth suggested he had several choice words for her mother, but he did as he was asked. That restraint coupled with the glance he gave her at the door before he stepped inside made her love him a little more.

"Jasmine—"

"Mother." She cut off the diatribe and faced the smaller woman with her head held high. "Before you launch into another tirade or start praying for my soul, let me remind you that I have done nothing wrong."

"Nothing?" She waved the papers in the air. "You call this

nothing?"

"I'm sorry you found out about my lifestyle in such a manner." Speaking of which, how did her mother find those photos? "I knew you wouldn't understand my choices, which is why I haven't mentioned them." And it appeared as if that instinct was spot on.

"Choices? You engage in these perversions by choice? Who taught you this? Where in my house did you hear about such things?" She began to pace back and forth, the papers in her hands turned into confetti as she shredded them while she continued to lament. "I knew it was a bad idea to allow to you to go to college. I should have forced you to stay home and find a husband. If you had just done what I asked, you would be happy now."

"No mother, you would be happy and I would be miserable."

Her mother paid her no heed. "I would have grand babies and a daughter who was respectable."

The ranting bounced on her last nerve. "Are you even listening to what you're saying? Look around you? You want to talk about normal and happiness? Most *normal* people would be proud to have a daughter who put herself through medical school and became a doctor. Who owns her own home and has friends and does what she loves. But not you. Oh no. You want a daughter who is a drone. A mindless baby factory with no other purpose in life but to serve others. That's called slavery mother and was outlawed years ago. I deserve more from life."

"Is that what you think I am? A mindless drone?" She turned to Bruno. "What is a drone?"

"I do not know." He shrugged. "Some kind of gadget-computer-thing."

"I am not a computer." Tears clung to her mother's lashes.

"You think I am nothing but a machine?"

A headache formed behind eyes. "I think you are a woman who is afraid of the world so asks little of it to keep safe. But there's more to life than being a wife and mother. You have a choice. That is the beauty of living in this country. Freedom of choice. That's why your family came here. You have the life you want and that's fine. And I have mine. I am not you and I don't have to be."

"No. Instead you live a life of sin and degradation."

Of course she would know the meaning of the word degradation but not drone. "Who isn't living in sin, Mother? Show me a person who claims otherwise and I will show you a liar." She folded her arms across her chest. "What are you really angry about? Are you really angry that I'm a dominatrix? That I like to dress in sexy clothes and make men beg for the chance to please me? Or are you really angry because you now have irrefutable proof that you have absolutely no control over me?"

The sharp intake of breath and the roaming of her mother's gaze confirmed it was the latter even as she sputtered. "That is ridiculous. Of course it's about this sexy business."

"Is it? Why? Is my lifestyle unusual? Not as unusual as you may think. I'm a trained professional in a controlled environment, and I screen all of my partners both medically and mentally. I can understand why you may be shocked, but if you have paid any attention to me at all during my life, this news should not be a surprise. But you've never paid attention to me, have you? Unless I exhibited some sort of behavior that was a mirror image of you, you didn't notice. And that's sad, Mother."

"You speak nonsense." Her mother sniffled and swayed on her feet. "You have let these vile perversions make you believe you can disrespect me in this way. No more. This ends now. You will pack your things and move home. You will marry a nice man and forget these disgusting ideas."

The sheer audacity of the demands blindsided her like a fistful of sand in the eyes. "Not happening. Ever. I'm not a child."

"You are my child," her mother roared. "You want a choice? This is your choice! Come home now or stay. If you stay…you will no longer be my daughter."

It was Jasmine's turn to gasp. Would her mother actually push her that far? In a voice barely louder than a whisper she warned, "Be careful what you wish for, Mother. I can make that happen."

Her mother took a step closer and lifted her chin. "Come with me or you are no longer welcome in my family."

Ice infused her veins and rooted her to the floor. She looked to Bruno, who watched them as if sitting ringside at a title fight. When he met her gaze, he lifted his hands and nodded, encouraging her to go along with her mother's wishes.

What the hell was happening? It was if a giant television had appeared before her and she was watching a horrible Lifetime Channel movie about a dysfunctional family in crisis. But this wasn't a movie and the horribleness was spewing from her mother's mouth. *Her* mother. A woman who was supposed to love her unconditionally.

Only she never did have a mother like that, did she?

In the future, when she looked back at this moment in her life, what would she remember? The clothes she wore? The wild look in her mother's eyes? The color of the walls or the time of day? Or the prickly numbness that one feels, like when their foot falls asleep. No sense of touch, but a million hot pin-pricks that brought tears to your eyes.

Maybe every detail. Perhaps nothing at all.

For certain it wouldn't be the walk to the front door. Before she realized she had moved, the cold doorknob was in her hand and the door pulled open.

She turned to face her mother. "I am hoping that it's only confusion and fear spurring your actions today. When you are ready to accept me as I am, I'll be waiting. Until then, you may leave my home."

As she spoke, the words sounded muffled in her ears. Absorbed by the cotton shell her heart wrapped around her for protection. The situation was too surreal to process in real time, if ever. Her mother had drawn an unreasonable line in the sand, and Jasmine refused to kowtow to fear. She was who she was. To behave otherwise was not an option.

Katarina drew up to her full five-foot-tall height and sniffed with indignation. With a nod at her husband, she swept out of the room like a queen bearing a long robe of self-righteousness.

Bruno paused at the door and looked toward his wife's retreating back then back at Jasmine. With a weary sigh, he continued down the hall without another sound save for the heavy tread of his loafers on the carpet. Not once did Katarina look in her direction, even as the elevator doors slid shut between them. The message was clear. From now on, Jasmine didn't exist in her world.

JASMINE STOOD WITH her back against the cement wall near the entrance of the parking garage as Marco searched his car for hidden explosives and GPS trackers. Of all the day's events, it was odd that this measure of precaution was not the strangest thing to have happened to her. And it wasn't even eleven a.m. yet. Yep, the morning had been one for the record books.

She pulled the lapels of her jacket across her chest, not because she was cold but because she liked the pressure against her body, much as she suspected was similar to the comforting embrace of a cocoon around a caterpillar. From the moment she closed the front door on her parents, her brain had shut down and gone on autopilot. Thoughts, words, ideas never fully formed as a numbness took up residency between her ears.

Was this really what it felt like to be disowned? The sensation was interesting, that was for certain.

"One more test and we'll be on our way," Marco said as he joined her at the entrance and pushed her further back into the hall. "Stand behind the wall, just in case."

He held his breath and pushed the ignition button on the fob. The engine caught and purred with a gentle roar. No boom. No fires. All appeared as it should.

If it had been the day before, she would have thought him paranoid, but after the day's events, anything was possible. Marco was nothing if not completely serious when it came to his job. If he felt there was a threat against their lives, he was not going to take chances. She couldn't fault him for being cautious.

Marco grunted with approval and placed his arm around her shoulders. "Ready?"

She nodded and stuck close by him as they dashed to the car and slid inside. In seconds they were on the road.

Marco surveyed their surroundings with quick turns of his head while she stared out the passenger window as they passed block after block of concrete and glass structures. Out in the city, people were going about their day wrapped in the drama of their own lives. Could any of them claim to have had as a tumultuous day as she had? God bless them if that was the case.

She still didn't know where they were going, and truthfully, she didn't care as long as Marco was at her side with his quiet strength. Not once did he make a pithy remark or a generic comment of sorrow on her behalf as most people might. Instead he had allowed her to gather her things and prepare for their journey with silent support and respect for her dignity.

"I liked it when you called me your boyfriend."

"What?" She turned to him with a surprised giggle. What a funny thing to say.

He shrugged and gave her a half-smile that brought out the dimple in one cheek. "Earlier, when you told your parents I was your boyfriend. I know that word is kind of juvenile, but I liked that you claimed me as someone who is more than your friend."

"Do you want to be more than my friend?"

He reached for her hand to place a kiss on her knuckles, then placed it on his thigh. "Sweetheart, I want to be mean much, much more to you than just a friend."

"If you continue to call me sweetheart, that's never going to happen." She batted her lashes and squeezed his quadriceps.

For once the nickname didn't make her want to pull her hair out. In fact, she wanted him to pull over to the side of the road so she could climb onto his lap and have him hold her tight for a really long time. If there hadn't been a vindictive crime lord threatening them, she knew he'd do it in a heartbeat. He'd offer her the comfort of his arms for as long as she needed, then fall to his knees if she asked. He was that type of man.

Giddy laughter tickled her lips. What a time to realize she was in love with the captain. His strength. His compassion. His honor. Even his sense of humor made her want to smile when she felt like doing anything but. She never thought she'd have a person in her life who she'd consider as her rock, her port in a storm, but Marco was all of those things and then some.

She held her breath and waited for the panic to seize her around the throat. To place one's heart into the care and trust of another was frightening, which was why she had never done so before. Whether he knew it or not, Marco had the power to crush her, not just destroy her, but crush her. No, she'd never allow another the power to enact an all-out decimation of her soul, but he definitely held sway over her thoughts and actions. Dangerous, dangerous territory.

The car trundled over the roadway without a rumble. Marco's thigh was warm and solid against her palm. The breath whooshed in and out of her lungs with ease and the panic never came. Despite the upheaval in her life caused by those photos, she felt at peace, secure, truly comfortable in her skin and with who she was for the first time in her life.

Marco flicked a glance in her direction and whatever he saw on her face made him do a double take. His posture relaxed and that adorable half-smile winked at her as he covered her hand with his.

It looked as if it took a great effort to tear his gaze away and focus back on the traffic. He cleared his throat and said, "So. Those were the parents."

She closed her eyes. "Yes. That must have been awkward having to listen to…that. I'm sorry."

"Don't apologize. I was so proud of you. Your mother is a trip. I was about ready to come in and lay down the law, but you did a much better job than I would've done. For the record, I think you're great, just awesome and the best woman, person, on the planet."

His stuttered statement made her smile and when she opened her eyes, she saw that his cheeks had turned a lovely shade of pink.

He caught her gaze and shrugged. "It's true."

"Thank you." She leaned forward and kissed his jaw. "And thank you for leaving me to fight my own battles."

"Let me tell you, it wasn't easy holding back." He made a right turn, then another, doubling back the way they came in what she suspected was an effort to spot anyone who might be tracking their whereabouts. "How are you feeling? Really? You don't have to tell me if you don't want to, but I'm willing to listen."

"The truth? Funny as it sounds, but I feel…" She sighed. "Free. I don't have to pretend anymore. No more hiding. No more fake smiles or deflections. Did I want my secret life revealed this way? Of course not. But now I know. Now I know."

Tears burned the back of her throat and his handsome face wavered in her vision as she continued, "It's funny, but the world sends this message that family is everything. Blood is thicker than water. Above all else, your family will stick by you through joy and tragedy. Good and bad. But we've both have witnessed firsthand how that's a crock of shit. We've seen what families do to each other, how they tear each other apart under the fallacy that because they share DNA, common courtesy doesn't apply. We've seen it. *I've* seen it, yet I still bought the lie. I still believed that no matter what, my mother was going to love me because I was her child. And she doesn't. And that—that really sucks." Her voice broke and she pressed her lips together.

With nowhere else to go, the pent up anger over the betrayal seeped from her eyes in fat tears that trickled down her cheeks. She focused her gaze on the street sign ahead until it flew past in a blur then looked ahead to the next, and the next one after that, and the next one after that, refusing to allow the pain free rein, but helpless to stem the tide.

Marco picked up her hand to place a tender kiss on her knuckles and held on tight. The rest of the journey was made in silence as he guided them across town to an industrial area of the city.

The garment district was composed of strip malls and warehouses that catered to the art and design communities. Furniture stores, fabrics, textiles and more were located within blocks of each other for one-stop wholesale shopping.

The building Marco drove them to looked no different from the others on the street. Bulky, tan, devoid of any character and rather desolate in appearance. Even the signage was sad with the words *New & Used Llantes—Cheap* written on particleboard in white spray-paint and resting against the side of the building.

"A tire shop?" she asked in surprise.

He smiled and withdrew his phone from his jacket. "We're here," he announced to whoever answered on the other end of the call.

Around the back were three oversized garage bay doors. One of the doors lifted as they approached and Jasmine quickly wiped at her wet cheeks with the sleeve of her jacket.

Lieutenant Coulter stepped from the shadows with a wave while Marco parked the car, then went to secure the door behind them.

"Hey." Marco caught her around the wrist and leaned close until the tips of their noses touched. "When this is over, we're going away. I don't care where. I don't care for how long. I just want to spend time with you in any way you'll have me."

"Even though I've brought shame to my family?" she asked in half-jest.

His smile widened and a wicked gleam winked in his eyes. "I'm hoping that what you'll do me will make the biggest sinner on this planet blush. I want every wicked bit of you."

The warmth of his affection chased away the ice left by her mother's departure and she felt an answering smile curl her lips.

"Get to it, Captain. While you're saving the day, I'll be planning your ruin in the most debaucherous of ways."

He pressed a kiss to her lips. "Yes, Mistress."

CHAPTER THIRTEEN

J ASMINE JUMPED AS two strong arms encircled her from behind. The knife in her hand skipped off the potato, barely missing her finger. "Be careful please. These fingers save lives."

"Sorry," Marco chuckled and brushed a kiss to her cheek. "You're killing us out there. Whatever it is you're cooking smells fantastic. Way better than what Santiago whips up. You didn't have to go to so much trouble."

"I don't mind. It's keeping me busy. Otherwise I probably would have spent the day fuming over my job or watching you look through evidence and surveillance paperwork."

"I thought you liked watching me look through evidence. At least that's what it looked like when I caught you staring at my ass. Repeatedly." He nipped her earlobe and chuckled.

Guilty as charged. "You're a sexy man when you're doing your thing. But you're even sexier when bound and at my mercy."

"Lucky for you, I live to be at your mercy."

He dipped his head as if to kiss her, then paused, silently seeking her permission. The potato and knife clattered in the sink before she turned to tunnel her fingers into his hair and take his mouth with a hunger destined to leave no doubt that his kiss was always welcome. Marco's answering moan tickled her lips and his fingers dug into her hips as he lifted her onto the counter and forced his body between her thighs.

"Whoa!"

Coulter's startled shout broke them apart with a gasp.

His held up both hands with a grin. "Don't stop on my account. Please, continue. I'd love to be witness to another scene. The last one was hot, especially since it's not every day I get to see my boss stripped naked and whipped."

"You were there?" she asked in surprise.

Beneath her hands Marco's shoulders tensed. "Yeah, Coulter's a frequent visitor to The Cavern. He happened to be there the other night when you put me in my place."

"Really?" How had she not noticed the cute blond man at the club before? Madeline would eat him alive and make him love it. "Sorry, handsome. You'll have to wait for another time for a public performance. I promise it will be good." She ran the edge of her teeth along Marco's jaw and felt a surge of arousal as both men shuddered.

"Damn," Coulter sighed. "Anyway, I came to say two things, Cap. One, dinner smells great. When can we eat? And two, they're here."

They?

"They?" Marco parroted her thought. "He brought back-up? Thank God." Marco helped her down off the counter and tugged on her hand. "I want you to meet someone."

Another surprise? Whoever "they" were must have been trusted friends if they were expected guests. Marco and Coulter had gone to great lengths to find a secure location accessible only to those who needed to know.

The lieutenant and sergeant from the SWAT team and two other of Marco's men had joined them. The rest of Marco's team were out in the field, acting as if there wasn't anything out of the ordinary about to go down. The entire operation was top secret, even to top police brass.

The store they were housed in was owned by an uncle of one of Marco's men and had housed the entire Sanchez family until all the children grew up and moved on to own their own homes. The empty rooms were the perfect size to set up their base of operation and was not on the list of the police department's known safe houses. Marco told her that after the first year on the Smithwick investigation, he had pegged this location as a possible safe house in case the police fell to the crime boss's coercion. Even though there wasn't any evidence of misconduct, Marco wasn't taking any chances, and truthfully, Jasmine was thankful for the extra caution.

She held on to Marco's hand as he led her down the hall but stopped him in his tracks as she caught sight of the two newcomers shaking hands with the other men. One was dressed in a costume straight from a comic book while the other was a familiar face.

"Bale? What are you doing here?" she blurted out in complete shock.

Amaryllis' bodyguard crossed his thick arms over his chest and smirked. "Greetings to you too, Mistress Jasmina. Amaryllis and Ari will be happy to know you are doing well."

"Jasmine." Marco said her name in a way that cautioned her to mind what she might say next. He gestured to the man next to Bale. "I'd like you to meet the Chameleon."

The Chameleon? Seriously? She shifted her gaze to the masked giant and promptly bit her tongue. A black cowl covered most of the man's face, and a tunic in shimmery fabric refracted the light to make his torso blend in with the interior, but even so, she recognized Lucian Kilsgaard the moment he offered her a smile. There wasn't a woman in the club who hadn't imagined those strong lips skimming over her most intimate of places, and she'd know those lavender irises anywhere.

"Dr. Jovanovich." The Chameleon bowed. "It's a pleasure to meet you."

She looked to Marco with confusion. What was going on here? Did he honestly not recognize Lucian? And what was with the costume? Out of all the things that had happened to her that day, she could honestly say seeing her friend's husband dressed like a superhero was the last thing she expected.

"Um, hello?" she responded when it became apparent they were waiting for her to reply.

Marco placed his palm on her back. "Jaz, *the Chameleon*, is here to assist us. He's been a consultant for my team and is familiar with Smithwick and his operations in the Cascades."

By the way he stressed the nickname, she understood she was to play along. "Oh. Great?"

"It's good to see you, Bale." Marco extended his hand and was met with a firm handshake. "I'm surprised, but in a good way. Does this mean you're ready to take up the sword again?"

A look of longing filled his eyes before he shook his head. "I made a promise, Captain. You know that. I'm only here to ensure that he—" he nodded at Lucian—"returns in one piece."

At the mention of a sword, Jasmine's spine straightened. Several months ago the city was all abuzz over a hooded vigilante who patrolled the streets with a giant sword. When Marco had discovered her Mistress Jasmina alter-ego, he had been at The Cavern investigating the case, and Bale had drawn his attention. Not much longer after that, the man the press had dubbed the Claymore disappeared.

If Bale was the illusive Claymore, then Lucian dressed as this Chameleon with a sword strapped to his hip, no longer seemed that farfetched. Were the two a crime-fighting duo?

Questions filled her head, and she hungered for the answers of every one of them. To hold her tongue was almost painful as she batted her lashes at Marco in a way she hoped he understood as Morse Code for "You will tell me everything."

He winked in reply. "Gentlemen, let me fill you in on what's going on, and how you can both help us out."

As the two gentlemen gathered around the collection of notes and surveillance material, Marco leaned close to whisper into her ear, "Were you aware that you were acquainted with two, maybe three, very powerful people?"

"In what way?" she murmured in response.

"You may yet to see with your own eyes. Let's just say I don't think the owners of The Cavern are from Sweden like they claim."

"What does that mean?"

Marco smiled and Lucian turned to look at her from over his shoulder with a wink.

She grabbed Marco by the sleeve. "When do I pitch a fit and make you tell me?"

He chuckled and bussed her cheek then turned away to address the group. "Cam, I need every detail you remember about the house on the lake." And just like that, Marco was in full police captain mode.

Dinner nearly became a burnt mess as she ran back and forth between the kitchen and war room. The exchange of power amongst the men fascinated her as each lent their own level of expertise to the operations.

Marco was the conductor, orchestrating each man's contribution in just the right proportion. He listened with an attentive ear as Lieutenant Kirby of the SWAT team laid out his plan of attack.

Several times her gaze wandered toward Lucian and Bale. Bale appeared as large and as menacing as ever with his ever-present scowl, but it was clear to her by the way his eyes constantly scanned the room and how he held his hands at his back while standing just behind Lucian that he considered the other man his superior.

Just what was their relationship? She knew Lucian had once worked in his family's sporting goods and excursion shop in a small town called Cedar, but the way he moved and spoke hinted at a strong military background.

The entire exchange made her curiouser and curiouser, but the time to delve into that mystery was going to have to wait until the operation was over.

The wait for the main event made her antsy and she wasn't the only one feeling the effects. Anticipation of finally getting their man had the testosterone pumping at a rapid pace. When dinner was served, they attacked the roast like warriors and displayed more of their caveman ancestry. Gestures grew more animated and speech reduced down to grunts and short sentences. The men were ready for battle.

"All right, gentlemen." Marco tapped at his watch. "We reconvene in six hours. That's oh-one-hundred. You know your marks. The only outside communication is between team leaders. Do not let myself or Lieutenant Kirby catch anyone making unauthorized phone calls or sending messages to anyone. I'll break more than your phone. Understood?"

"Yes, sir," the men replied in unison.

Jasmine stood. "I'm going too."

Eight pairs of eyes turned in her direction.

Marco blinked several times before his brows rose to his hairline. "What?"

"I'm going too."

His chuckle died a quick death as he realized she was serious. "Are you insane?"

"Far from it." She crossed to his side. "Hear what I have to say before you get your boxers in a bunch and say something stupid and male. I'm not saying I want to storm the castle with you, but I want to be there. You'll need medical support."

"That's why the paramedics are on standby."

"And I will be with them. Are you objecting because you doubt my skills as a doctor or because we've had sex?"

The men let out a collective groan and Marco flinched. "Geez, Jasmine. Did you have to pull the sex card? If that's how you want to play, fine. I don't want you anywhere near the danger. I don't want you to even look at or be within breathing distance of anything that might harm you in any way, shape or form."

"That's sweet." She patted his cheek. "I'm going."

"I'll stay with her," Bale offered. "I'll patrol the perimeter and if anyone tries to leave the ring that shouldn't, I'll push them back in. She'll be safe, Captain."

"I don't like it," he grumbled.

Jasmine laid her palm against his chest. "But you understand why I need to be there. I need to help somehow, someway."

"I still don't like it." He pressed a kiss to her forehead and slid his arms around her waist to draw her flush against his body. "You'll owe me one."

She snorted. "*I'll* owe *you?* On what planet?"

"You know that you're going to be on my mind the entire time. Once this is all over, I'm going to need an outlet for all of that worry." His eyes narrowed and glittered with devious intent as his voice lowered to a near growl. "And I know exactly what I'll need. Now do *you* understand?"

Heat raced over her skin as her throat tightened. "I do."

He nodded twice then claimed her mouth in a desperate kiss.

Marco feared for her. His worry was in the possessive grip of his hands and flick of his tongue as he sampled the inside of her mouth, but by no means did the concern run in one direction. She crushed the fabric of his button-down in one hand and gripped the back of his neck with the other as she kissed him back with all the emotion she couldn't yet put into words. Did he not think she was just as concerned for his safety as he was with hers? He put his life on the line every day, and if they were to continue on as a couple, moments like this were destined to become commonplace. The best thing either of them could do for each other was to stay strong, keep the home fires burning and never give up until they returned to each other's arms.

"Hey. Get a room, you two," Bale said. "You're making me miss my Ari."

"I wish I had an Ari," Coulter chimed in, then gasped as Bale's expression turned murderous. "Not your Ari, but an Ari. I haven't had a girlfriend in much too long."

"Mistress Madeline is looking for a new sub," Jasmine suggested.

He laughed. "Neither of us is prepared for that match-up."

"You think you can top her?"

"I *know* I can top her," he replied with a cocky grin.

"I'd pay to see that," Marco said as he pulled her in the direction of one of the bedrooms. "But later. I want alone time with my girl first."

"A power nap will probably do us some good."

"Nap?" He stopped so quickly she ran into his back. "I'm planning on doing more than nap with you."

"Captain DeWinter. Are you suggesting that I would engage in illicit activities under the same roof and within ear shot of your co-workers mere hours before an important tactical operation?"

Pink darkened his cheeks. "Well…yeah."

She shook her head and clicked her tongue. "You are greatly

mistaken. For that, you shall be punished."

His eyes brightened. "Now?"

"Later. When you least expect it. Come." She tugged him the rest of the way into the bedroom. "You may hold me while we nap."

"You will so owe me," he muttered under his breath.

"I'm looking forward to it."

CHAPTER FOURTEEN

"T HE SUSPECT IS not on the premises."

"Bullshit," Marco spat into his headset and stepped over the remains of the mansion's front door. "He's here. Keep checking."

To his left and right, members of the SWAT team invaded each room on the main floor and restrained the few men who had been guarding the grounds and entrance. Coulter and the rest of his team followed behind him with guns drawn.

"I want every piece of paper bagged and tagged," Marco shouted over the sound of shouting and the occasional pop of gunfire in the distance. "Garbage, books, bag the whole goddamn building, if you can."

He took the stairs two at a time up to the second story. It killed him to go slow, but he forced his feet to take measured steps down the hall, scanning the interior of each room before moving on to the next.

Lieutenant Kirby approached from the opposite end. "This floor is clear, Captain. No Smithwick."

"Sorry. I don't believe that. Surveillance saw him arrive this afternoon and he hasn't left. The little bastard is hiding here somewhere."

"We've checked both floors. No Smithwick. No girls. It looks like they left in a hurry. Maybe they were tipped off."

"Keep looking. They're here. I know it."

He left Kirby and continued to the end of the hall where the double doors hung askew from the hinges after being kicked in. The bed sheets were rumpled and pillows were scattered across the floor as if they had been knocked aside.

"He was here. I bet his stench is still on the bedding," Marco said to Coulter, then spoke into the mic on his shoulder. "Cam. talk to me. Help me out here. Smithwick's hiding."

Lucian replied from his perch on the roof. Remaining true to his vow of not interfering, he had agreed to stand sentinel and assist only when the situation became dire. "There is a large swell of emotion coming from the lower level."

"No shit," Coulter replied. "There's a lot of men kicking ass on the first floor."

"No," Lucian countered. His voice coming in loud and clear on their headsets. "The lower level. Below the first floor."

"Below?" He exchanged a confused glance with Coulter. "The blueprints of the house show only two stories."

"I speak the truth, Captain. There is another level beneath you."

"Secret tunnels?" Coulter whispered. "That's how he escaped from that building the last time."

"Check the bathroom. I'll try the closet."

Marco dashed into the huge walk-in and started yanking clothes of their hangers. Once the floor was littered with every thousand-dollar suit he got his hands on, he attacked the ceiling-high shoe rack.

Coulter ran in a moment later. "Bathroom's clear."

"There has to be a door here somewhere."

He reached for the tie rack and pulled. The entire case of shoes jolted and a soft popping sound released.

With two fingers he gently nudged the side of the cabinet and held his breath as the entire console swung open in his direction. Tiny lights along the ground revealed a circular staircase that wound down.

"Oh, we're on to you now, you little shit." He readied his weapon and took a step into the dark hallway.

"That is so cool," Coulter whispered and followed at his heels.

Each step down the staircase made his pulse pound louder in his ears, and when the secret door snapped shut behind them, his heart about jumped out of his chest.

"Is there a latch on this side?" he asked Coulter in a soft murmur.

After several seconds of fumbling around in the near dark he answered back just as quietly, "If there is, it's not readily accessible."

Marco spoke into his mic. "Kirby, Sanchez. Anyone copy? This is DeWinter, I repeat, anyone copy?"

"The signal may be blocked."

"We'll try again in a minute. Let's keep moving."

The staircase led into a hallway that was about four feet wide. Ten paces farther the hall split in two directions.

Marco gestured with his head. "You go left. I'll take right."

"We go together."

"Don't be ridiculous. We'll cover more ground."

"With all due respect, Cap, but the last time we separated, I had to have your carcass scraped off the asphalt. You need back-up."

"We need to cover more ground," he gritted out between clenched teeth.

"Three. Story. Fall."

"Cass—"

"Marco." Coulter leaned in so close, Marco could smell the man's toothpaste. In the dim light, his gaze narrowed and his blue eyes sparked like a struck match. "You're too close. If you go alone, either you or Smithwick is going to end up dead. I'm going with you."

Marco drew in one breath, then another. "That might have been true before, but not now. I've worked too hard to let anything jeopardize this case. I can keep my cool. Besides, there's a pretty lady waiting for me that is damn good with a whip. She'll hand me my ass if I fuck this up."

Coulter shook his head. "I don't like it, Cap."

"I don't either. Every few feet, try to make contact with Kirby. In fifteen minutes, we'll turn around and come back here. If you don't hear from me, or I you, we'll go after each other. Don't make me order you, Lieutenant."

Coulter drew back and looked him in the eye for several seconds they didn't have, then nodded. "Fifteen minutes."

"Good luck." Marco clapped him on the back then set off down the dark hallway.

He couldn't find fault with Coulter's worry that once he had Smithwick in his crosshairs, he'd go off half-cocked. If the situation were reversed, he'd have the same questions, and be more vocal about his objections to boot. Funny how staring death in the face changed a man's perspective.

Another hundred paces and the tunnel split off again. To the left was the same line of lights along the ground that disappeared around a corner, but to the right the darkness wasn't so black, and a cool breeze bathed his heated cheeks. His arm ached from having held his weapon aloft for so long, but he didn't dare drop his hand as he made his way toward the source of light.

This end of the tunnel also turned a corner. As he drew near, he heard the murmur of voices. He paused at the bend then slowly eased his head around for a peek.

Fuck, yeah.

At the end of the tunnel was a big, solid door, complete with a cross barricade and keypad that required a passcode to unlock. Just the thing to slow a criminal in his path.

Smithwick stood before the door in all his sleep-interrupted glory. Barefoot, rumpled and dressed in pajama bottoms and an untied bathrobe, he stood still as stone as one of his guards set the heavy crossbeam to the side.

The crime boss was a classic example of why not to underestimate a person based on their size. Smithwick was a small man. At about five-foot-seven, he couldn't weigh more than one-seventy soaking wet. He didn't look like a man who inspired an army of crooks and thugs to follow his orders, until you looked into his eyes. The man was as cold and brutal as an Arctic winter. Rumor had it he had sold his own family to a group of Islamic extremists in exchange for passage to England and enough cash to go to school. The leader was willing to listen to the then-fourteen-year-old because he had taken a cue from their text book and walked into their encampment with a bomb strapped to his chest and his siblings chained like a prison work crew. Man, woman or child, it didn't matter whom he had to crush to obtain what he wanted.

To Smithwick's right, he held a woman by the back of her neck. Draping her shoulders was the matching top to his pajama set. Beneath the hem, her knees shook as she attempted to stifle her whimpers.

Along each side of the tunnel stood three sets of jail-cell-type doors. Several hands gripped the metal bars, yet no one inside the cells made a sound. One would expect at least a little excitement or murmurs of interest, but it was as if the occupants had been trained to remain silent in even the most extreme circumstances.

Marco's vision narrowed down to high-def focus. This was

it. The moment he had been dreaming about, obsessing over, imagined too many times than was mentally healthy, over the last three years. There was nothing but air between him and his prey, and this time triumph was his destiny.

Before he over-thought his course of action, he stepped out into the tunnel. "Stop! Police. Hands in the air. Hands in the air."

The silence of before was like a drum line competition in comparison to the lack of sound that followed his command. All movement stopped and Smithwick's shoulders tensed beneath the silk of his robe. Even the curls on his female companion's head stopped their sway.

Smithwick glanced at him over his shoulder. The corner of his mouth turned up into a smirk. "Captain DeWinter, I presume?"

"Turn around slowly and put your hands in the air." He crept closer with each word.

"And if I refuse?"

"Then I'll make you."

"Will you?" He chuckled. "I don't think so. I've done my research on you, Captain. You're too much of a cop to shoot a man in the back."

Smithwick's man shifted ever so slightly. His eyes flicked to his boss's then he blinked twice. The fool reached for his sidearm as Smithwick pulled the woman in front of him as a shield. Marco reacted with reflexes born from years of training.

He fired off two quick rounds, straight into the bodyguard's chest. The woman jumped with a scream as the goon slid to the floor, leaving a trail of blood on the wall behind him.

"I said hands in the air. Who taught your men to be such idiots, Smithwick?"

The light shimmered off his bald head as he turned and

faced Marco with a blindingly white smile. "Stanislov was my quickest draw. It appears you are faster."

"And obviously smarter." He nodded to the woman. "Honey, run back down the hall. You'll run into my partner. He'll get you out."

She didn't need to be told twice and raced past him while her compatriots trapped in their cells cheered in her wake.

Smithwick raised his hands. "What now, Captain?"

"First, you're going to stand in that corner and face the wall. Hands on your shiny head and move slow."

He snickered and did as he was told. "You can arrest me, Captain, but know that I will be free before the sunrise. There isn't a cage strong enough, or a man I can't buy, that will keep me behind bars."

"I guess we'll just have to see," he replied and stepped forward to secure Smithwick's hands in a set of cuffs. He cinched the metal with an extra vicious pinch, then let out a sigh. His ears popped as if he just breached the ocean's surface and his lungs filled with clean air.

He got him. Fuck yeah, he got him.

Sure, the little shit was probably telling the truth and he'd buy his way out of prison and be back in business before the ink dried on the police report, but nothing was going to take away this moment when DeWinter caught his man.

"Tell me, Captain. How is your lady friend, the doctor?"

Marco's spine straightened with a snap.

"Lovely creature," Smithwick continued with a snake oil salesman's grin. "Strong. Sexy. I bet she's even more beautiful when broken and submissive."

The implied threat hit him as real as a fist to the gut. Maybe he was bluffing, but Marco wasn't dumb enough to ignore the warning. Smithwick wasn't sitting at the top of the food chain because he lacked initiative. Even if only out of spite, Smithwick might burn through all his resources just to get back at him.

"I'm listening," was all he said and crouched down to rifle through the guard's pockets in search of any other weapons the man might have stashed upon his person. A ring with several shiny keys in all shapes and sizes was attached to his belt.

Smithwick's smile grew. "You're a smart man. I'm sure you've already put it all together. Let me free. In fact, come with me. I can use a man with your skills. And as a gift, I'll give you your woman. You can teach her how to behave like a proper whore. I can give you all the women you want. Take any here if you wish."

It took all of Marco's strength to not burst into laughter. The man was certifiable. "And if I refuse?"

His expression fell into a mask of ice and malice. "Then the good doctor pays."

"You seem to think I'll care about what happens to her."

"I know you care, Captain. My man filmed you at that club she frequents. I saw the video, how she brought you to your knees. And how you loved it. You care."

Fuck it all. Talk about damned if you do, damned if you don't. What options did he have, really?

"Well, then." He spun the key ring around his forefinger once, then clasped the keys tight in his grip. "I guess you've made my decision easier to make."

He glanced to the cell on his left. Five girls crammed into the tight space behind the door, watching their exchange with a mixture of hope, hatred and fear on their faces. They were all young, dirty, and barely dressed in short gowns or underwear. To his right he met more gazes that flicked between the keys in his hand and the door that stood slightly open with the promise of freedom. He swore he could hear their thoughts. Would he take the offer or set them free?

He glanced at Smithwick with a raised brow and asked, "Any woman I want?"

Smithwick rocked back on his heels with a chuckle. "Any woman."

As he approached the cell door, the women shrank back. Well, all but one. With her blonde, wavy hair, pink cheeks and bruises on her arms and legs, she reminded him a bit of Jenny. A snarl flirted with her upper lip and her narrowed glare dared him to try take her. She didn't say a word as he unlocked the door and looked her in the eye, but her chest rose and fell with her escalated breathing, and he knew if he took one more step, she'd fight him for survival. Freedom was too close not to at least make an attempt. It was an outcome he was counting on.

For several seconds he held her gaze, then gave her a slow wink. She blinked in surprise as he backed away from the doorway.

"You do drive a hard bargain." He withdrew the key for the handcuffs from his pocket and stepped behind Smithwick. As he unlocked the cuffs, he leaned forward to speak into his ear, "I choose option three. Justice dealt by the hands of those you have wronged."

He shoved Smithwick into the cell. The blonde released a battle cry then jumped upon the man's back, driving him to the ground. Emboldened by their cellmate, the other girls dove into the melee with fists and feet flying at Smithwick's huddled body.

Pandemonium erupted as the women in the other cells shouted and banged against the walls their encouragement, drowning out the sound of their tormentor's screams of pain.

Marco unlocked the next cell and the moment the door swung open, the women inside rushed into the adjoining cell to aid in the punishment.

"Marco! Marco!" Jasmine's voice echoed above the din.

He turned to see her round the corner with Coulter and Kirby with the SWAT team leading the way.

The moment she was within reaching distance he pulled her into his arms. "What are you doing down here?"

"Did you really think I'd stay away if I heard you were involved in a shooting? No one knows how to save your ass better than me."

He smoothed his thumb over her cheek, then looked over her head at Coulter. "Took you long enough to get here. How far down the hall were you?"

"I came as soon as I heard the shots fired. A brunette ran into me saying you had shot a man, then collapsed at my feet in hysterics. I had to pass her off to someone else before I could continue."

"Where's Smithwick?" Kirby asked.

"In there." He pointed to the pile of writhing bodies. "I was just about to pull him out."

"What the hell are you waiting for?" Kirby shouted.

"What? Oh…right. Coulter, let's get in there."

Coulter shook his head with his lips pinched together then joined him in the fray, pulling girl after girl away to get to the mass at the bottom of the pile. Kirby released the rest of the women from their cells while Jasmine directed them down the hall to waiting officers.

When the last girl was dragged away with blood staining her hands, Jasmine fell to her knees besides the quivering form and began assessing Smithwick's injuries.

The once elegant and dapper man looked as if he had been stung by a million bees as his face swelled to the size of a pumpkin, and one of his arms was bent at an odd angle.

"Holy shit," Coulter ran his hand over the back of his neck.

"Is he alive?"

"Well, he has a pulse," Jasmine replied and searched for a vein to prep for an IV. "We need to get him out of here now, and that staircase is going to be impossible to traverse. What's on the other side of that door?"

"I'll go check," Coulter disappeared through the doorway.

Marco watched as the woman he wanted to protect from the horrors of the world worked to save the life of one of the vilest humans on the planet. His hands clenched in an effort to withhold the urge to spirit her away to someplace safe, but he knew she'd break his legs if he tried to stop her. If only it were any doctor other than Jasmine covered in the slime bag's blood. For that atrocity alone, he'd feed Smithwick to the angry masses all over again.

A better man might have felt sorry for being the instigator of an act that caused so much physical damage. But the only thought running through his mind was that it was about fucking time.

Kirby clapped him on the shoulder. "Care to explain how our suspect was found in the middle of a donnybrook?"

"Donnybrook?" Marco snorted. "You're showing your age there, Lieutenant."

The SWAT lieutenant folded his arms over his Kevlar-covered chest and encroached on Marco's personal space.

Marco shrugged. "While I was cuffing Smithwick, one of the girls reached through the bars and took the keys from the victim's belt. By the time I saw the movement, the girls rushed us."

Kirby's brow made a slow glide to his hairline. "That's your story?"

"That's my story."

"Good luck explaining that one." He scoffed and continued

to secure the scene.

All around him controlled chaos swirled with men, woman and equipment battling for space. The calm in the center of the storm was Jasmine working away as efficiently as if she were in the middle of an operating room and not in the dungeon of a mansion.

She looked up and caught his gaze. With a soft smile and a tiny nod, she stood and bellowed, "Where's my transport? We need to move."

Marco wanted to laugh. As with everything, Jasmine was rock solid with her laser-like focus. Completely in control while he felt his emotions wavering like strips of tattered cloth in a hurricane.

More medics arrived from the doorway Coulter had gone through to explore, and assisted her in strapping Smithwick to a stretcher. His lieutenant appeared right after them and joined him.

"The tunnel leads to a boat house about a hundred yards away. We found a vessel ready to depart. The driver's detained. Captain? Captain? Hey." He waved his hand in front of Marco's face. "Are you all right?"

"What?" He blinked. "Yeah. Just comprehending that it's all over."

"Phase one anyway. Next comes the clean-up."

He mumbled an agreement and kept his gaze on Smithwick's body as the medics wheeled the stretcher past him. Only Jasmine's tug on his hands garnered his attention.

She cupped his face between her palms. "I'll keep you posted on his condition. As soon as I'm able, I'll come to you. Promise you'll do the same?"

He placed his hands over hers and absorbed her ability to focus through her touch. With her as his beacon, he'd always be able to find his way home.

"Promise." He risked delaying her for the second or two it took to brush a kiss to her lips then sent her on her way.

"Right." He slapped his hands together and turned toward the men left in the hall. "Let's wrap this up, boys. Our work has just begun."

CHAPTER FIFTEEN

THE SCENT OF beef and rosemary stopped Marco in his tracks as he entered his home. "Abby? Are you here?"

"It's just me." Jasmine's voice came from the kitchen, and a smile spread across his tired face. He dropped his bag and coat on the floor and made a beeline toward the delicious smell.

Jasmine stood before the sink looking like a domestic wet dream dressed in a purple bustier and his favorite black miniskirt. Steam rose from the rushing tap water and formed a halo above her head in defiance of her devilish attire.

He sighed and leaned against the doorjamb, weakened by her beauty. "Are you really here or am I dreaming?"

"You did give me a house key. Or was that only for emergencies?" She laughed and turned off the water to dry her hands on a dish towel. "Do you have to hurry back to work?"

"I'm officially on administrative leave for at least three days. You?"

"Me too." Her smile grew and she crossed to his side to hug him around the waist. "However shall we spend the time?"

"Trust me, darlin', I can think of lots of things." He nodded at the project she had going on the stove. "Can that wait?"

"Those are dirty pots I was about to wash. I put everything in a slow cooker, so it will be ready when you are."

Could she be any more perfect? "Holy hell, woman. Are you really mine?"

She stepped back and the cool, in control dominatrix mask fell over her features. "Am I yours, Captain?"

Absolutely.

Without the slightest hesitation, he dropped to his knees and placed his hands on his thighs and lowered his gaze. The sight of her bare feet sent a jolt of electricity to his cock. Immediately the exhaustion caused by thirty-six straight hours of questioning, reports and more questioning evaporated.

"How may I please you, Mistress?"

After all they had been through, she was still his Mistress. That hadn't changed because she agreed to take their relationship to the next level. If anything it only strengthened his conviction to be the man she needed him to be whenever she wished.

"Good boy." She circled him once and dug her fingers into his hair, drawing a groan.

After another rotation she cupped his face in her hands and lifted his chin. As she gazed into his eyes, she stroked his lips and cheeks with her thumbs, and he melted like whipped cream on hot skin.

"What, oh what, shall I have my boy do for me?" she asked as she feathered kisses across his forehead.

"May I make a suggestion?"

"You may."

"I'm calling in my favor."

She drew back with a puzzled frown. "What favor?"

"You owe me for letting you come on the raid."

"Ah…that favor. Are you certain you want to cash that in now?"

"Positive."

She straightened with a smile. "And what is this favor you will have me do?"

He shot to his feet and pulled her against his chest. "Whatever I want."

The struggle as to whether she'd concede all control swirled in her dark eyes. He held his breath and allowed her the chance to decide without his influence if she'd acquiesce.

She blew out a long breath and softened in his arms. "What will you have me do?"

Heat raced from his head to his toes as the power of those words ignited powder kegs of lust in his veins.

Anything and everything was his initial response, but at the top of his list was to confirm the fact that she was there in his arms, and for one solitary moment there was nothing and no one to interrupt them for the foreseeable future.

He captured her lips in a deep, bruising kiss and cupped his hands under her butt, lifting her against his pelvis and the erection she created. If he had been a professional Dom, he'd probably have some smooth moves to slowly crank up the heat until they both couldn't take it any longer, but he wasn't that guy. All he wanted was to immerse himself in his woman. Taste and feel and take what he wanted for as long as he wanted. Debonair and suaveness could jump off a cliff.

Not that Jasmine appeared put off by his caveman handling. She wrapped her arms around his neck and tried to climb up his body, only to be stopped by the tight skirt keeping her legs from parting.

"I've got you, sweetheart," he muttered against her lips and lifted her into his arms.

"Is calling me sweetheart part of the deal?"

"I'm going to call you all sorts of things. Sweetheart is one." He carried her into the bedroom and dropped her onto the mattress with a little bounce.

With the control in his hands, he realized he now had the

opportunity to say all the things she forbade when they were in her dungeon. Man, he only hoped he could maintain the brain power to form a coherent sentence.

He brushed the backs of his fingers against her cheek. "Mine is another. You're mine, Jasmine. Your mouth is mine. Your pussy is mine." He reached into the cup of her bustier and pinched her nipple. "Your breasts are mine, too. Now, be a good girl and show me my tits."

Heat flared in her eyes as she sucked in a breath at his vulgar language. Yeah, his girl liked it naughty, even when she wasn't the one leading the charge.

Her hands shook as she worked the catches of her bustier and pulled the sides away. The soft mounds of her breasts pooled into his waiting hands where he rolled the soft flesh in his palms.

"I love your breasts." He bent down and alternated taking the hard buds into his mouth. "The first time I saw you in the club, and you were wearing that sheer top, my God, I've thought of these babies every day since then. You don't share them with me enough, you tease."

Judging by the sly chuckle she tried to hide, the little witch knew exactly how much she tortured him. In retaliation, he sucked the skin on the inside of her left breast between his teeth until a purple bruise formed. By morning he'd make sure she bore more of his marks on her flesh.

"Lie back and take off your skirt," he instructed and tackled the buttons of his shirt. "Look at you with no panties. Damn, that's sexy."

"Aren't you Mr. Chatty." She smiled and tossed her skirt to the side.

"You never let me talk. I'd be talking non-stop, if you gave me a chance." His pants joined her clothes on the hardwood floor.

"I'll keep that in mind."

"You do that. Now, get on your knees."

With a sensuous sway of her hips, she rolled to her hands and knees and offered her backside with a playful wiggle. Her teasing laughter ended with a gasp as his hand landed with a hard whack to her right butt cheek.

"Ow." She glared at him over her shoulder. "What was that for?"

"That was for all of the times you've teased me until I lost my mind." Smack. "And that one was for making me like it."

He alternated smacks, loving the way her flesh rippled and turned pink. "And this is for asking to be placed near danger. And that's for thinking I would want to change anything about you. And this one is for pushing me away."

"Marco," she cooed and arched her back.

He kneeled behind her and rubbed the length of his cock between the slick lips of her sex, then he popped her on the butt again. "And that one is because you love it this way."

"Please, Marco," she panted and wiggled her reddening ass. "Please. Fuck me."

"I don't know." He worked two fingers into her drenched sheath. "Maybe I should tease you like you tease me. Keep you on edge until you scream."

"No, no, no. Please don't. Please, please."

"You beg so prettily." He leaned down and bit her hip. "I want to hear more."

His fingers plunged and rubbed, teased and tormented. He leaned down and ran his tongue down her spine as his free hand stroked her body from neck to clit. With each cry and moan, he absorbed the sounds of her pleasure until his teeth ached.

When her cries became sobs and her sheath fluttered around

his fingers, he withdrew from her body. His legs trembled as he crossed to the night stand for a condom. With the foil-wrapped packet in his hand, he turned his attention back to Jasmine and froze.

She waited for him on all fours, her cheeks a lovely shade of pink and her eyes glowing with fire as she stared up at him with so much passion, she about burned him alive. Her breasts swayed as she shivered and her lips were puffy from his kisses. She was a bitch in heat. His bitch. Eagerly waiting for him to claim her.

As the cream from her pussy cooled on his skin, he realized that aside from their shared bath, this was the first time they were completely naked with each other. There was no cloth separating their skin. They were stripped to their core, and he wanted to keep it that way.

He held her gaze and set the condom onto the nightstand, then stepped away. She watched him as he climbed back onto the bed and settled the bare knob of his cock against her entrance and held his breath. Her expression shifted from confusion to understanding. Her tongue swept over her lower lip then she lowered her shoulders to the mattress and lifted her hips into the air.

He dug his fingers into her flanks as he set his jaw and slid his cock home in one slow glide. "Fuck, baby," he groaned and his eyes crossed as her wet heat enveloped him in a tight grasp. "You undo me. You absolutely fucking undo me."

Any thoughts of going slow and steady dissipated in a heartbeat. His pelvis took over and set a punishing pace as his body weight drove her into the mattress. Jasmine responded by grinding against him, her moans and grunts encouraging him to take her harder, faster.

"Fuck, you're so wet and tight." He fisted the sheets near her head and bore down. His lungs burned as he panted in her ear. "You drive me crazy. Out of control. Can't. Get deep enough. Inside you."

"Marco." Trapped beneath his punishing lunges, she bucked and rolled and gazed at him with wild eyes framed by strands of her dark hair that stuck to her sweaty cheeks. "Marco."

"That's it. Say my name. Me. I'm the only one who can give this to you. I'm the only one that can take away your control. And keep you safe. Admit it."

Her pussy tightened around his cock as she gasped, then a slow smile curled her lips and she went lax beneath him as she mouthed the words he didn't expect.

"I love you."

The declaration zapped the remaining energy in his arms, and he pressed her deeper into the mattress. He rubbed his forehead against hers as his heart felt as if it were about to explode. "Damn, sweetheart. I'm wrecked."

"That's why I love you."

Nothing else mattered but submerging himself in his woman. He gathered her in his arms and felt the fire of release burn down his spine as his cock swelled in her sheath. Between biting kisses and gasps for breath, he grunted, "Love you."

Jasmine's eyes widened before she screamed into the mattress as she came. Her sweet pussy squeezed his turgid length in hard draws, sucking the cum from his cock as he flooded her sheath with his seed. His entire body was aflame, leaving him deaf, blind and a quivering mass of flesh and bone. Even if he wanted to move, he lacked the coordination to do anything more than twitch with residual adrenaline.

"I love you. But. Can't breathe." She slapped at his head with a weak hand.

"Sorry," he mumbled and managed to roll to his side, keeping his arms wrapped around her until their breathing slowed to normal and the sweat cooled on their skin. Goose bumps erupted across her arms as she shivered in his hold.

By then he regained enough of his strength to drop kisses across her shoulder and around to the curve of her breast as he pushed her onto her back. She watched him with a sated gaze as he continued with a line of kisses down her torso and the soft pad of her belly. Her thighs parted with the slightest nudge, revealing the ripe fruit of her sex. He saw her hold her breath then release it in a rush as he touched his tongue to her clit before moving lower to lap up their combined release. She giggled and worked her fingers into his hair.

He took his sweet time building her up into another orgasm, soothing her swollen flesh with the flat of his tongue and soft caresses. He worshipped at the altar of Jasmine. Paid homage to the woman who made him want and hunger in ways he didn't know were possible. Who cut him to the bone with one look and the sound of his name from her lips.

When he had asked, with all his naivety, for her to take him on as her submissive, he sensed that she'd be able to provide him with that intangible something he sensed was missing in his life but didn't know what to name. Not only did she deliver on her promise in spades, but he in turn learned how to be the man she needed. The man who'd cherish her drive to be in control, but give her the safety and solace when asked to lower that hard-won guard.

Their combined flavor burst across his tongue in a savory cocktail that made him smile. He'd eagerly lap up his cum from her skin every time just to watch her head toss back and forth on the mattress and her hips roll, trying to move his mouth against her sweet spots. She stroked his scalp with one hand and plucked at her nipples with the other in a wanton display that brought the steel back to his cock.

"You are so sexy." He thrust his fingers into her sheath in a smooth, steady glide. "You're even sexier when you come. Will you come for me again? Please?"

He took her clit between his lips and sucked on the sweet berry until she moaned and squeezed his fingers in a rhythmic pulse of release, pushing more of their cum into his mouth.

As she floated down from the heavens, he trailed the tip of his tongue up her torso and between her breasts. She grabbed his head and brought him down for a kiss to share their taste.

"Thank you," she said and snuggled into the curve of his body.

He slid his arm beneath her head and brushed the hair off her cheeks. "Ah, Jasmine. I'm gonna say all this now, and please know it's not the sex talking, but I love you. You are it for me. My one and only. I know that at times I'll probably do the stupid man thing and take you for granted and not tell you enough, but I love you. You. Exactly as you are."

"Don't make me sound as if I'm perfect." She pressed kisses to his chin. "After a three-day shift I'll be cranky and want to forget all about it by tanning your backside. But know that with every lash, I'll be loving you."

"I'm counting on it, sweetheart."

She chuckled and pushed him onto his back then straddled his lap, lowering her pussy down his erect shaft. "Let's get one thing straight. Stop calling me sweetheart."

"You like it. Your pussy flutters every time I do."

"Keep it up and I'll have to punish you." She reached out and twisted his nipple.

"Ow," he cried and his cock jerked in her sheath. "Does this mean you're back in charge?"

"I've always been in charge. That's why I've come twice and

you only once."

"You are an evil genius."

"Who loves you."

"Thank the lord."

"Now, for your punishment, sweetheart." She cupped her breasts and rode up and down his shaft. "Reach up and grab the edge of the mattress. Don't move, or I'll bring out the ball-gag and strap-on."

The idea that she'd take him up the ass excited him in ways he didn't ever think were possible and his hips jerked as if she had already penetrated him. Maybe he should disobey her just to unleash the full force of her genius.

Her raised eyebrow warned him that she knew his thoughts and expected better of him.

He settled into the bed as he gripped the mattress as instructed, and was rewarded with a sexy smile. His Mistress would take care of all his needs.

"Good boy." She slammed her hips down on his cock. "You're catching on."

"I live to serve, Mistress."

About Anna Alexander

Award winning author Anna Alexander is the author of the Heroes of Saturn and the Sprawling A Ranch series. With Hugh Jackman's abs and Christopher Reeve's blue eyes as inspiration, she loves spinning tales of superheroes finding love. Anna also loves to give back and has served on the board for the Greater Seattle Romance Writers of America as chapter president and on the committee for the Emerald City Writers Conference.

Sign up to receive news about Anna's latest releases at
http://eepurl.com/Q0tsz

Anna welcomes comments from readers.

Website

annaalexander.net

Facebook

facebook.com/pages/Anna-Alexander/282170065189471

Twitter

twitter.com/AnnaWriter

Newsletter

http://eepurl.com/Q0tsz

Also by Anna Alexander

Cavern Series
A Night at The Cavern
Only at The Cavern

Heroes of Saturn Series
Hero Revealed
Hero Unleashed
Hero Unmasked
Hero Rising

Men of the Sprawling A Ranch Series
The Cowboy Way
The Marlboro Man
To Have Faith
Sweetest Kisses

Elite Metal Series
Bound by Steele
Adamantium's Roar
Vibranium's Truth

Learn about Anna's latest release by subscribing to her
newsletter at
http://eepurl.com/Q0tsz

www.ingramcontent.com/pod-product-compliance
Lightning Source LLC
Chambersburg PA
CBHW031713170626
46808CB00005B/1733